Under

A

Broken Sky

Ed Harvey

Under A Broken Sky
Copyright © Ed Harvey April 2013

All rights reserved
ISBN: 978-0-9568207-6-1

Imprint: Ed Harvey

Printed by www.createspace.com

Available from Amazon

Contact email: edharvey28@icloud.com

Cover image:
Copyright © Petr Malyshev
www.shutterstock.com

'Under A Broken Sky'
is set in modern-day Spain.
All places and characters are fictitious and any
resemblance to actual persons is purely
coincidental.

Dedicated to Mike Macpherson

Stolen from us when our backs were turned

Acknowledgements

'Under A Broken Sky' was originally entitled 'The Whore's Companion'.

Thank you to everyone who read 'The Whore's Companion' and were generous enough to pass on their thoughts, particularly Jean Macpherson who read an earlier version of the manuscript and offered editorial advice.

This version has been revised and edited with the help of Akiyah Clements and Marcia Redmonds.

Additional thanks to:

Dave Tadd, my forensics guru and the Reverend Canon Alan Bennett, my ecclesiastical consultant.

And my darling Sue for her love, advice, support and patience.

1

Juan Gonzales had been unwell for much of the night and was up long before the rooster's strangled call. His doctors had told him this would be his last summer but, at eighty-three, he was thankful to have the opportunity to kill one last time.

As the sun rose, he sat in the shadows of his small terrace and sipped coffee and smoked the last of his cigarettes. He looked beyond the village church to the maze of alleyways and narrow streets and watched those who still had work as they made their way to the fields.

During the rest of the morning, he wrote a letter to his son and then completed preparations for this, his final mission. At twelve, he checked the bolt action on his rifle, loaded five rounds into its magazine, and then wrapped it in an old rug. He had no doubt it would still work but, as a precaution, he took a handgun from the behind the lintel above the front door.

At two, he noticed an angry storm out at sea, but overhead the sun seemed to defy the gathering clouds. He retreated to his bedroom and stood before the fading photograph of his wife. He offered up a simple prayer.

As the village settled into its siesta, he pushed the handgun inside his waistband, covered it with his shirt and glanced around his modest home.

He collected his rifle and stepped out, under a broken sky.

*

Antonio Fernández sat in the oldest bar in the City. He sipped beer and glanced at the match being screened on a TV. This was his local and few things entertained him more than watching men unwind at the end of the day. He was amused by the intensity of their asides and, like a fly on the wall, his eyes skipped from one group to another as he watched reactions to the game.

Bars like this attracted few women. Occasionally, daughters would be sent to extricate their fathers and tourists would be drawn there by its reputation.

The walls were plastered with images that summoned the passions of Spanish men - bullfighting, flamenco, hunting, and football – and alongside the public phone the telephone number of the local taxi firm was pinned next to the contact details of several brothels.

Fernández ran his hand over two-day stubble, pushed long, dishevelled hair off his forehead, rubbed the back of his neck, and caught a face staring back at him from the mirror behind the bar – his face - eyes red rimmed, underscored by dark rings that betrayed his need for sleep.

He smiled at two men arguing about a refereeing decision. He understood that, when times were tough, distractions such as sport, the camaraderie of a bar, and a few beers, could mean the difference between coping and going under.

He ordered another beer, glanced at the TV and saw a familiar face agonising over a missed chance on goal.

'José Castaño playing for the reserves?'

'Yeah,' the bartender said. 'Making a comeback after breaking his leg. He's on the fringes of the first team. He was born in Los Mineros, wasn't he?'

'I think so.'

It was a small lie. Fernández had known José well and had dated his sister, Ana-Maria. He'd heard she'd married, but wasn't sure if she'd moved from the village.

The bartender placed his drink in front of him.

'You're early this evening, Inspector.'

'I've got three days off. First for months. Just hope the rain holds off.'

'Anything planned?'

'Nothing, except a matanza on Sunday.'

'I'll take any part of the slaughtered pig. Give you a good price.'

'It'll be divided amongst the family, as always.'

The bartender nodded, as though knowing there was no point arguing. 'She well? Your mama?'

Antonio Fernández hadn't seen his mother for several weeks. Work meant he rarely had time to be with her. 'She's fine.' He got up and slid his hand into the hip pocket of his jeans. He'd left his wallet in his car. 'Can I pay later?'

'Yeah, but you'll all have to settle up soon. The bank manager's looking over my shoulder. This is on the house, but don't leave it much longer.'

The bartender poured him a complimentary brandy and, as he placed it in front of him, most men in the bar bellowed in celebration. Malaga had scored, cancelling out José Castaño's earlier goal for Real Madrid's reserves.

Several other men came in, ordered their drinks with a nod towards the bartender and, as they settled to watch the match, the shrill of Fernández's mobile cut through the air. He sighed, stepped outside, and crushed his cigarette on the cobblestones.

The storm had passed. The evening was warm, shops had reopened, and pavements were alive with families strolling in cool shadows cast by a low sun behind the city centre's ancient buildings.

'Yes?'

It was Cabo Leo Medina, a recent recruit to the Policia Nacional's plain-clothes division.

7

'Sorry to disturb you, Sir.'

'What is it, Leo?'

'A Major Incident, Sir. In Los Mineros.'

'Look. I'm off duty. There must be someone else.'

His annoyance was nothing to do with missing a few days leave. Murder rarely had the decency to keep office hours, but an investigation in the village where he was born was the last thing he needed.

'The Comandante specifically asked for you, Sir.'

'Oh, really?' He struggled to stifle his sarcasm, but was resigned to this unwelcome addition to his caseload. He lit another cigarette and said, 'Tell me.'

'There are four corpses...'

'Four?'

'Yeah. Three men have been shot and it looks like the gunman committed suicide.'

'Where are you?'

'At the crime scene. A building site in the campo behind the village.'

'You've shut everything down?'

'Yeah, and I've contacted Cientifica. The white suits are on their way, but I'm finding it difficult to locate the duty pathologist.'

'Try the bar or the brothel.' He turned his back on the busy square. 'OK. Secure the area until I get there. Who reported the bodies?'

'Klaus Dagmar, an ex-pat. He alerted Guardia Civil and they contacted us.'

'What time?'

'Sir?'

'What time did Dagmar phone in?'

'About four thirty.'

'Did he say what he was doing there?'

'His dog died yesterday. He used to walk her across the campo, same time everyday. You know what these ex-pats are like, treat animals like one of the family.'

Fernández shook his head, dragged on his cigarette and exhaled forcefully. 'OK. Hold him. Assume he's a suspect and don't prime him by asking questions.'

He ended the call and walked back into the bar just as the teams were leaving the field for halftime. He downed his brandy and checked the handgun stowed beneath his crumpled linen jacket.

His Seat was parked three blocks away. The lack of convenient parking was one of the few disadvantages of buying an apartment in Almeria's old quarter. He chose to live in the city because of its anonymity, its relative sophistication, and the edge he felt each time he looked at the anti-fascist graffiti scribbled on walls. His favourite proclaimed a simple message: *'Policia! No!'*

He drove north, towards Los Mineros.

The road wound across the coastal plain before it sliced through a valley and rose steeply into the hills near the village. He passed his mother's cortijo - the smallholding she'd managed single-handedly since his father's death - and resolved to try to stop by and see her later.

Los Mineros had retained much of its natural beauty. Crescent-shaped, it nestled on the lower slopes of a hill and was protected from prevailing winds. It enjoyed stunning views north to the peaks of the Sierra Nevada and south across the vast plains that swept towards the golden beaches of the Mediterranean. It had garnered a reputation as a picture-postcard village and the villagers took pride in their humble homes with their white walls and terracotta roofs, and bougainvillea clambering from the narrow streets. Even the church with its crumbling façade attracted a small congregation to Sunday services.

As he approached the outskirts of the village, he saw a carpenter working on a pergola at the entrance to one of a rash of villas that pockmarked the hillsides.

9

He lost concentration, rounded a bend and found he was heading straight for a stream of goats crossing the empty road. He slammed on his brakes, swerved and careered into a shallow ditch. 'Shit!' he reversed and sat back, and watched the herd amble past, unhurried, despite the attention of two mangy dogs scurrying back and forth, snapping at their hind legs.

He drummed on the steering wheel, knowing that there was nothing on God's earth that would hasten this almost biblical of scenes.

He imagined the goatherd, dressed in a blue gandoura, carrying his staff, his feet shod in sandals, but Pepe appeared, similarly unhurried, wearing a grubby hat, stout working boots, brown corduroy trousers, and a long sleeved shirt buttoned to the neck. He carried a small bamboo cane and used it to prod the last of the goats as they scurried across the road.

Fernández forced a smile.

As a child, he'd listened with a mixture of fascination and revulsion to the story of how 'simple' Pepe had had his tongue cut out by Fascist soldiers, and he'd often wondered what, if anything, went through the goatherd's mind as he tended his flock in the hills around the village.

Pepe stood his ground in the middle of the road for a moment, his eyes boring through the Seat's windscreen. He began to gesticulate wildly, stabbing his cane at the road leading up to the village and at the car.

Fernández shrugged, lent out of the car window and shouted, 'For God's sake, Pepe, I'm in a hurry.'

Again, Pepe pointed at him, his eyes wide, as though desperate to be heard but having no way of making clear what he had to tell. And, then, just as suddenly, he appeared to give up, shook his fist and clambered over the bank to catch up with his goats.

Fernández sat, holding the steering wheel, irritated by the delay. 'Poor bastard,' he muttered, then drove into the village and parked on a grass verge near the football pitch.

He clambered out and checked the damage to his car. One of the headlights would need replacing but it would have to wait. The first few hours after a homicide were crucial and he was impatient to get started. The village was settling into the rhythm of the evening and the sun had slipped behind the hills. It was only a matter of time before word would get round. He climbed an old stonewall and made his way across the campo towards the construction site.

Leo Medina was leaning against the doorframe of the new-build, dressed in a leather jacket, a dark polo shirt and beige chinos. When he saw the Inspector, he stooped to ease his way through the doorframe and walked down the gravel path to meet him.

Born in Los Mineros, Medina had married Roz, a local girl. They'd bought a dilapidated, two-storey house and spent a couple of years restoring it before he joined the police force. Despite his lopsided grin, Leo Medina cut an imposing figure beneath short, military style hair. At six-four, he towered over most and had a reputation for a fiery temper, storing his passion, powder-keg-dry, just below the surface of a very thin skin. Early signs suggested he would make a good detective if he curbed his tongue and channelled his aggression.

'Very quiet, Leo?' Fernández said. 'No press, no locals?'

'Tried to keep it quiet, Sir. But the Guardia decided to escort Dagmar back home.'

'Did they? I thought I made it clear that I wanted him kept away from the village.'

'They thought it best.'

'Oh, really?' He pulled a pack of cigarettes from his jacket. This was Leo Medina's first big case and having a senior officer jump down his throat could make him defensive and kill any initiative.

'I think I know when it happened,' Medina said.

'The shooting?'

'Yes, sir. As I see it, several shots must have been fired. I was at home, with both my boys and Roz. We'd just sat down for lunch when several rockets exploded above us.'

'Rockets?'

'Fireworks.'

'What time?'

'Must have been about two. There was a break in the storm. Felipe must have...'

'Felipe Romero?'

'Yes. Thing is sir, the fiesta's not until tomorrow.'

'I thought he fired rockets on the day of the fiesta? Not the day before. So, why today?'

'God knows.'

'It's our job to know, Leo. We'll chase Felipe later, and see what he has to say for himself.' He took a drag, wincing when the smoke stung his eyes. 'OK. Contact the Guardia. Tell them to bring Dagmar here. They're to keep everyone else away. Understand?'

Whilst he waited for Leo Medina to make the call, Fernández surveyed the carnage.

He recognised the dead men, knew their names and understood exactly why the Comandante had assigned him to the case. There were three from the same family: the grandfather, Alberto, his son, Bartolomé, and his grandson Matias.

'Two weapons were used.' Medina stood beside him. 'Both ancient. The rifle's a Mauser 98, the handgun's a Walther P38.'

'Really?'

Medina grinned.

'As kids, we played war games and collected pictures of old guns. For me, it turned into a bit of a hobby. That and bullfighting.' He hesitated. 'It looks like Gonzales used the handgun on himself. Could be history between the two families.'

'Possibly.'

Fernández knew that Juan Gonzales was detested for the part he played in Franco's purges after Spain's Civil War, but this early in the investigation he was reluctant to drag up the past. He looked over at the SOCOs in their white suits and asked. 'Is this all Cientifica could manage?'

'Yes, sir. Waiting for your orders, sir. I thought you'd want to examine the area yourself before they started.'

'Did you contact the pathologist?'

'They're sending a replacement. Seems he ignored his doctor's advice to lose weight, stop smoking and lay off the hard liquor. He had a heart attack. The funeral's scheduled for Saturday.'

'Along with four others.' Fernández shook his head and dragged smoke deep into his lungs. 'What a fucking mess.'

'And one you'll want cleaned up, Inspector.'

A woman's voice cut through the sultry air. She was tall and casually dressed in jeans and a white blouse, her long auburn hair tied tightly into a ponytail. She placed a black case on the ground and held out her hand. 'Doctor Julieta Santiago, duty pathologist.'

She pulled the cigarette from his mouth. 'Don't want our boys at the lab adding you to the list of suspects, do we?' She smiled. 'Shall we suit up?'

He followed her over to the SOCOs who were quick to extinguish their cigarettes. He removed his jacket, adjusted his holster and pulled on a white forensic suit, finding the ritual as irritating as ever.

Santiago passed him a facemask, but he didn't put it on immediately. She stepped through the entrance to the new-build and surveyed the bloodbath.

She moved silently, as if she was making an initial assessment, and stopped at each body before joining him at the door. 'So, what do you think?' she asked.

'Medina reckons it happened earlier this afternoon. Unfinished business between two old men.'

'And you?'

'It's possible, but it's never that simple, is it?' He turned his back and concentrated on the four bodies strewn across the floor. 'The Comandante will want this wrapped up quickly. Kids will be on holiday in a few weeks and the whole area will be flooded with tourists. The last thing he'll want is this splashed over the front pages.'

'Unfortunately, the timing couldn't be worse,' she said. 'It wasn't that long ago that the right-wing were celebrating the seventieth anniversary of the end of the war and the start of Franco's dictatorship. Trust me, the press will be all over it. We'd better make a start before we lose the light.'

'Sir?' Medina said. 'Klaus Dagmar? The ex-pat who found them? He's here.'

'Suit him up and bring him in,' Santiago said.

Medina glanced at Fernández who raised an eyebrow, shrugged and nodded.

'Is there a problem?' Santiago asked.

'My team run everything past me,' Fernández said. 'They would have assumed this was my investigation and my crime scene.'

'Oh, I see.' She hesitated. She didn't know him but in her experience some Spanish men didn't relate easily to assertive women - *women with balls,* as her mama would say. She knew she came over as tough and resilient - and that that didn't endear her to everyone - but the truth was that she'd been as nervous as always as she'd driven from the hospital in Almeria. 'I'll have to make sure there are no misunderstandings in future, won't I?' she said. 'Now, if you don't mind, we have work to do.' She walked to where Matias had fallen and began examining his wounds. She then spent several minutes with the body of his father, Bartolomé, before checking his grandfather, Alberto.

Fernández took time to untangle the strapping of his facemask, then pulled a pack of cigarettes out, put one between his lips, and looked up in time to see one of the SOCOs wag a finger at him. He shook his head and replaced the cigarette, pulled on his mask and crossed to where Doctor Santiago was standing over the corpse of Juan Gonzales.

She sidestepped blood coagulating in a large pool and knelt down, lifted Gonzales's head and brushed flies away. She examined the bullet's exit wound and the star-shaped laceration on his right temple. 'This is where the bullet entered,' she said.

Klaus Dagmar was brought into the room. Santiago stood up. 'You found them like this?'

'Yes, exactly as you see them,' Dagmar said. 'I knew it would be wrong to touch anything.'

'And you were sure they were dead?'

'Yes.'

'You didn't bother to check?'

'Well, it was pretty obvious they weren't going to get up,' Dagmar said. 'I'm sorry, it was such a shock.'

Santiago walked over to him.

'I know how distressing this must be but, if this goes to court, any contaminated evidence would destroy the prosecution case. If you've compromised the scene in any way it might mean the difference between catching whoever is responsible and...'

'But I heard that young detective say that the old man committed suicide.'

'That's precisely my point.' She took a couple of moments to compose herself. 'I'm sorry,' she said, 'but we won't know exactly what happened here if you don't tell us the truth.'

Dagmar rocked from one foot to the other.

'I did move him.' He pointed at Bartolomé. 'I found him curled up, on his side.'

'That's it?'

'I rolled him on his back. I wanted to make sure he was dead. I mean...'

'We know what you mean,' Fernández said, and removed his mask. 'I'm sorry to hear about your dog.'

'Old age. Had her put down.'

'You'll have to stay away from here. Understand?' He smiled. 'Oh, and keep your mouth shut. We'll need time to inform the next of kin. I'd really hate them to hear it from anyone else.'

Before he handed Dagmar over, he took Medina to one side. 'Detail a SOCO to process him...fingerprints, gunshot residue. Tomorrow, run a background check. It's unlikely, but we can't dismiss the possibility that he killed all four men.' He watched as Medina spoke to one of the forensic scientists and they escorted Dagmar to a large tent that served as a field laboratory.

He turned to Doctor Santiago. 'I'll need a couple of SOCOs to check Gonzales's home.'

'Fine, as long as you leave me enough to do my job.' She glanced at the men from Científica. 'I'll be here for most of the night. I'll need a generator, lights, and a full forensic team. We'll carry out a thorough search of the area tomorrow morning.'

She looked around the crime scene. 'So, you want to tell me what you think happened here?'

He pulled on his mask, walked to the other side of the room and knelt between the corpses of Matias and Bartolomé. He noticed the discarded orange peel, empty tins of tuna, the remains of a sandwich, and an empty water bottle. He looked across at Santiago. Insecurity wasn't a familiar sensation but she'd unsettled him and, as he spoke, he was uncharacteristically hesitant.

'Early days, obviously,' he began, 'but I'd say they'd had lunch and settled down for the siesta. If we assume that Juan Gonzales shot Matias and Bartolomé with the Mauser and used the P38 to kill Alberto…'

'It looks like he used the handgun on Bartolomé.'

He returned to the body of Bartolomé and examined wounds to his throat and forehead. 'But why shoot him twice?'

'Presumably, because he wasn't dead.'

He heard one of the SOCOs snigger. He glanced round and the man melted into the brickwork.

Santiago replaced her mask and joined him.

She took the dead man's head, eased it off the floor, and turned it gently. There, she found a small, gaping crater with a distorted rim encrusted with subcutaneous tissue, splinters of bone and hair matted with drying blood. 'There are two exit wounds here,' she said. 'The first shot in the throat shattered the cervical vertebrae and the spinal chord. Any higher and he would have died instantly. But he probably survived until the second shot entered his forehead.'

She moved to Juan Gonzales, spent time examining the handgun that lay just out of reach of the old man's right hand, and then concentrated on where the bullet had entered.

'This is a contact-range gunshot wound.' She looked at Fernández. 'He could have taken his own life. We'll

17

collect fingerprints from the rifle and handgun and get ballistics to check striations on any bullets we recover, as well as firing pin indentations on spent shells. It'll be important to match bullets to the guns - we don't want to stand up in court to find that these weren't the weapons used, do we?'

'Gunshot residue? Ferrozine?' he said, impressed by her meticulous approach.

'Yes. Good idea,' she said, and he felt sure she was looking at him like a schoolteacher...pleased that the pigheaded boy at the back of the class had volunteered something. He was beginning to warm to her.

'We'll take swabs from each victim's hands. It'll also be worth running ferrozine tests to check for traces of metal absorbed into the skin.'

She stood up and removed her mask, discarding it into her bag and taking a fresh one. 'That's probably it, for now. Rigor mortis is advanced enough to suggest that Cabo Medina could be right. It happened sometime during siesta. I'll know more once I get the bodies back to the morgue in Almeria.'

'I'll let you get on, but I'll need a video record of the scene and as many photographs as possible.'

He stepped outside the shell of the building and removed his forensic suit.

'I hope your department's got deep pockets,' she said. 'Forensics, ballistics, fingerprints, video, and DNA aren't cheap and the recession's meant money's harder to come by.'

He shrugged. 'Balancing the books has never been my priority. You'll let me know as soon as you have anything?'

'Drop by the morgue tomorrow, late morning. I'll bring you up to date.' She paused. 'Anything else?'

'No, no thanks,' he said.

They'd be working together over several weeks and he wasn't sure how she felt about that but, he had to admit, she was refreshingly different from other medics he'd worked with. He lit a cigarette, drawing deeply, exhaling forcefully.

'Inspector?'

'Yes, I know, it a crime scene, but I need this before I carry out my favourite part of the job - breaking the news to three women who are waiting for their men folk to come home.'

Ana-Maria smiled as she sauntered down the narrow alleyway where she'd played as a child. A carbon copy of her mother at the same age, Ana-Maria was tall, with full breasts accentuated by a dress that hugged her waist and billowed over her hips. Her hair was dark and fell below her shoulders and framed her sun-kissed face and hazel eyes.

The whitewashed walls of the humble houses seemed familiar and yet far removed from the life she and Paul had created together. And with the taste of coffee and chocolate cake lingering in her mouth, she knew that their life was light years from the hand-to-mouth existence of the women she'd spent the afternoon with.

Ahead, she saw her father Enrique. She stopped and waited. He'd been working in the fields and sat down wearily outside the family home, removed his hat and boots, and relit the stub of a cigarette. He was short and stocky, his powerful arms and broad chest testimony to a lifetime's toil on the iron-hard land he'd inherited.

She hid from him like a child, watching him draw a last gasp from his cigarette before snubbing the fag end between his fingers, hauling himself to his feet and shouldering his way past the heavy front door.

She made her way down, placed a hand on the metal latch and paused, savouring a few moments of peace, and then pushed her way in. She stumbled over the granite sill set in place over two centuries ago, cursed as she removed her high heels, and then smiled when she heard her mother, Inocenta, reproach her younger sister.

'Sofia, wait for Ana-Maria.'

'But I'm hungry.'

'Let her be, woman,' she heard her father say. 'She's a child. Let her eat like one and give us all some peace.'

Ana-Maria walked into the kitchen where the table had been laid for supper. 'Sorry I'm late.'

Sofia ran towards her and she lifted her high in the air, making her squeal. At six years old, Sofia Castaño was slight and smaller than girls of her age, and her unruly, dark hair fell across her face.

'It's a fiesta, isn't it?' Sofia said. 'Did you hear Felipe's rockets?'

'How could I *not* hear them?' Enrique grumbled. 'He ought to be lynched, disturbing the siesta like that.'

Ana-Maria glanced at her mother and rolled her eyes. 'Well, something smells good.'

'Chicken and chorizo, one of your favourites. Come on, let's eat.'

They sat around the roughly hewn wooden table and, after Enrique had filled his plate, Inocenta spooned out the rest of the casserole.

After a few moments Sofia asked, 'Will you take me to the fiesta?'

'It's tomorrow,' Ana-Maria said gently. 'The shops will be closed and everyone will go to the square late in the evening to celebrate the summer solstice - the longest day of the year.'

'But you'll be here, won't you?'

20

'Of course. I'll stay the night, if mama and papa don't mind.' She turned to her mother. 'I'm meeting Paul in Almeria. I'll drive the Mercedes back, but he'll probably stay at the apartment.' She sighed and shrugged, turned to her mother and said. 'He's tendering for Almeria's regeneration project. Keep your fingers crossed. Things are getting desperate. This damn recession's driving everyone out of business.'

'What does *damn* mean?' Sofia said.

'It means we'll have to be very careful with our money, but if we're lucky we'll be able to buy a car for mama and papa and a new dress for you.' She took a piece of bread, dipped it in olive oil and offered it to Sofia, catching her big brown eyes, wide with expectation and trust.

Sofia looked at her mother and pushed the bread wilfully into her mouth. Ana-Maria knew Inocenta had learned to pick her battles, and guessed that this was one time she'd save her energy for later. She rubbed Sofia's back and smiled when Inocenta asked, 'Did they enjoy the cake?'

'Of course. We all had coffee and a slice, except Juanita. She had two and wanted a copy of the recipe. Chocolate cake never fails, does it?'

Both women laughed before Inocenta said, 'Thanks for going in my place.'

'It was nothing. They're good people.'

'You were a long time.'

'We had lunch and a glass of wine. Madalena loves to gossip. She and Matias are trying to start a family.'

'But that's wonderful. Bartolomé will be thrilled. His first grandchild. And Alberto will be a great-grandfather. Imagine the fuss they'll make of it.'

'He's doing well, isn't he, Alberto? There can't be too many men his age still working.'

'I'm not sure he contributes much, unless it's to give unwanted advice.'

Mother and daughter laughed again, then Ana-Maria turned to Sofia and said, 'Laura will be here for the fiesta.'

'When are they getting married?'

'Sofia.' Ana-Maria shook her head playfully. 'José and Laura have only been going together for a few months. We must give them time. Maybe, one day, your brother will ask her to marry him.'

'And I'll be a bridesmaid?'

Enrique put his fork down and sighed heavily. He spoke gently. 'That woman has the devil in her.'

'Papa,' Ana-Maria protested. 'Laura is one of my closest friends and could be your daughter-in-law soon.'

'She has an eye for your man.'

'Paul? Nonsense.'

'I've seen the way she looks at him.'

There was a long silence and Inocenta began to clear the table, carrying the dirty dishes to the sink. Ana-Maria went to help her.

'What's so important that you've got to be in Almeria this evening?' Inocenta whispered, slipping an apron round her waist.

'I've got another check-up at the hospital.'

'I heard that,' Enrique said. 'The hospital? Are you sick, woman?'

Ana-Marie smiled and looked at her mother.

'You'd better tell him,' Inocenta said. 'He'll worry me to death if you don't.'

'Papa...' She went over to the table and knelt down beside him. 'God willing, you'll be a grandfather, come November.' She blushed as she did when he challenged her as a teenager.

'About time,' he said.

He got up, walked into the front room and slumped onto the soft cushions of the sofa, his legs dangling over the end. He closed his eyes and Ana-Maria saw a thin smile flicker at the corner of his mouth as he mumbled, 'Didn't think he had it in him.'

She joined Inocenta at the sink and took a tea towel to dry the dishes.

Sofia trailed behind. 'I was afraid when I heard the rockets. Bang! Bang!'

Ana-Maria took her hand, walked her to the bedroom and lay with her, comforting her, until, just before sleep overtook her, Sofia muttered, 'I saw Gloria playing hide-and-seek with that old man.'

'Gloria?'

'You know,' Sofia said, and looked, as if imploring her to understand. '*Gloria.*'

Ana-Maria shook her head and pursed her lips, trying to recall Sofia's friends, but was unable to remember anyone called Gloria. She smiled, stroked hair from Sofia's eyes and whispered gently, 'Hush, nena. Go to sleep.'

2

Early, before the sun had time to chase away the light summer dew, Fernández returned to where the bodies had been found and tried to reconstruct the killings. He walked the route Juan Gonzales would have taken and wondered if anyone had seen the old man from any of the houses that overlooked the campo.

He slipped under the crime scene tape, stepped inside the shell of the new-build, glanced up through the void where the roof would be and sat on a pile of cement bags covered in polythene.

Subject to confirmation from Doctor Santiago, he felt confident that they'd established the modus operandi. The weapons used had been dusted, bagged, and handed over to ballistics and there seemed little doubt that Juan Gonzales had killed all three men.

What nagged at him was motive. Why? Why had Juan Gonzales shot three men and turned the gun on himself?

He'd grown up without ever being aware of the *pact of silence* that denied successive generations access to the truth about the appalling atrocities of the Civil War and Franco's reign. The media had exercised a level of self-restraint that amounted to suppression and schools turned their backs on the past, modifying the curriculum so most people still had no idea what really happened.

The Comandante had given him until the end of the month. 'Not a difficult one to solve, Inspector, so don't waste time and resources.'

It looked straightforward, he had to agree, but he mistrusted anything that appeared to be too easy.

He'd already decided to set up an Incident Room in the Town Hall and arrange for administrative backup - Valencia Ramoz, top of his list.

Without local refrigeration facilities, the bodies had been taken to the hospital in Almeria, and the Coroner had been warned that, after the autopsies, he'd have four bodies to sign over for cremation.

As the church clock struck nine forty-five, he eased himself from the stack of cement bags and strolled across the campo. Deep into the village, he came upon a crowd, thirsty for information, outside houses that had been home to the men slaughtered less than twenty-four hours before. He took a final drag, stubbed out his cigarette, knocked and eased open the front door to the first house.

Consuela Ramos sat on the large sofa that dominated the cramped sitting room. The family's matriarch was flanked by daughter-in-law, Juanita, and her grandson's wife, Madelena – each of them, widows before their time. They stared blankly at the fireplace and toyed absentmindedly with rosary beads. Fernández sat in the only other chair and waited a few moments, giving the women time to acknowledge his return. When he spoke, he did so gently, calmly, sentences measured and punctuated by pauses that hung in the air. 'I'm deeply sorry for your loss.'

The women remained impassive.

'Your bereavement has touched us all.'

There was little more than a flicker from the youngest, Madalena, as her fingers hesitated over the rosary beads.

'I cannot imagine what you're going through.'

Consuela Ramos lifted her head, looking at him through small, moist eyes. 'They were good men,' she said, her voice cracked and fragile.

'Men respected by everyone in the village,' he added.

'The man who..?' Juanita moved her hand across to hold her mother-in-law's. 'He is dead?'

'Yes.'

25

'Pity. Fascist bastard. They should have killed him years ago when he came back to the village. He only had one thing on his mind...' She fell silent.

'To avenge the murder of his parents?'

'Obvious, isn't it?'

'And you think Alberto had something to do with their death?'

Consuela showed no emotion as she said, 'If my husband did kill them, he would have had good reason. But, if he did, he's kept it from me all these years.'

'May I attend the funerals?'

All three women began to rock gently, as if realising their nightmare wasn't over - coffins paraded through the streets on Saturday, the service and the cremation, the ashes placed in the cemetery at the entrance to the village.

'Why not?' Juanita said, sadness sweeping across her face. 'Most of the village will be there.'

'Inspector,' Consuela said, quietly, 'why are you here?'

'I came to offer...'

'Yes, yes. We know that. You're a police officer and you did your duty last night when you came to...' she appeared to struggle to find the words, 'when you came to tell us what had happened. I presume you're back in your official capacity?'

'Yes.'

'Then there are things you're still investigating?'

'There are questions that need answers, to understand why this happened. Your men deserve that.'

Silence filled the room. Hushed voices from outside filtered through the window. Somewhere a donkey brayed and the church clock struck ten.

Tears trickled down Madalena's face.

'They'd be stopping for breakfast now,' she said. 'It would have been my turn to take lunch to them today.' She turned to Juanita. 'It was your turn at yesterday, wasn't it? But you didn't go, did you? None of us did. If we had…' She sobbed uncontrollably and collapsed into Consuela's frail arms. Juanita stood up and, gently, pulled Madalena from the old woman's lap and led her upstairs.

Consuela was alone, her small frame swallowed by the sofa and Fernández eased himself from the fireside chair and sat next to her. She looked up and laid her hand gently alongside his face, tracing a small scar high on his cheek.

'I remember the day you were born, Antonio. Your papa was so proud. He was drunk for a week.' She tried to laugh, but didn't seem able to summon the strength. 'And then he was taken from you, and your mama has been without him all these years.' Her hand caressed his cheek. 'We have missed you, Antonio. How long has it been?'

'Ten years since I moved out of the village.'

His words slipped through the open window and they sat in silence until Consuela said, 'You'll have to watch your back, you and anyone who helps you.' She wiped away a tear. 'There are those who will try to stop you. The village has grown silent over the years, but silence only masks the legacy of the Civil War and Franco's barbarity. We may have to accept my husband, my son and my grandson are the latest casualties.'

Her hand dropped, as though her arm could no longer support the weight of her despondency. 'You could be next,' she said.

He took her hands and in them he saw his mother's long, slender fingers and deeply veined skin - delicate and fragile like ancient parchment upon which a lifetime had been recorded.

He spoke gently. 'I hear you, Consuela, and I will be careful. But, for now, you must tell me what happened yesterday...everything, no matter how insignificant.'

He realised she might need prompting.

'It was Juanita's turn to take them their lunch. Is that something you did every day?'

'Most days.'

'So what kept her away yesterday?'

Consuela sighed. 'Coffee and chocolate cake.'

'A cup of coffee...I'm sorry, I don't understand.'

She wiped her eyes. 'Ana-Maria brought a cake, fresh from Inocenta's oven. We had coffee, Ana-Maria stayed for lunch, and then she and Madalena spent a couple of hours together.' She looked at him and her hand returned to his cheek. 'You know she's married, don't you?'

'Yes, I'd heard.'

'She broke your heart, didn't she? Ten years ago?'

Fernández left Consuela and drove back to Almeria. The despair of the widows punctuated vivid impressions of his time with Ana-Maria. It was rare, he realised, for a day to pass without her face and her smile intruding.

He went to the morgue, but was redirected to a local square where Doctor Julieta Santiago was taking her first break for several hours. The market was in full swing and, as bargain-hunting crowds streamed past, he saw her sitting at a table outside a bar. He didn't know if she lived locally, but hadn't seen her before they'd met at the crime scene. He smiled, and felt sure that if he'd seen her, he would have remembered.

He walked across the square towards her, but saw an elderly woman with a young girl in-tow.

28

He watched as the child jumped onto Santiago's lap and threw her arms around her neck.

They embraced tenderly.

He went inside the bar and ordered a black coffee.

'I'll pay their bill,' he said.

The bartender smiled. 'She's very beautiful, no?'

'A professional colleague.'

'Yeah, right.'

Fernández watched as Santiago listened to the child's chatter and smiled when she got down and performed a clumsy pirouette.

It didn't tax his deductive skills to conclude that they were mother and daughter. They had the same auburn hair, generous mouth, and long legs.

The bartender had been right: Julieta Santiago was a beauty.

'She local?' he asked.

'Seen her around here for a couple of months. Some sort of medic, judging by the white coat.' The bartender took Soberano off the shelf and offered him a slug.

He declined the brandy, took his coffee outside, and sat at a table as far away from the crowds as possible. He watched as Santiago pulled the young girl onto her lap and cuddled her.

Moments later, she looked up and saw him. She said something to the elderly woman, handed over the young girl and they left, swallowed by the throng of the market.

She walked over to join him.

'Your daughter?' he asked.

'Yes. That's my Holly.'

'She wants to be a dancer?'

'Like her mother: trying to learn flamenco.'

'Flamenco?'

'Why don't you come and watch us? There's a tablao tomorrow evening…eight o'clock at El Morato. I'm dancing with your friend, Ana-Maria.'

He lit a cigarette and scuffed his feet on the ground. Moments before, he'd been watching her from the haven of the bar, but now he felt exposed, awkward, like a lover who'd been found out in a lie. It was as if he'd been asked, 'What are you staring at?' and, in trying to dismiss the image of Ana-Maria from his mind, he'd replied, 'Nothing'. He couldn't deny he found Santiago attractive, but began to wonder how he would feel watching her dance alongside Ana-Maria.

'Well,' Santiago said, as if puzzled by his reticence, 'the invitation's there. Come if you want to.'

'Yes. Thanks. It'll depend on how much progress I make.'

She shrugged and sipped her coffee. 'So, how much progress have you made?'

'I went to see the widows this morning. Three women who'd woken up yesterday without a care in the world and spent the day gossiping over homemade chocolate cake, only to find themselves condemned to sleep in empty beds.' He rubbed his eyes, dragged hands down his face and said, 'What time did you get away?'

'I had the bodies removed at about one this morning and came back here, to the lab.'

'You look tired.'

'You don't look much better yourself.' She leaned forward. 'But, you'll be interested to know that you were right to reserve judgement at the crime scene.' She stood up. 'Come on, I've got something to show you.'

She walked briskly and stopped outside large double doors, punched an entry code into a security pad and pushed her way in.

She ignored the lift and walked down three flights of stairs into the pre-op room, where they scrubbed up and dressed in blue protective suits.

The lab was an acre of stainless steel, lined with cupboards, and sinks, and work surfaces, and trays of surgical instruments. In the centre of the room were two, height-adjustable operating tables.

A mortuary technician removed two corpses from a refrigerator and then left them to it.

'I haven't completed the autopsies,' Santiago said, as she pulled back the sheet covering Bartolomé Ramos, 'but thought you'd be interested in the work we've been doing over night.'

She slipped on latex gloves, adjusted her facemask and used a probe to trace a tour of Bartolomé's injuries. 'The first bullet was fired from the rifle at a distance of about three meters. It smashed through the cervical vertebrae and exited here, at the back of the neck. The second bullet was fired from the handgun, within a meter. It entered the forehead and exited here, high on the back of the head.'

'So, he must have survived the first bullet?'

'Looks like it.' She covered Bartolomé, and then uncovered Juan Gonzales. 'I opened him up and found signs of bleeding - a malignant brain tumour. You'll need to check his medical history with his doctor.' She turned the head and pointed at the star-shaped laceration on his right temple. 'This is a close-contact entry wound. And, this,' she pointed at a circular imprint, 'is caused by super-heated gases burning an impression of the muzzle into his temple when the handgun was fired.'

'Which would indicate that Juan Gonzales did commit suicide?'

'I doubt it. There are two complications.' She pulled the sheet further down and took Gonzales's right hand. 'When a gun has been fired, we use ferrozine to detect traces of metal absorbed into the skin. When a revolver is used in a suicide, it's quite common for ferrozine to reveal metal deposits on the thumb of the hand holding the weapon. It's assumed that those who commit suicide hesitate, priming their weapon several times before pulling the trigger.' She illustrated, using her thumb. 'The handgun was found by Gonzales's right hand, but there were no deposits on his right thumb.'

'So, he didn't hesitate. Just put the gun to his head and pulled the trigger?'

'Yes, that's what I assumed, but the tests revealed significant traces of metal on his left hand.'

'He held the handgun in his left hand?'

'Evidence points that way, yes. At least when he shot Alberto and Bartolomé.'

'Then why switch the gun to his right hand to commit suicide?'

'I'm not sure but, if someone was going to commit suicide, do you think they'd trust their non-dominant hand?' She didn't wait for an answer. 'That's not all…' She held gun-shaped fingers to her temple and asked, 'If I put a gun to my head and pull the trigger, where would you expect the exit wound to be?'

He stood, momentarily unsettled by the mock suicide, and then touched her head on the opposite side.

'Yes. Parallel, or maybe slightly higher.' She rolled Gonzales's head, exposing an exit wound just below the cheekbone on the left side of his face. 'This exit wound is much lower than we'd expect. The bullet would not have followed that trajectory if he'd shot himself.'

'So where does that leave us?'

'You're the detective. But, it's not difficult, is it?'

He stalled as the only option surfaced. 'Someone else was there?' he said. 'Someone who shot him and tried to make it look like suicide?'

'It's a possibility.'

*

Usually, a fiesta wouldn't spark into life much before eleven in the evening. Any earlier and villagers might gather, have a drink and wait for the music to begin. But this evening few had an appetite for fiesta. Four men were dead. They'd known the victims and the man who'd slaughtered them, and understood the tensions that lay beneath the gentle facade of the village.

This evening, it would take more than a few glasses of beer to lift spirits.

Soon after ten, several children dragged their parents to the square outside the Town Hall, where they spent a few euros at sideshows and watched itinerant jugglers and a fire-eater.

Most women sat on white plastic chairs. Widows wore black and younger women, some loaded with the next generation, supped wine.

Men stood at the makeshift bar and drank beer.

Soon after mid-night, the band had completed sound checks and were ready, but the villagers sat silently as Antonio Fernández, Leo Medina, and officers from Guardia Civil, Policia Local and Policia Nacional moved among them. They were there in the hope that someone would come forward with information.

Sofia Castaño skipped along between Ana-Maria and Laura. She was dwarfed by their striking height. She was proud of her big sister and her big sister's best friend. Three years ago, Ana-Maria had married a man from England and he had promised to buy Sofia a new dress. Sofia longed for a new dress because, in a new dress, she'd be the most beautiful bridesmaid at her brother's wedding to Laura. She loved Laura. Laura made her laugh until her tummy hurt and they shared secrets, secrets Sofia had promised to keep, but was bursting to tell.

As they walked across the square, Ana-Maria smiled and nodded at friends she'd known all her life. Friends she'd left behind when she went to live in the villa overlooking the beach. Friends who might be pleased for her or resented her good fortune, she didn't know which and was past caring.

When Laura went to buy a couple of glasses of wine, Ana-Maria stopped to talk to a friend who'd been in the same class at school. She'd just given birth to her second child and, Ana-Maria thought, she seemed contentedly middle-aged.

Ana-Maria looked at Sofia, smiled, and then glanced across at Laura standing at the bar. She was sharing a joke with one of the men. As Ana-Maria watched her friend, her father's words came back to haunt her...'*She has an eye for your man.*'

Sofia slipped away and went over to a group of men who'd gathered at the bar. She stood and listened to them and stared at their faces. They seemed so full of anger and pain. The men were arguing, but their words were not accompanied by the smiles of friends and Sofia sensed they were worried and she became uncertain, frightened.

One of the police officers came to over the bar, a giant, taller than anyone else, and she heard him ask them several questions before he struck the counter with his fist and shouted, 'There must be someone in the village who saw the old man, for God's sake!' The giant glowered at the men. One by one, they turned their backs on him and returned to their beer.

The giant shook his head, slapped the bar again, and made his way down a steep, narrow alleyway that led to the small square where the doctor held his surgery each day.

Sofia saw him take a packet of cigarettes from a pocket and light up. She chased after him, unaware of the alarm she'd caused when Ana-Maria turned to find her missing.

'Don't worry,' Laura said, pressing Ana-Maria's forearm. 'She's down by the old olive press, talking to Leo Medina. I'll fetch her.'

Laura took her time, enjoying the few moments of peace and, when she thought of how she'd spent her afternoon, a broad smile broke across her face. Sex, she realised, always made her happy. As she approached, she noticed Leo Medina glance at her and guessed he'd be lusting after her, as he always had - her legs and her come-to-bed blue eyes, her golden hair - unusual enough in this part of Spain to have made her even more striking, and even more irresistible.

'You with Elliot?' she said.

'Elliot?' Medina looked puzzled.

'We watched the movie together. Remember? Elliot Ness, the FBI guy who tracked down Al Capone? Your Inspector Fernández has that scar on his cheek…'

Medina shook his head, and she assumed his mind had raced back to their youth when they'd been close and had taken those first, awkward steps into an adult world they weren't destined to share. She remembered a lot of things they'd done together, but wasn't surprised he couldn't remember the movie - those days of sexual awakening made watching movies no more memorable than washing dishes.

Sofia tugged at Medina's sleeve. 'I saw an old man. He was with Gloria. They were playing hide-and-seek.'

'Ignore her, Leo.' Laura smiled. 'She's got such a vivid imagination.'

'How are you?' he asked.

She flashed her engagement ring.

'So, it's true?'

'This time it's for real.' She took Sofia's hand. 'It'll be the biggest wedding this village has seen for years.'

'And I'm going to have a new dress,' Sofia said.

Both adults laughed.

'Look, I'd better get back,' Laura said. 'It was nice seeing you again.'

'Yes,' he said. 'Congratulations, by the way.'

'Thank you.'

She lent forward, kissed him on the cheek and led Sofia back up the hill. Just before the square, her mobile trilled at the arrival of a text. She stopped, pulled the phone from her belt, and opened the message. 'Sofia,' she said, 'it's a message from your brother.' She read it and punched in a reply.

'I saw an old man.' Sofia folded her arms. 'I saw an old man, and Gloria was playing hide-and-seek with him. But no-one wants to listen to me.'

Laura stowed her mobile phone and knelt down.

'Gloria?'

'Yes. You know. *Gloria.*'

'Where did you see them, nena?'

'In the campo, when Felipe fired his rockets. I was on the terrace. I saw them.'

'When was this?'

'Yesterday.'

'You're sure it was Gloria?'

'Yes!' Sofia stamped on the cobblestones.

'And the old man? Was it Señor Gonzales?'

'Yes. He was carrying a carpet under his arm. I think they were going to sit on it when they had their lunch. Why doesn't anyone believe me?'

Laura pulled Sofia to her breast and calmed her, and stroked her hair and rubbed her back.

'I believe you, Sofia, but you must keep it a secret. You can keep a secret, can't you?'

'Of course I can. I'm six-and-a-half, and mama says I'm very grown up.'

'Yes you are, and you're a very good girl, but you must promise that you'll never tell anyone about Gloria.'

'Why?'

'It's a very special secret. Remember?'

'Yes.' Sofia giggled.

'And the game they were playing?' Laura said. 'I expect Gloria wanted to surprise the old man and if you tell anyone it won't be a surprise anymore, will it?'

'S'pose not.'

Laura took her arms and squeezed, gently, as though she wanted to intensify the significance of what she was about to say...'You must promise. Promise not to tell anyone and I'll buy you something very special to go with your bridesmaid's dress. Promise me, Sofia.'

'OK, I promise.'

Laura kissed her forehead, stood up, unclipped her mobile again, punched in another text message and sent it. She turned to Sofia and took her hand.

'Now, come on. Let's find Ana-Maria. I've got some great news to tell her.'

'What is it? I can keep a secret, you know.'

'I know, but this is not about Gloria or Señor Gonzales. This is something I want to share with the whole world.'

They found Ana-Maria and stood breathlessly before her.

'What is it?' Ana-Maria asked.

'José's just sent a text. He was pulled off at half time in last night's reserve game. He's made the first team squad for Sunday's exhibition match.'

'But that's fantastic.'

'I know. He wants me to fly up to Madrid to be with him.'

The two women hugged.

'I must go home and pack,' Laura said. 'I'm booked on the early flight tomorrow morning.'

'I'll give you a lift to the airport.'

'No, it's OK. You have enough on your hands.' She knelt down and looked into the young child's eyes. 'Be a good girl won't you, Sofia? Ask mama if you can watch your brother play on Sunday.' She stood up and saw Medina standing nearby. 'Crack open a beer on Sunday, Leo, and I'll wave to you from the Director's box.'

3

Back at his apartment, Fernández dragged a lung full of smoke from his cigarette. It had been thirty-six hours since the discovery of the bodies and enquiries during the fiesta had produced nothing concrete. As expected, the men in the village had put a wall of silence around events. They would want to deal with what happened in their own way, in their own time. The women had shrugged and turned their backs, deferring to tradition, knowing that Juan Gonzales' death had robbed the men of the chance to put things right.

The autopsies had been completed on each of the bodies and DNA and fingerprints had been taken and stored. The three Ramos men had been handed over to funeral directors in preparation for today's service and cremation, and Juan Gonzales's body had been collected by his son and was to be cremated elsewhere.

But, Fernández was coming under pressure.

It wouldn't be long before tourists swamped the area and every available officer would be needed to police the beachfront. As far as his superiors in Almeria were concerned, the old man had killed three members of the same family in a fit of revenge before turning the gun on himself. End of story.

But, for Fernández, things didn't add up.

He'd been a cop for more than eighteen years and although domestic disputes and bungled burglaries still counted for a substantial part of his business, there had been a dramatic increase in number of criminal gangs from Eastern Europe and this had been accompanied by an exponential rise in ruthless and callous crimes. But these hadn't been contract killings. They lacked the hallmarks of a professional hit, and hired gunmen weren't exactly renowned for executing their targets and then turning the gun on themselves. So what was it that had driven Juan Gonzales to kill three men and then blow his brains out? Or was Doctor Julieta Santiago right and someone else had been there?

Results of background checks on Klaus Dagmar, the ex-pat who'd alerted the Guardia, hadn't come through. But, he hadn't been ruled out. It wouldn't be the first time a killer was drawn back to the scene of the crime, taking perverse delight in watching the investigation unfold. Had Dagmar orchestrated the killings? Had he turned the gun on Juan Gonzales and tried to make the old man's death look like suicide? And, if he had…why? What would have been Dagmar's motivation?

He hadn't interviewed Felipe Romero and was still waiting for ballistic and forensic reports, but Fernández knew that unless someone was prepared to talk he might never find the answer to his questions. If he was lucky, one of the Ramos women might remember something but today he knew their minds would be elsewhere.

Leo Medina had mentioned the exchange he'd had with Ana-Maria's six-year-old sister, Sofia. She was the only person in the village who'd said she'd seen an old man. But which old man had she seen? The village was full of them. When had she seen him? Where? And who the hell was Gloria?

He looked at his watch. It was four o'clock. The sun wasn't up and he decided to try to get some sleep for a few hours. Later, he would go back to the village in time for the funeral and see if he could stir things up.

*

Fernández stood opposite steps that led down to the small square outside the village church. As a child, he'd been baptised, taken to hear Mass and attended his First Communion. But, once he'd reached his teens, he'd been unable to reconcile the proclamations of the Church with stories he'd heard of its past and he'd lost his faith long before he'd moved out of the village.

Today, he stood as a stranger, with eyes that searched for clues, for someone, for anything that would uncover the truth about the murders that had rocked this small community.

It was noon and the church bells were summoning villagers to a muted celebration of three lives cut so brutally short. The funeral procession had started at the Town Hall and at least a hundred villagers followed behind. The path was well worn and snaked along narrow streets to the top of the village. It passed mourners who threw flowers onto the coffins as they stood in their doorways, and then it made its way down, past the bakers and the post-office, towards the church square. The three coffins were carried on the broad shoulders of men closest to the deceased and the widows clung to each other, staring ahead, as if unable to acknowledge those who'd lined the streets to pay their last respects.

The cortège passed between the huge oak doors at the church's entrance and the young, peripatetic Priest, Father Gabriel, welcomed the mourners, his face grave and sincere as he shook hands and administered words of comfort.

Fernández knew the Priest would be hoping that, just this once, men would come inside but, as the coffins were lowered onto a-frame supports before the alter, most had stepped aside, as resolute as ever to mark their protest and wait outside.

41

Father Gabriel nodded and beckoned him inside, but Fernández looked at the men assembled on the steps and shrugged his apology - not today, Father.

As the church organ fell silent several women hurried across the square. Among them were Ana-Maria and her mother.

Ana-Maria had been a restless and temperamental child whose teens were littered with discarded suitors. But, at twenty-two years old, Antonio Fernández and the arrestingly beautiful Ana-Maria had become lovers. For a time, they were inseparable and he'd assumed that they were destined for the altar. But her restlessness returned. She was, she told him, determined to escape the tedium and the limitations of village life and she cast aside the ardent but impecunious police officer. She found no one else in the village able to match her ambition and had elected to marry a wealthy Englishman, ten years her senior.

When she saw him, Ana-Maria left her mother's side.

'Antonio,' she said. She seemed genuinely pleased to see him and smiled the most disarming of smiles. 'It's been such a long time.' She kissed him on both cheeks.

'You're looking well,' he said.

'Thank you.'

'Life's good?'

'But for this awful tragedy. You're here for the funeral?'

'I'm on duty.'

'Ah.'

'You'd brought them chocolate cake?'

Momentarily, she looked confused, and then nodded. 'Sofia was playing up and the weather looked unsettled. Mama asked me to take it round to them. Is that when it happened?'

'Yes. During a lull in the storm. Perfect cover.' He lit a cigarette, knowing he'd have to question her further, knowing this was not the right time. 'Your husband's not with you?'

'In Almeria. On business.'

'And doing well for himself?'

'He works hard. He's put in a competitive tender for the regeneration project in Almeria. It'll be a godsend if he's successful.'

'The recession biting deep?'

She sighed.

'Most construction companies are struggling or have gone out of business. If Paul does secure the Almeria contract it will not only help us through the downturn, but it should also put serious money in the bank.' She turned and pointed at the scaffolding along the south side of the church. 'He's also doing his bit for the community, supervising the church renovation.'

The church bell tolled.

'Look, I'd better...' She lent forward and pressed his forearm. 'It's really good to see you again. I hope you find whoever did this.' She hesitated, as if remembering something. 'By the way, I'm dancing at the El Morato tonight. You must come. Please say you will.'

He was – inexplicably - cautious about telling her that Julieta Santiago had already invited him. 'I'm not sure I'll be able to.'

She held her fingers like a gun and pointed it towards him. 'Eight o'clock, this evening. Be there, Inspector.' She laughed, straightened her skirt, and hurried over to the church.

He watched her disappear inside. She was beautiful - more beautiful perhaps, if that was possible - and, whilst flamenco might stir painful memories, he had to admit that the prospect of watching Ana-Maria and Julieta dance together might well prove irresistible.

As the service began, he walked across the small square. He stopped so that, at a glance, he was able to see all of the men on the steps. He lit another cigarette and offered them around, but there were no takers. 'Most of you will know me and know why I'm here.' He took his time and looked at each of them. There were those who'd seemed ancient when he'd been no taller than the handrail they stood against. There were others who were barely out of their teens. 'I only wish circumstances were different,' he said, but they didn't respond. He tried again. 'I grew up with some of you, or stole fruit from your orchards. I've helped you at harvest, and stood alongside you in the bar.' His voice trailed off and he sought respite in his cigarette, hoping the delay would give them time to realise he wasn't going away. 'I understand why you want to remain silent and find your own way to deal with this tragedy.'

An old man pushed away from the youngster who'd escorted him into the square and said, 'Then you'll also understand why you need to keep your nose out of our business.'

Fernández shook his head. 'Unfortunately, my friend, it is as much my business as it is yours. I want to find out why we are burying three men today and why Juan Gonzales took their lives in such a brutal, premeditated way.'

'Because he was a fascist bastard,' the old man said.

'I know something of the dreadful atrocities this village suffered many years ago.'

'You know nothing,' another man shouted, his face seemingly suffuse with anger, his fury breaching the dam.

'That bastard was born with violence in him.'

'Yeah, his father was no better.'

'They killed hundreds, for God's sake.'

'Bragged about executions they'd carried out. How many men, women, and children they'd murdered.'

'Fucking bastards!'

The bitter words hung in the air until Eduardo Gomez spoke.

His voice was barely a whisper, but he commanded the respect that age, and three tours as Mayor, had earned. 'You'd be too young to remember, Antonio. The Civil War tore our country apart and for forty years Franco made the people of Andalucia pay a high price for backing the wrong side.' He drew on his cigarette. 'Juan Gonzales inherited his father's thirst for violence.'

Fernández knew he should curb his impatience, but he wanted to provoke them, to prise the door open still further. 'So, what you're telling me,' he said, 'is that Gonzales lived in the village for thirty-five years and then woke up on Thursday morning and decided that that was the day he'd avenge the death of his parents?'

His sarcasm struck home and he sensed that their smouldering resentment was about to erupt in violence.

They began to shout and curse, and faces contorted with disgust and anger, until a woman hurried from the church and demanded their silence.

In the uneasy respite, Fernández walked over to Eduardo Gomez, intent on finding common ground.

'You're right to say I have no memory of those times. We all rely on those of you who do remember. But, I don't believe Thursday's tragedy can be explained away solely by history. Yes, Juan Gonzales may have been driven to act because of the murder of his parents, but...'

'They got what they deserved. His parents and the fucking Priest,' someone shouted.

Fernández stubbed out his cigarette and turned to face them.

'But, I'm much more interested in why Gonzales chose Thursday, at the time when one of their women should have brought them lunch. Can you explain that? Can you explain how Juan Gonzales *knew* the men would be alone?'

'If the woman had been there, he'd have killed her as well.' The old man cleared his throat and spat.

Eduardo Gomez held up his hand and the men fell silent.

'And what,' he asked Fernández, 'makes you think this has been anything other than a cruel act of revenge?'

'I'm waiting for reports from the pathologist and scene of crime officers. You may not like what I have to say but, if my suspicions are correct, Juan Gonzales did not kill himself. Someone else pulled the trigger.'

'Please God, it had been me!' Someone shouted and the men applauded.

Fernández called above them, 'And his killer may still be living among you.'

'He'd be welcome at my house, anytime.'

This sentiment was greeted with universal approval and the men fell into a raucous denunciation of everything Juan Gonzales stood for.

'Inspector?'

A strong, calm voice came from behind him. He turned, and recognised Rodrigo Perpiñán. He was short, slightly built and wiry, his face was swamped by a bushy moustache. He was twelve years older than Fernández, a scholar and an expert on Andalucian history.

He spoke with measured intelligence. 'You will tread a lonely path if you can't guard your tongue. We have all lived in a world of silent denial for many years. You will not shake them out of that. Your main suspect blew his brains out. That alone has denied them a chance to face the truth.'

Fernández stared over Perpiñán's shoulder. The men had turned away and were arguing forcefully with one another. He whispered, 'and, you have no doubt that Juan Gonzales pulled the trigger? That he shot three men and then turned the gun on himself?'

'You have another explanation?' Perpiñán said.

'I will find out.'

'If you look under too many rocks, you may find more than you bargained for.'

'Not if I have you to turn them over for me.' He stubbed out his cigarette. 'I need your help. I need to know what happened here around the time I was born, and why these men won't enter the church? I want to understand why Gonzales came back to the village, with vengeance burning inside him, then waited thirty-five years before carrying out this massacre?'

Rodrigo Perpiñán sighed heavily. 'It would be so much easier if these murders were the work of a lunatic.' He looked around at the men who'd fallen into an awkward silence. 'Look we can't talk here, not now. Meet me tonight, at twelve, in the church.'

'I don't like wasting time, chasing shadows.'

'You will not be doing either, Inspector. I can tell you now that Juan Gonzales did not wait thirty-five years before avenging his parents.'

'What do you mean, he didn't wait?'

'Oh, for God's sake, Antonio.' He hesitated, as though struggling to find the words. 'You don't know, do you?'

'Know what?'

'Thursday's killing spree started thirty-five years ago and your father was caught up in it.'

*

With Rodrigo Perpiñán's words jangling in his head, Fernández watched mourners disperse and, as the square emptied and fell silent, he found himself struggling with his impatience, desperate to know what part his father played in the murder of Juan Gonzales's parents and the village Priest.

He grabbed a coffee at the bar and then decided to return to the scene of Thursday's murders. The area was cordoned off. A uniformed police officer was guarding the entrance and forensic technicians were searching the area.

He went inside and stood in - what would be, one day - someone's lounge, and looked at the chalk outlines that marked where the four bodies had fallen. After several minutes he heard footfalls on the gravel outside.

He stepped back into the shadows as the steps drew nearer. There was a moment's hesitation and hushed words before a middle-aged woman, her head covered by a black shawl, stood in the doorframe and looked about the room. The uniformed officer led her to two of the outlines and identified each before withdrawing.

Juanita Ramos was holding white Madonna lilies to her breast and Fernández watched her draw back her veil and place one of the lilies against the wall where her son had fallen. She stood in silent prayer, her head bowed, before making the sign of the cross and moving over to the empty hearth. There, she placed a second lily, for her husband, and looked down at where he'd collapsed, fighting for his life, before a second bullet ended it.

Her body began to tremble and she appeared to be fighting back her tears. She grasped at a crucifix on a gold chain around her neck, brought it to her lips and kissed it gently.

She turned, as though trying to locate the place her father-in-law had fallen, and must have seen a figure standing in the shadows. 'Madre Mia, you startled me.'

'I'm sorry to intrude upon your grief.'

'The funeral was just too impersonal and I couldn't face the lamentation. I just wanted to say goodbye to each of them, in private.' She looked across at the wall where she'd laid the first lily. 'For my son,' she said, and nodded towards the fireplace. 'For my husband.' She searched amongst the rubble that was strewn across the floor.

'We found Alberto here.' He showed her where her father-in-law had fallen and she knelt to place the third lily and offer up a solitary prayer. She lifted the crucifix and kissed it. 'Thank you,' she said, looking up at him, tears in her eyes. She managed a smile. 'Has it helped?' she asked. 'Being here?'

Of the three widows, it was Juanita who'd shown the most anger and who would, he hoped, be ready to offer an insight into the tragedy.

'It's been good to talk to you.'

'Doesn't take a genius to know what happened,' she said, her anger apparent and voice stronger. 'The bastard murdered my father-in-law, my husband and my son, and then turned the gun on himself. What more do you want?'

'The truth. We know when, where and how, but we still don't know why.' He moved closer to her. 'I need your help, Juanita. I need to know about the men in your family. Their friends, problems with neighbours, which bars they used, and what business they had with Juan Gonzales.'

Juanita laughed hollowly. 'They'd have nothing to do with him.'

'But you knew him?'

'We all *knew* him.'

'But didn't speak to him, or pass the time of day?'

'No.'

'Do you know of anyone in the village who'd have spent time with him?'

'Inspector. That man butchered innocent people. He may have lived among us, but no one would have had anything to do with him.'

'No one?' He allowed the question to hang in the air and watched her face.

'Oh, God, I don't know. Maybe someone new to the village. Foreigners. Kids. Kids of foreigners who know nothing of our history.' She breathed out heavily and then said, 'I need a few moments alone. Do you mind?'

'No. No, of course not.' He stepped into the blazing sun, lit a cigarette and had just begun to stroll back across the campo when he saw Sofia Castaño waving at him from their terrace. He waved back and smiled. She'd been conceived about seven years ago - a shock for parents who thought they'd done with rearing. He heard her shout and watched her mother hurry on to the terrace to see what was exciting the child. Sofia waved again. Inocenta stood behind her and then bundled her inside.

He shrugged and scanned the rest of the village. Most homes faced away from the hill, as though preferring the views towards the sea and the mountains in the distance. Very few had terraces that overlooked the campo. But the Castaño home did and Sofia had said she'd seen an old man.

Fernández returned to his apartment in Almeria and sat on the balcony. He was impatient for the hours to pass. He wanted, above all, to tackle Rodrigo Perpiñán about his assertion that Thursday's deaths began thirty-five years ago and that his father had been involved.

50

He took a photograph of his parents' wedding from the mantelpiece, wondering why the hell he was feeling so anxious about uncovering the truth about a man he'd never known.

He looked at his father and wondered if this was the face of a murderer...*a man who had killed a Priest, for Christ's sake. As well as a man and a woman.* He wondered if anyone else had been involved and if they were still alive and lived in the village? He wondered how many people knew of his father's involvement and why his mother hadn't told him?

And then, quite suddenly, he felt sick as he realised he was assuming that his father *had* killed that night, thirty-five years ago. He wondered why he'd jumped to that conclusion, so readily?

In contrast to his own anxiety, the evening was unfolding without urgency and from his balcony he saw several old men make their way unhurriedly across the square. One carried a newspaper tucked under his arm. Another stopped to light a pipe. A third wore a fading red scarf around his neck. Each one had come from a different corner of the square and they met under a huge ficus tree trimmed into the shape of an annular - reminiscent of a bullring.

He watched them greet one another with a barely-disguised Republican salute and then exchange simple greetings. They then sat in silence, as though words were no longer a valued currency, and he wondered if they'd ever known his father.

As a clock chimed seven, he retreated inside, but left the wooden shutters open to allow sounds of the evening to drift in. He poured a glass of red wine, slumped onto the sofa and tried to relax. He sighed heavily and stared at the ceiling fan.

An hour later, he woke with a start and checked his watch. He was still undecided whether he would drive north of the city and watch Ana-Maria and Julieta Santiago dance. It would be worth the effort, he tried to convince himself - watching Ana-Maria dance flamenco was, after all, one of the most sensual experiences that he, or any man, could have. They'd had something special, for sure, but she'd dumped him and they'd drifted apart. Today's funeral was the first time he'd seen her in ten years and tonight she'd be going home with another man, her husband, and lying in his arms, making love with him.

Why, he asked himself, was he even thinking of going? Whilst he'd always enjoyed flamenco at village fiestas and concerts, he preferred a lonely beach, with a small group of friends and a few beers. The air would be filled with a lone voice and a soulful guitar, and the rhythmic body of one of the girls swaying in the moonlight. He wondered if Ana-Maria still danced on the beach and found himself wondering about Doctor Julieta Santiago - had she ever danced beneath the moonlight, on a deserted beach, accompanied by a lone voice and a soulful guitar?

He looked at his watch again and shrugged, got off the sofa, shaved, showered and dressed. He stopped at his local bar for a shot of brandy and then drove across town and parked as close as he could to El Morato.

*

Fernández had read somewhere that El Morato was reputed to be Almeria's *most authentic* flamenco venue. Set in a natural cave, the passion of the music is trapped beneath its low ceiling and the audience is never far from those performing...an intimacy that's hard to beat.

He picked up a programme from a trestle table at the entrance and crossed to the side of the cavern just as the full-house applauded dancers on to the stage for one of the last of the evening's schedule. He glanced round and recognised Holly, Julieta Santiago's daughter. She was standing on a chair at the end of the third row from the front. She was holding the hand of a young girl on the chair next to her. The elderly woman he'd seen at the bar earlier that day was sitting next to Holly. Neither girl seemed able to contain her excitement. They giggled and pointed, whispering animatedly as though swept away by the urgency of the music. Several times the elderly woman raised her forefinger to her lips to silence them.

The other child was Sofia Castaño. Her mother sat nearby, but seemed to be trying to ignore the girl's antics and concentrate on the performance. He watched a man, probably in his mid-forties, move quietly to the end of the row and place Sofia on his lap. He whispered to her, calming her as the *fandango* reached its climax, and clapped with her as the dancers bowed.

Then, two women took to the stage. Ana-Maria was wearing a cream Sevillana that contrasted well with her dark hair. Julieta Santiago was in midnight blue. They shook their dresses and waited for everyone to settle.

The difference between the two women was marked. Ana-Maria's breasts were accentuated by the décolleté of the dress. Her large, fiery eyes shone in defiance as she thrust her rounded hips provocatively to the side, and she smiled that same, self-assured smile he'd seen outside the church. Santiago, by contrast, was tall and slight. Her auburn hair hung like a velvet curtain as she reclined her head and looked self-consciously over the heads of the audience. He did what most men would have done and compared them. But, as he did, he felt concerned that Julieta Santiago would not be able to hold her own in the company of a woman who knew every trick in the book and could command a man's attention with the slightest movement of her head.

Out of the corner of his eye Fernández saw the man, who'd moved to sit with Sofia, get up, scoop both of the girls into his arms and carry them to the side of the cave. From there, they watched Julieta and Ana-Maria dance a classic lament, a *petenera,* telling the story of a beautiful girl who brings tragedy to herself and to her village. Although their movements were slow and lyrical and contrasted with the rest of the programme, he sensed the audience was enjoying the sensitivity of the piece and its gentle emotions.

There was no doubt in his mind which of them was the more sensual and Santiago's inexperience made her vulnerable. It was as if, at any moment, she might falter, or forget which way to turn.

He spent the performance willing her to succeed.

The dance was distilled into a final tableau, applause resounded around the cave and, as they embraced, the rest of the cast joined them on stage for the finale: *a fandangos grandes*.

He left the cave and walked towards the water's edge, lit a cigarette and waited for everyone to file out.

'Antonio.' Julieta Santiago called as the audience eased through the double doors, Holly skipping at her side. 'Why didn't you tell me Ana-Maria invited you?'

'I wanted to,' he said, lamely.

'Were you in time to see us dance?'

'Yes, of course.'

'And? What did you think?'

He didn't answer, but stubbed out his cigarette and knelt so that he was at eye-level with Holly. She slipped behind her mother as though hiding from the man with the scar on his face.

'What do you think?' he asked her. 'Not bad, eh?'

'My mama was beautiful,' Holly said, burying herself in Santiago's Sevillana.

He smiled. 'I agree. Even the dancing was pretty good.'

'Pretty good?' Ana-Maria called as she joined them. 'Antonio Fernandez, how could you tease Julieta and Holly like that? We were sensational.' She placed an arm around Santiago's shoulder and hugged her. 'We did well, didn't we?'

'We did, didn't we?' Santiago's face lit up.

Ana-Maria turned to Fernández. 'There should have been three of us. Scarpetta here, Laura and myself...'

'Scarpetta?' he said.

'Laura has a thing about nicknames,' Santiago said. 'She decided mine should be Scarpetta. The pathologist in Patricia Cornwall's books. It's a harmless bit of fun, but...' She looked across at Ana-Maria. 'She doesn't tell *everyone* what his or her nickname is, does she?'

'She hasn't told me and I don't want to know.' Ana-Maria laughed. 'You're Elliot, by the way,' she said to Fernández. 'Elliot Ness? Put Capone away.'

'Capone?'

'Scarface?'

'Ah.' He hesitated. 'Laura couldn't make it tonight?'

'No. She's flown up to Madrid to watch José make his first team debut.'

'Well, you did just fine without her.'

The voice came from behind and Santiago introduced the older woman who'd been at the bar earlier in the day. 'This is my mama, Pedra.'

'You have a very talented daughter.'

55

'You seem surprised.'

'Mama. Behave. Antonio's a colleague of mine and a friend of Ana-Maria's.'

'He's a man, isn't he?'

'Mama.' Santiago wagged her finger at her.

Then Sofia appeared, carried aloft on the shoulders of the man who'd swept both of the girls into his arms.

'Holly,' Santiago said, 'why don't you take Sofia and play in the square?'

'Do you want to play?'

'Yes, please.'

'Come on, let's play chase.'

'Don't go outside the square,' Ana-Maria called, and turned to Fernandez. 'You'll remember my mother?'

'Of course. Inocenta. It's been a long time.'

She looked older, he thought, more than the ten years that had passed.

'You look a mess, Antonio. You need a good woman to look after you.'

'If only you weren't spoken for...' He took her hand and kissed it. 'Sofia must be a joy.'

'She's a headache, but I wouldn't be without her.'

'And this is my husband, Paul,' Ana-Maria said. 'Paul Turnbull.'

He was fractionally taller than Fernández and his broad shoulders suggested that he was used to manual labour. His receding hairline accentuated a furrowed forehead.

Fernández shook his hand and said, 'You seem to have a way with Sofia.'

'She's a good little girl.' Turnbull smiled, watching the girls chase each other. 'Ana-Maria tells me you're busy with the deaths in the campo. An easy case to solve, I'd guess, with the murderer blowing his own brains out.'

'Colourful, but inaccurate. My money's on murder, on all four counts.' Usually, he didn't dislike someone quite so quickly but, given the circumstances, he sensed he'd make an exception. He wondered if Ana-Maria had told him about their relationship (and guessed she hadn't) but experience taught him that, if her husband knew where to look, the signs were always there. 'Is your business always straightforward?' he asked.

'Construction is never straightforward, especially in Spain, especially during a recession. There are too many conflicting interests. But everything I'm involved in is legitimate.'

Fernández held his tongue.

'I only deal with reputable companies and suppliers.'

Fernández dragged on his cigarette.

'Let's not talk business all evening,' Ana-Maria said. 'Besides, we've got good news of our own, haven't we darling?' She pulled Paul Turnbull towards her. 'We'll be starting our own family soon, won't we?'

'Congratulations,' Fernández said, unsure if he was jealous or apprehensive. He'd known what it was like to be with Ana-Maria. They'd even talked of starting a family of their own. He looked away, searching for a distraction. He watched Sofia cover her eyes and count to ten as Holly hid behind a palm tree. Leo Medina's words jangled in his head...Sofia Castaño had seen *an old man carrying a carpet.*

Julieta Santiago called the girls over.

Inocenta took Sofia's hand and led her to a Toyota Landcruiser. Ana-Maria smiled and said, 'we must do this again sometime. We could have dinner at our villa. What do you say?' She looked at Julieta Santiago, then Fernández and then her husband.

'Yes. Yes, of course,' Turnbull said.

'Work permitting, of course.' She took his arm and, as they walked towards the Landcruiser, she turned and called, 'Julieta, give me a ring tomorrow.'

'I'll try.'

Holly took her mother's hand and they watched as the car pulled into the evening traffic. 'It was good of you to come tonight, Antonio,' Santiago said. 'I'm sure Ana-Maria appreciated you being here.'

He nodded, awkward, unsure what she expected him to say.

'You like cake?' Holly asked him.

'Not particularly.'

'I think Holly's inviting you for tea tomorrow. Her idea, not mine.'

'I can't.'

'No, of course not.'

'No, no. That's not what I meant. I can't tomorrow. It's a family thing. A matanza.'

'The slaughter of a pig?'

'Sounds gross,' said Holly. 'Can I watch?'

'She takes after her mother.' Santiago smiled. 'Eight years old and already fascinated by the gruesome and the grisly.'

'You can come, if you'd like to. Everyone starts arriving at about four. It's a bit short notice, I know.'

Holly looked up at her mother, eyes pleading.

'It would seem there is a rare gap in our social diary. We'd love to be there.'

'Good.'

'We'll suspend hostilities for the afternoon?'

'Yes. Yes, of course. I...'

'I'm kidding, Antonio.'

'Oh. Yes. Of course.'

'See you tomorrow, then.'

'Yes.'

'Bye,' Holly grabbed her mother's hand. 'Come on.'

*

Rodrigo Perpiñán had suggested they should met in the church, long after the setting of the sun and once the village had withdrawn for the night. It was just before mid-night and the bar had closed and stragglers filtered through the narrow streets after a skin-full and an update on the gossip surrounding the investigation.

Fernández arrived early and took time to enjoy the tranquillity the church offered - cool and quiet and dark and perfumed by incense. Although he'd struggled with his faith since adolescence, he found a special solace in a church. He stared at the simple alter in the middle of the Chancel, the figure of Christ on the cross dominating the semi-circular apse, the pulpit to the left.

He lifted his head towards the high, vaulted ceilings. Time to talk to God? He wasn't sure. Time to ask that his mother and his sisters would enjoy good health. Time to hope the families of the bereaved would find comfort in one another. Prayers of a sort.

He lit a candle the entrance to the vestibule.

'For your father?' Rodrigo Perpiñán's voice filled the church as he walked down the nave. 'The candle? For your father?'

'I never knew him.'

'He was a good man. My father was fortunate to have him as a friend, a man he could trust.'

'A product of their times, perhaps?'

Fernández shook the scholar's hand. They sat on an ancient pew as yellow streetlights filtered through the stain glass and cast strange shadows across their faces.

'I understand that the restoration is proceeding well,' Perpiñán said, 'although Father Gabriel has told me that Paul Turnbull believes the foundations are crumbling.'

'Ana-Maria's husband?'

'Putting his own money into it, apparently.'

59

'Hoping his generosity will help him in his bid for the regeneration project?'

'Sowing seeds.'

Both seemed to welcome this light-hearted prelude, but then Perpiñán said, 'Outside the church today, I told you that your father was involved in a killing spree that started thirty-five years ago?'

'I had no idea.'

'You'd only just been born.'

'But, my mother...'

'Should have told you?'

'Why wouldn't she?'

'It might help if I explained what happened, why it happened, and how our fathers got involved.'

'Our fathers?'

'Your father wasn't alone...' Perpiñán drew air, filled his lungs, and exhaled forcefully before saying, 'I asked you to meet me here because you need to understand the significance of the church and its Priest, thirty-five years ago.'

'Father Emanuel?'

Perpiñán nodded. 'You'll know that for centuries the clergy sided with the landowners and exploited the poor. The Priest lived in the big house at the top of the village and each morning he'd walk down to the square to meet with the landowners and men who managed the mines. They'd select the labourers who'd work that day.'

'Deciding who'd eat and who would go hungry?'

'A pattern repeated across much of Spain. It was only a matter of time before their frustration and resentment erupted into violence and when the landowners and the church sided with the Fascists in 1936...'

'The poor backed the Republicans.'

'The Civil War tore families and communities apart. It was never as simple as rich against poor but if a man's family is dying of starvation, how would you expect him

60

to react if you offered him an opportunity to 'redistribute wealth'?'

'Was there much bloodshed here?'

'Yes, but compared with other areas we were spared the worst of Franco's purges. There's only one date that need concern your investigation. January 1974.'

'But that was long after Franco finished eradicating opposition to his regime.'

Perpiñán's features were cloaked by shadows.

He smiled weakly and Fernández offered him a bottle of water. Perpiñán sipped at it, distracted, distant.

'You're right, of course, after the War Franco set about crushing any opposition. Early reprisals were on a massive scale. A list of Republican sympathisers was compiled in Salamanca and everyone on it was hunted down and executed with little more than a summary trial. Accurate figures have been very difficult to obtain, but prisoners of war were put into concentration camps and dissidents were sentenced to hard labour. Homosexuals and other 'deviants' were locked up in mental asylums. The Jews suffered here just as they did elsewhere in Europe. A list of six thousand names was handed over to Heinrich Himmler. Estimates vary, but the death toll ran to tens or even hundreds of thousands. To this day, we are still uncovering mass graves.'

'And Juan Gonzales was part of that tyranny?'

'Yes. As soon as he was old enough he became one of Franco's assassins.'

The church clock struck twelve-thirty.

'You asked if there was much bloodshed here. The answer is simple. Yes, there was, and there are clues to the atrocities throughout the village.'

The scholar paused.

'In the winter of 1974, something dreadful happened It was an incident that will not only help you understand

61

what drove Gonzales to shoot three men last Thursday, but will also help you judge our fathers.'

Perpiñán sat and stared out at the blackness of the night. The village streetlights had been turned off and most homes were in darkness. Only the scream of cats fighting or a lone dog barking cut through the still air.

'By the mid-1950s, most organised resistance had been eradicated. During the 1960s, when tourists flocked to the Costas, Spain prospered.' Perpiñán sighed. 'And then, in December 1973, Admiral Carrero Blanco was assassinated by ETA. He'd been chosen to succeed by Franco and had only been Prime Minister for six months. Most people outside the Basque area didn't agree with ETA's use of violence, but the assassination made everyone realise just how serious they were. Five of them spent months excavating a tunnel under a street the Admiral used on his way to Mass. The blast catapulted his car over the church and onto a second floor balcony on the other side.'

'Spain's first astronaut,' Fernández said, recalling reports he'd read – the black humour of a nation weary of the Dictator's repressive regime.

Perpiñán exhaled forcefully. 'Franco's response was restrained, at first, and this was interpreted as a sign of his frailty. But, how wrong they were. The assassination prompted his most violent reprisals. He was determined to hunt down those responsible and unleashed his death squads. They ranged throughout Spain and across the border into France. Hundreds were tortured and killed. In January 1974, news reached us that a death squad was closing in on two ETA fugitives and was on its way to the village. As it neared, anyone considered a likely target was hidden in a safe house...'

'Members of ETA were here?'

'No, but that was of little consequence. Franco would have seen it as an opportunity to mop up any remaining opposition. We watched the convoy as it snaked across the plain – there were no roads, of course, just dirt tracks, and dust billowed behind them like smoke from a gigantic fire. It made quite an impression on a ten year old, I can tell you.'

'It must have been terrifying.'

'The tension was palpable, but very few words were spoken. It was as though everyone was resigned to their fate. As though they knew something awful was about to happen and felt powerless to stop it.'

He sipped water.

'When they arrived, they searched every house and barn. One man was lucky to escape serious injury when they beat him for not returning the Nazis salute Franco had adopted. Pepe, the goatherd, was a teenager, but they cut his tongue out.'

'Why?'

'They mistook his stupidity for insolence.'

Perpiñán paused. 'And then we saw Father Emanuel and Jésus Gonzales…'

'Juan's father?'

'Yes. Both were Francoists and, in hindsight, what they did next should not have shocked us. But, it did. Father Emanuel and Jésus Gonzales led soldiers to a safe house where we'd hidden two fugitives.'

'Fugitives responsible for the assassination?'

'No. Republican sympathisers and members of the Resistance. Both men had slipped away, but the widow in the safe house, her son and a neighbour were taken to the square outside the Town Hall. They were forced to kneel. When they refused to tell the soldiers where the fugitives were, they were shot, back of the head, gunned down like dogs, their bodies left as a warning to us all.'

'My God.'

Perpiñán took another sip.

'The death squad left and, later that evening, three men from the village attended Mass. After the service, they waited until the church had emptied and followed the Priest home. They broke into his house and two of them took Father Emanuel 'for a stroll', high into the hills. They tied him alongside a disused mineshaft, slit his throat and left him to die. They went back for Jésus Gonzales and took Jésus and his wife, Teresa, to where they'd secured the Priest. They slit their throats and threw the bodies down the mineshaft.'

'Our fathers did this?'

'Yes.'

'But how can you be sure?'

'I was ten years old, Antonio. I followed them. I saw everything that happened that night. I watched my father kill Father Emanuel and Teresa Gonzales, and I watched your father kill Jésus Gonzales.'

They sat in silence.

Fernández was unable to stop a mixture of emotions surging through his body. His breath was shallow and rapid as he struggled to justify what his father had done. Everything he'd stood for was crumbling before him: the distain he felt for anyone who took another's life; the dedication he'd shown tracking down anyone suspected of murder; his inability to countenance any justification and his contempt for bleeding-heart excuses. But he *could* justify what his father had done that night, he told himself, couldn't he? *Jésus Gonzales had betrayed his neighbours, for Christ's sake. Three innocent people had died, the back of their heads blown off. What sort of Priest is it who sends his own flock to slaughter? Both men deserved to die.* But then he pictured the terrified face of Teresa Gonzales. He tried to imagine how she'd felt, dragged from her home, shocked and bewildered, unable to comprehend, made to watch as her husband was slaughtered. *Did Teresa Gonzales deserve to die?*

He found himself gulping in air as arguments raged inside him and it was several minutes before he lifted his head and looked at Rodrigo Perpiñán. 'You said there were three men involved that night?'

'Three men, Antonio. Your father, my father and...'

'Alberto Ramos?'

'Yes. His involvement has been shrouded in secrecy for thirty-five years until...'

'Someone found out and told Juan Gonzales.'

'Yes.'

Fernández realised there must be more.

'That wasn't the end, was it? There were reprisals? More bloodshed?'

'When we spoke outside the church earlier, I told you that Thursday's killing spree *started* over thirty years ago.'

'Yes.'

'My father was murdered a year after they'd killed the Priest, and Jésus and Teresa Gonzales. He was found in an outbuilding, his throat slit. And your father...'

'Died in 1976, a hit-and-run accident.'

'Your father wasn't killed in an accident, Antonio. You were probably told that to hide the truth from you. His throat was slit.'

'My God.' He sat silently for a few moments. 'Why would my mother lie to me?'

'And then what? You go after Juan Gonzales and the cycle of violence continues?'

'She must have known I'd find out, eventually.'

'It couldn't have been easy...her husband's murder and three children to fend for.'

'And Alberto?'

'Would have been next. He was in his mid-thirties and had just been elected Mayor.'

'But, as Mayor, he could have arrested Juan Gonzales for the murder of your father, of my father...'

'And implicate himself in the death of the Priest? No. Besides, Alberto knew that if Juan Gonzales found out he'd been involved he would have come after him.'

'But, he survived.'

'As far as I know, there were five people who knew what happened that night. Our fathers, Alberto, me…'

'And?'

'And a young girl. The Priest's whore. She was with Father Emanuel, when our fathers burst in and took him away. Alberto stayed with the girl.'

'So, he wasn't actually involved in…There must have been other people who knew what happened that night?'

'Possibly.' Perpiñán hesitated. 'Come on, let's get out of here.'

They left the oppressive confines of the church and crossed the village to Perpiñán's home where they sat on the terrace and opened a new bottle of Soberano brandy. They sank a shot each and recharged their glasses.

'We're assuming that someone betrayed Alberto.'

'The Priest's whore?'

'After Mass that evening, Father Emanuel came back to his house. He was unaware he was being followed. I used shadows for cover. I climbed a tree and saw her, naked, in the Priest's bed, waiting for him.'

'She knew what our fathers had done?'

'She was not a witness, as such. Alberto stayed with her. She didn't actually see what happened.'

'But?'

'It was rumoured that a couple of months after the Priest was killed not only did she marry a local man, but was carrying the Priest's child.'

'She was pregnant?'

'So it was rumoured. But Alberto's involvement was hushed up, and so was her identity.'

'You saw her that evening. You know who she is.'

'It was dark, the room lit by candlelight. Her face was turned away from me.'

'And, presumably, the man she married was unaware that she was carrying someone else's child?'

'Probably. But suppose, after all this time, someone found out and threatened to expose her? Threatened to tell her husband that the child he'd cared for all these years was not his own? Threatened to tell the child that the man she thinks of as father, isn't really her father? Suppose someone threatened to tell the child that her real father was a Priest who'd betrayed innocent people. A Priest killed in retaliation - his throat slit, left to bleed to death and thrown down a mineshaft?'

'You said, *she*. The child was a girl?'

'I believe so. Find the Priest's whore, and the Priest's child, and you may begin to unravel this tragedy.'

4

Fernández drove home and after several fitful hours he gave up trying to sleep. He poured himself a glass of water, sat on his balcony and watched the day unfold. The sounds of the city were distant and vague, his body sluggish and inert, his mind numb and impassive. He no longer felt anything...was no longer shocked, ashamed, confused, or angry, just so tired that all he wanted to do was sleep. Except that he knew he wouldn't be able to, even if he tried. He shuddered as the chill morning air wrapped around him and he withdrew to the sofa in the lounge. He stared at the ceiling, his mind melting in the confusion of images staging repeat performances each time he tried to close his eyes.

At nine, he drove to the village, parked, crossed the road and, leaning heavily on the door, pushed his way into a packed bar.

The cascade of conversation trickled to nothing, as if a dam had been installed above a waterfall.

Everything was exactly as he remembered it...a long, wood-panelled bar with glass-fronted cabinet displaying homemade tapas; the floor strewn with cigarette butts and paper serviettes; square tables, and chairs with high-slatted backs; men, standing, one foot on a metal rest, the other planted on the floor, sipping coffee, anise or brandy. There were additions...a cigarette machine, a one-armed bandit, a flat screen TV, and a pool table...but Fernández couldn't decided whether they did anything to improve the bar.

Gradually, the men returned to their breakfast, and Fernández walked over to the bar, lit a cigarette and ordered a double espresso. He glanced at the display of village photographs on the wall – miners with blackened faces stepping into the daylight, a donkey carrying water

68

or salted fish, a goatherd cradling a newborn kid, and proud villagers dressed for Sunday. Above the cigarette machine, a poster featured several images of a bullfight at The Plaza de la Maestranza in Seville and, next to the television, someone had pinned a photograph of José Castaño in Real's white strip, smiling self-assuredly at the camera.

Fernández noticed Enrique, José's father, standing at the far end of the bar and then turned his attention to a group of Brits who'd congregated around several tables. He assumed that they lived in the village or in a villa on the surrounding hills and came to the bar to pass the time of day and to gossip. He had no doubt that they would see themselves as integral members of the community, but he knew the locals would refer to them as *guiris* - a term of contempt - its meaning long forgotten, but a dictionary might define simply as *foreigner*. He decided the Brits would keep, but knew he'd have to talk to them sooner rather than later, if only because Klaus Dagmar, the man who'd reported the bodies, was sitting mid-way down on the far side and seemed to be the focus of their attention.

As the barmen enlisted help to rearrange the furniture for the afternoon's big match, Fernández asked what the excitement was about and was told that José was playing in an exhibition match - Real Madrid v's an all-star South American line up - and that his inclusion was seen as an opportunity for him to become a regular in the first team.

He finished his brandy, left the bar, and walked into the village where he found a teenage girl sitting on the doorstep of the general store. She was stroking a dog that had been barred from entering the store.

The dog appeared to appreciate her attention and had rolled over to expose his tummy, inviting her to tickle him. She'd obliged but Fernández thought she seemed bored, resentful and sullen.

He wasn't to know, of course – he would find out later - but her world had fallen apart six months earlier when her parents decided they'd had enough of each other and she'd found herself sitting next to her tearful mother on a budget flight to 'sunny' Spain. She would like Spain, her mother had tried to reassure her. She'd be able to swim in the sea, learn a new language and make new friends. Trouble was all she wanted to do was stay with her friends in Edinburgh, sit her dance exams and snog Mickey, her first serious boyfriend. As if the wrench wasn't enough, she'd had to go to a Spanish school where she couldn't understand a word the teacher or her classmates were saying. And, to top it all, her mother didn't waste much time before she met Danny, a tattooed plumber who'd left Glasgow to live in Spain three years ago.

Life was not sweet. The dog had it better. At least he got his tummy rubbed.

She sat, her chin resting on the palm of her left hand, mouth glum, eyes glazed, her mind back in Scotland, where she'd be snogging Mickey.

'Mind if I join you?' Fernández asked in his heavily accented English and sat next to her.

She shuffled away from him, resting against the door jam.

'Your dog?'

'I wish,' she said. 'Our apartment's too small. Would nay be fair to keep a dog, so Danny says. Me mum don't argue. So that's that.'

'School out?'

'Yeah. Thank God.'

He looked at her blue eyes and fair, freckled skin.

'What is it they say? School...the happiest days of your life?'

She snorted. 'School sucks.'

'Yes. I know what you mean.'

'At least you can speak the language.'

He laughed. 'I've had to work hard to lose the accent. Even visitors from other parts of Spain have difficulty understanding what the locals round here say.'

She smiled and looked at him for the first time. 'I know how they feel.'

'New to the village?'

'Aye. It's like wearing new shoes.' She looked at him. 'It's what my gran used to say. Painful.'

'What did your gran call you?'

'Aimee, when she was sober.'

'You know who I am?'

'You're the cop who's investigating those murders.'

'And what have you heard?'

'The old man shot three men from the same family and then blew his brains out, right?'

'You knew the old man?'

'Señor Gonzales? Aye, s'pose so. Most of the kids in the village swore at him. But he was OK. I'd feed his cats and his chickens. He couldn't speak English, so we didn't talk much - all sign language and the odd word, you know?' She looked down at the dog at her feet. 'I'd wash the dishes and he'd teach me how to care for his canaries. He liked to play games.'

'Games?'

'Board games, cards, dominoes.'

'And which hand did he use to throw the dice or pick up a card?'

'Left, I think.' She hesitated. 'Aye. He made a real show of rattling the dice before he threw. I'm pretty sure he was left-handed.'

He lent forward and rubbed the dog's tummy. 'Thank you for talking to me.'

'I was nay rushed off me feet, Inspector.'

He stood up. 'I've sure your mama's a good woman, and would really appreciate it if you made an effort to be happy.'

'It can't get much worse.'

He turned to go and then remembered something he meant to ask, 'Do you know a kid called Gloria?'

'Gloria? Here, in the village?'

'Yes, probably a young girl, about six years old, I'm not sure.'

'She part of your investigation, then?'

'She's a friend of Sofia Castaño's.'

'I know Sofia, but I've not seen her pal. *Gloria*, you say? She pursed her lips and shook her head. 'It's no good. I dun nay know the wee lass. They witnesses or summat?'

'I'm not sure.'

'You're not sure about a lot of things, are ye?'

'You like jigsaws?'

'That's what you do, is it? Join all the pieces together before it makes sense?'

He laughed. 'Yes, something like that. Look, if you do come across Gloria, you'll let me know?'

'Aye, if you think it'll help.'

Fernández found the small house near the top of the village and ducked under the crime scene tape. As he pushed open a wooden gate it splintered away from its top hinge, crashed to the flagstone floor, and sent several cats scurrying for cover.

He eased open the door into a lean-to that doubled as a chicken coop and toilet and guessed that this must have been one of the few homes by-passed, quite deliberately, when mains water and mains sewage were installed in the village. Over time, effluent had nowhere else to go but to seep into the surrounding hillside.

The smell inside the lean-to was almost unbearable. Dead chickens lay strewn across the dirt floor - probably the victims of a fox - whilst others continued to scurry and scratch out their meagre existence. On top of a long table, caged canaries struggled from one side of their cage to the other and screamed as though demanding to be fed. It had been three days since Juan Gonzales executed three men. Three days and, after SOCOs had finished, it was obvious that no one had thought to check on his animals.

He unlatched the door leading into the kitchen and was greeted by the stench of rubbish rotting in the bin next to the sink. He pushed the bin's pedal and the top flipped open, releasing flies and wasps that had gorged on chicken giblets and discarded cat food. He took out his handkerchief, covered his nose, pulled out drawers under the work surface and rummaged through them. He found nothing to indicate that Juan Gonzales was left-handed.

He moved into the sitting room with its low, beamed ceiling and stone, whitewashed walls. He was surprised by its order and neatness - the home of a man, he supposed, who'd been meticulous and precise.

The room narrowed significantly where the open hearth and chimneybreast jutted out. There were only two pieces of furniture – a leather armchair in the corner and a small, drop-leaf table. Abandoned on top of the table was a lined note pad and fountain pen. He picked up the beautifully crafted, gold inlay pen, and assumed that Juan Gonzales had stolen it from someone he'd executed. He opened the pad, and then cracked open the case of the pen, unscrewing the two parts until he was able to apply light pressure to the bladder inside. A droplet of ink oozed onto the nib and dropped onto the table. He reassembled the pen and tried to write his name on the pad. The nib caught and scratched the surface of the paper. It was a left-handed nib.

Julieta Santiago's assertion was looking irrefutable.

Juan Gonzales did not turn the handgun on himself.

Someone else must have been there.

Fernández pulled his Beretta from its holster and felt its weight. He switched it from his left hand to his right, and the back again. He repeated this several times and then stood in front of the mirror over the fireplace. Using his left hand, he raised the handgun to his left temple and held it there. His hand trembled slightly, as though the muscles in the wrist were struggling to manage the gun's weight. He lowered the gun and passed it to his right hand. He raised it to his right temple. In his right hand, the gun felt much easier to handle, much more natural. This was how he would blow his brains out - holding the gun in his dominant hand - and, in that moment, he knew there could no doubt that he was heading a murder inquiry.

His mother lived in a rambling, white-walled cortijo that had, over the centuries, been farmed by labourers paid 'in kind' when money was short. Since her husband's death, Adelina had scaled down the extent and diversity of the farm and, despite recent poor health, remained almost self-sufficient, tending goats, pigs and chickens and growing enough fruit and vegetables.

Twice a year, in mid-December and around summer solstice, the family would gather and she would preside over the matanza. The slaughtered pig would provide food for months...the choicest cuts hung to produce the leanest hams, whilst the rest - flesh, bone, blood, trotters, head, offal - made soups, stews and sausages.

Nothing was wasted.

New regulations, introduced in the name of health and safety, made it illegal for anyone to slaughter a pig unless they were a designated official. The rules were widely ignored, but a portion of meat would be taken to the vet where it would be tested and, if it was clean, he'd gratefully accept his 'cut' and the family feast could begin.

Adelina shuffled from the door, stooped, frail, and weary, but overjoyed to see her son as he parked his car. She would often boast that he was 'chief of police' and held up long, slender arms and pulled him firmly into her body.

'Mama,' Fernández said, 'you're looking well.'

'And you've never been able to lie, Antonio. So don't start now.' They held each other, tenderly.

'Are Inez and Olivia here?' he asked.

'And my grandchildren.'

She rarely missed the opportunity to remind him that time was running out for her. 'You're late, as always.' She looked at him, brushing thick, dark hair away from his eyes. 'You look tired. You work too hard. You'll make yourself ill.' She smiled, pulling him to her once again.

As they embraced, another car pulled up and parked. 'Mama,' Fernández said, as Santiago and her daughter walked hand-in-hand towards them, 'this is Julieta.'

Adelina looked confused and he instantly regretted not warning her.

75

It had been a long time since he'd brought someone home and he sensed his mother's cautious appraisal of the tall, graceful woman with her long, auburn hair and green eyes.

'You look like you could do with a good meal inside you,' Adelina said.

'Mama.'

'What? The woman's a bag of bones.'

'Mama, Julieta is a colleague and my guest.'

'No, you're right,' Santiago smiled. 'I haven't been taking as much care of myself as I should.' She eased her daughter gently in front of her and placed her hands on her chest. 'This is Holly.'

Holly walked tentatively towards Adelina, held out her hand and said, 'I am very pleased to meet you.'

Adelina chuckled, raised her hands, framed Holly's face, brushed her copper hair to one side, looked deep into her eyes and said, 'You're very beautiful, like your mother.'

'Are you very old?'

'Am I..?' Adelina cried with delight. 'I would say I'm the oldest woman in the whole of Spain.'

'Really?'

'I have been on this earth for over two hundred years.'

Holly giggled and Adelina stroked her cheek with the back of her hand and said, 'you will need to stay out of the sun. Your skin is fair and the sun is fierce. Come with me. I have a hat for you to wear.' She led Holly into the house.

Santiago looked across at him. 'How does she do that? People fall in love with her everywhere we go.'

'Well, it can't be genetic, can it?' He raised an eyebrow and tilted his head slightly.

'A truce, remember?'

'A ceasefire...as agreed.' Fernández smiled. 'Holly has an accent. Your Spanish is flawless, but you weren't born here were you?'

'Mama's Spanish. Papa's English. A physician. I was born in Malaga. They brought me up to be bilingual.'

'And Holly's father?'

'A holiday romance that blossomed then turned sour. I should have known better. It lasted three years. He left without knowing I was pregnant and he hasn't been in touch since. Not entirely his fault. I was ambitious and I'd decided to move to London to complete my training. Holly was born there.' She smiled ruefully. 'Come on, introduce me to the rest of your family.'

They walked round to the yard at the back of the house.

His sisters were together, talking - an art they'd taken to astonishing heights, practising as they did for many hours each day. Their husbands were drinking beer - stomachs testifying to their dedication. A pig foraged, unperturbed, in a large holding-pen built onto the side of the cortijo. Children were playing chase among the small outcrop of olive and almond trees. 'Uncle Antonio,' one cried, and they all hurried over to him, bounding around like puppies and badgering until he produced the shiny euro coins he'd always brought with him - a token offering and compensation for his long absences.

He shook hands with his brothers-in-law and kissed his sisters tenderly on the cheek. He introduced Santiago and she was led away, into the cabal that characterized his sister's social gatherings.

'These murders? A sorry business,' Julio, the eldest of the two husbands said, his face serious.

'Yes, indeed.'

'But from what I hear it's unlikely to tax your powers of deduction,' Carlos mumbled, wiping beer froth from his moustache.

'Then your sources are better than mine,' he said. 'Is that cold?' He took a can of beer from the icebox and pulled at the ring. 'Salud.'

'You'll stay for supper, this time, Antonio?' his sister Inez asked, as she strolled over to join them.

'Of course, but I can't stay long. I need to get back to work. I'm sorry.'

'You must find time for mama. She will not always be with us.'

His mother came from the kitchen with Holly.

A straw hat, edged with a full brim, shaded the young girl's face and Adelina called her grandchildren to her. As they gathered round to look at the stranger clinging to their grandmother's arm, the eldest girl held out a hand and said, 'Come on. Don't be shy.' Holly didn't appear to need a second invitation and it wasn't long before her shrieks rivalled those of her newfound friends.

Others began to arrive - friends, neighbours, and relatives from the extensive family network - and soon the yard was full and noisy. The men prepared to drag the pig onto the table where the slaughter would take place. Weighing in at fifty kilos, more or less, and with a temper to match, this saddleback was built like a rhino and did not take kindly to being manhandled.

After they'd chased it round the holding-pen several times, it became obvious this pig's sacrifice was going to be hard-won and, after Carlos was upended and Julio tumbled on to his backside, Fernández and other men were drafted in. It was this part of the ceremony that dignified the pig's death - allowing it the opportunity to fight back - but it wasn't long before the men ran out of steam and patience and the pig was wrestled onto the table where the combined weight of its captors pinned it down.

As the men rolled the pig on to its side and pulled its head back to expose its throat, Adelina motioned to Inez and Olivia to place a stainless steel bowl on the floor under the pig's head. She drew a long bladed knife from its sheath, but did not look at the pig. Instead, she stared at hills in the distance and in her face Fernández saw something he hadn't expected.

There was, embodied in her, a serenity, a gentleness and a compassion that he'd only ever seen reserved for those she loved. It was as though this ritual was her way of honouring her husband; her way of confronting the horror that she'd had to live with for so many years; her way of paying tribute to the man she'd loved...she would carry on, remain steadfast, and take his place.

Even so, Fernández couldn't help wondering what went through her mind each time she held a knife, and cut a pig's throat and watched the blood flow.

He joined the other men and, as they subdued the pig, he wondered if her strike would be swift and deep enough, whether she still had enough the strength and the power. She stepped forward and, as if summoning all her strength, she sank the blade into the pig's neck, plunging it through the jugular and the carotid artery. As the thyroid cartilage severed, the pigs vocal cords vented in a scream that would live in the nightmares of anyone susceptible.

The men stepped away, leaving Adelina, alone. She dropped the knife and stood for several seconds, her head bowed, and then lifted her crucifix, kissed it, and walked slowly to the back door and into her home.

The death of a pig, slaughtered in this way, is never instantaneous. It suffers - life draining from it, squirming hopelessly, its hind legs tethered - before it's hauled upside down and each heartbeat pumps blood into the bowl sited below its head. As it drifts into death the body begins to spasm as though its brain has surrendered, but its muscles are reluctant to yield. As the final drops of blood drip from its body, there is a calm and a stillness, but no lament at its passing.

This is the way it has always been and, when it seemed that there was nothing more to see, most of the kids ran into the garden and left the adults to drink their wine.

'Don't be sad,' the child's voice startled him. 'It's only a pig.'

Holly was looking anxiously at him. He turned away, momentarily - his breath snatched from his throat by overwhelming sorrow, unable to shake the image of his father, his throat slit, hanging on to life as it ebbed away.

'Yes. You're right. It's only a pig,' he muttered. 'No one would treat a person like that, would they?' He summoned a smile, but felt anxious, not sure how to counter her innocence. Instead he asked, 'Where's your mother?'

'Right behind you.'

Julieta Santiago took Holly's hand. 'I thought you'd be playing chase with the other girls.'

'I was, but I wanted a drink and I saw him looking sad.'

'That's very thoughtful, my darling, but go on, off you go.' They watched Holly join the others. 'She's very perceptive,' Santiago said.

'She'd make a good cop,' he said, fumbling to light a cigarette.

'You OK?'

'There's something I need to tell you.'

'Need to tell me?'

He lifted his head and stared directly at her.

'Yes, but not here. Not tonight.'

*

80

He stayed an hour into the meal and, as he prepared to leave, his mother took his hand and led him towards his car. They embraced and she held on to him, stroking the back of his neck.

'Mama?'

She held him at arms length.

'What is it?'

'Juan Gonzales?' she said. 'He is dead?'

'Yes.'

'Then you know?' she said.

'Yes. Everything. And Inez and Olivia?'

'I'd prefer it if they didn't know the truth.'

They held each other, as though neither wanted to allow the moment to pass. Then Adelina stepped back, caressed his face and said, 'you have your father's eyes. You're not as good-looking, of course. And you've put on weight.' She hesitated. 'He was very proud of you, Antonio. He'd be very proud of you now, our chief of police.' She smiled, but the smile faded quickly. 'Don't leave it too long before you come and see me again.'

On his way home, he pulled into an almond grove and turned off the car's engine. He held onto the steering wheel, gripping it as though he needed to stop the world from spinning. He looked at the flood of light from the full moon and the gaunt silhouettes of the almond trees, and it was there in the stillness of the night that the tears came.

5

It was sometime after midnight, as thunder rumbled and monsoon-like rain hammered on the roof of his car, that Fernández turned the ignition, eased away from the almond grove and drove back to his apartment.

He lay on the sofa in the lounge and resolved that that would be the last time he'd succumb to the confusion of emotions raging inside him.

At ten, he showered, changed, grabbed a coffee at his local bar, settled his bill and picked up washing from the family-owned laundry next door.

He spent the next hour sitting on his balcony.

He phoned Valencia Ramoz, brought her up to date with his lines of enquiry and checked on the support she was getting from headquarters in Almeria. She was, she told him, primarily concerned about the growing media interest. Press and TV were camped outside the new-build where the four men had died. There was growing speculation that the murders were linked to past terrorist activities in the village and that an unknown assailant was still at large.

He phoned Leo Medina and asked him to go into the village and see if anyone had anything new to tell them - anything about the Ramos men, about Juan Gonzales, about the fascist's parents, or the Priest and his fifteen-year-old whore.

'Doctor Santiago apologised yet?' Medina asked.

'For what?'

'Taking control the other day and ordering us around.'

'I'm not sure I handled it as well as I should have.'

'Bloody typical - woman like that.'

'Thought you liked women, Leo?'

'She annoyed me, that's all.'

'First impressions can be very misleading.'

'If you say so, Sir.'

'I do. Besides, I find it's best to give new members of a team time to settle, don't you think?'

At twelve, he drove to the village, parked outside the bar and walked to the small house where he knew he'd find Felipe Romero. The torrential rain had stopped in the small hours of the morning and the sun had washed away any standing water.

Romero was asleep in the shade of a fig tree in a rubbish-strewn ginnel. Lying among weeds around the tree's exposed roots was an empty wine bottle.

Fernández sat on the ground and waited.

It wasn't long before Romero stirred. 'What d'you want with me?'

'I didn't see you at the funeral on Saturday.'

'So?'

'There are three more widows in the village, Felipe. Widows before their time.'

'I pray for them.'

He looked at Felipe, barely out of his forties, ravaged by drink and robbed of his youth. His skin was sallow, jaundiced. Hollow cheeks jutted beneath sunken eyes. His hair was thin, sparse, and matted to his head, and his mouth hosted festering sores and broken teeth.

'Three widows need answers to the same questions as I do. Without them, they will not be able to rest.'

Romero's dog pushed its way past Fernández and sat at its master's feet. Romero laid a hand on the animal's coat and smoothed it. He nipped a tick from the fur and flicked it away.

'Last Thursday, during siesta,' Fernández said, 'how many rockets did you fire?'

'I don't remember.'

83

'But, you'd be lynched for disturbing the siesta.'

'Another case for you to solve, then.'

'You're sure?'

'If I fired rockets, or I'd be lynched?'

'You heard the gun fire?'

'Fuck knows.' Romero wiped his eyes on the back of his sleeve. 'Sound travels. It echoes.'

Fernández stood up. 'Launch one for me.'

'A rocket? What now, days after the fiesta? You really do want to get me lynched, don't you?'

'They'll forgive you. Just one.'

Romero shrugged, struggled to get to his feet, and then disappeared into his home. Moments later he returned with a rocket in his hand. He lit a cigarette and moved away from his front door. He checked for obstructions overhead and, with the fingertips of his left hand, he grasped the body of the rocket and held it level with his eyes. He took the cigarette from his mouth and used it to light the blue touch-paper and turned his head away at the last moment. Within seconds, the missile launched from his hand and exploded over the village. Romero forced a smile.

'You fired several rockets around the time the Ramos men were murdered,' Fernández said. 'You must have been well prepared?'

'Always am.' Romero counted fingers on both hands. 'It's why I've still got ten. Pays to be careful. Now, will that be all, Inspector?'

'For now.' He began to retrace his steps up the ginnel when he turned and asked, 'Oh, by the way…do you remember the fifteen year old the Priest was fucking?'

'What?'

'The Priest, killed back in 1974?'

'Murdered. Father Emanuel was murdered.'

Fernández felt a rush of anger. Anger he'd vowed to control. Anger he'd have to suppress time and again if he was to make any sort of progress in the investigation. He knew that Romero wasn't provoking or goading him, just telling it as he saw it, but he found himself justifying his father's actions...'Father Emanuel was responsible for the death of three villagers, shot by fascist soldiers searching for those who blew the Prime Minister to bits.'

'Bloody terrorists.'

'If the Priest was having an affair, it would have been be difficult to ignore.'

'Don't know and I don't care. It was a long time ago. I was only a kid.'

'It may have been a long time ago, Felipe, but it seems inconceivable that you'd forget. Was she a whore, or one of his parishioners? What happened to her? Is she still alive? Does she still live in the village?'

'Fuck you. Fuck your questions.' Romero fell silent.

'How old were you?'

Romero didn't look at him.

'Well?'

'I don't know.'

'Oh, come on. 1974. How old were you?'

'Fifteen, I think.'

'Same age as the Priest's whore.'

'If you say so.'

'Did she sit next to you at school? At church? A girl from the village? Your age?'

There was silence.

Romero sat on his haunches, picked up a stick and began to draw absentmindedly in the dust, struggling, he guessed, with images of the past, misty in an alcoholic fog.

'There was a child,' Fernández said.

'A child?'

'A girl, born to the Priest's whore.'

'You're making it up,' Romero protested.

'Eight months after the Priest's death.'

He retreated into the shade and sat close enough to smell the wine that seemed to seep from the pores of Romero's parched skin.

'You're telling me the Priest fathered a child?'

'A girl.'

'A girl?' Romero continued to carve random designs in the earth.

'Do you know where they are now?'

'How would I know?' His eyes had lost their focus and he appeared to be grappling with his recall of events thirty-five years ago. 'I've told you all I know. I don't remember.'

Fernández grabbed him by the lapels and pulled him close. 'Don't remember, or won't remember? Which is it, Felipe?' He held him for several moments before he loosened his grip and pushed him back to the ground. 'I'll leave you to think things over, but I'll be back.' As he turned to go, he fished a five-euro note from his pocket and threw it on the floor. 'A glass or two of wine, but I expect to hear more from you, my friend.'

'I don't need your charity,' Romero said.

He staggered to his feet and stumbled into the blazing sun. 'Don't insult me.' He picked up the five-euro note and threw it after him. 'You won't buy me with that.'

Fernández watched the note flutter to the floor.

'Then, how much will I need? How much before you tell me what you know? What price the truth, Felipe? What price, peace of mind for three widows?'

*

Fernández found Rodrigo Perpiñán in his study.

He was pouring over a set of photographs donated to him in the will of one of the village's oldest inhabitants.

'How goes it?' Perpiñán asked without looking up from a print he was studying through a large magnifying glass.

'I could murder a coffee.'

'An unfortunate turn of phrase.' Perpiñán smiled as he rose from his desk and ambled into his small kitchen. He filled the kettle, placed it on the range and spooned several heaps of coffee into a Pyrex cafeteria. 'You still driving from the city each day?' he called.

'What option do I have? It's where I live.'

'Well, if it makes it any easier, you can always stay here anytime you need to.'

'Thanks.'

They took their coffee onto the terrace and sat on white plastic chairs. They took a few moments to enjoy the tranquillity, as if they knew their time together would be laden with the tragedy of the past and the horror of the present. As he finished his coffee, Perpiñán said, 'Juan Gonzales was murdered?'

'It looks like it. He was left-handed. The gun was found near his right hand. The bullet entered his right temple but exited through his lower jaw. Difficult, if not impossible, to self-inflict.'

'If he'd *not* been murdered, had it occurred to you that he may have turned his gun on us?'

'It crossed my mind but it's not relevant now, is it?'

'I suppose not, although who ever murdered *him*…'

'You want me to arrange protection for you?'

'No.'

'Even so, do watch your back.' Fernández poured another coffee and stared absentmindedly towards the sea. 'I'm finding it difficult to accept that my father, our fathers, were responsible for such a…'

'What are you going to call it, Antonio? Wicked? Evil? Or immoral, perhaps?' Rodrigo Perpiñán's eyes flared suddenly. 'You can't compare the desperation of Franco's years with today. For God's sake, how would you feel if your mother or your sisters had been dragged through the streets, made to kneel and beg for mercy before a gun was put to the back of their heads?'

Fernández nodded, but he was unable to let it rest. 'Doesn't make it right, what they did. Does it?'

Perpiñán hauled himself out of the chair. 'You asked for my help. If you want to solve these murders, you must cast aside all sentiment, all emotion, anything that will stop you seeing the truth for what it is…our fathers killed three people, but given similar circumstances we would have done exactly the same.' Perpiñán's anger was displaced, suddenly, by coldness. 'Juan Gonzales killed Alberto because he was with our fathers that night, but to think of your father, or of my father, as murderers is to deny the age in which they lived.'

The two men sat in silence, but after several minutes Perpiñán couldn't hide his impatience.

'If it had been us,' he said, 'you and me. We'd have reacted in the same way as they did. We'd have been at the forefront of the Resistance, no matter what the cost. You know it as well as I do.'

Fernández knew there was some truth in his friend's words - some wisdom, even. He'd grown up in a Spain struggling with its new democracy, and he was part of the unsophisticated machine that was easing its people away from the horrors of the Civil War and the tyranny of the Dictator, towards the Rule of Law. But, there were times when he'd investigated acts of violence triggered by revenge and he'd found himself empathizing with the perpetrator. If it had been his mother or his sisters, God knows what he might be capable of.

Perpiñán put his coffee down and wiped traces from his moustache.

'In time,' he said - his voice had moderated - 'you'll be able to put the barbarity of the past into some sort of perspective.'

Fernández didn't react immediately. He dragged air into his lungs, puffed out his cheeks, lifted his head and looked at his friend. 'You must have found it difficult, as a child, knowing what your father had done. It can't have been easy after you witnessed the slaughter. How did you cope?'

'I didn't at first. I couldn't speak to him. I withdrew, happy only when I was roaming the hills or reading. I don't mind admitting that I often cried myself to sleep. I had nightmares. I imagined I saw my father killing the Priest and Teresa Gonzales. But, when *he* was murdered, the tears dried up and I channelled all my guilt and anger into caring for my mother and two younger brothers. I've dedicated my life to trying to understand what drove him to act so...' He smiled. 'And the more I know, the less I understand. You were right when you said they were products of their time. Thank God those days are behind us.'

Fernández looked at him. 'I spent some time with my family yesterday. Mama's frail. She knows I know.'

'She's probably relieved. Feels lighter for it.'

'I left soon after I'd told her, but on the way home I had difficulty...'

'Crying's not a sign of weakness, Antonio.'

'Yes, I know.' He breathed out heavily. 'Once they'd started, I couldn't stop. I was exhausted by the time it was all over. Trouble was, I didn't know whether the tears were for papa, for mama, or...'

'For yourself.'

'Sounds pathetic, doesn't it?'

'Yes.'

He looked up.

Rodrigo Perpiñán was grinning.

'You bastard.'

Perpiñán retreated to the kitchen. 'So, where do we begin?' he called.

Fernández joined him. 'With the Priest's whore?'

'I was ten when he was killed. He'd surround himself with youngsters, heard our confessions, encouraged us in our faith and spent time with us. I think he enjoyed our company.'

'And that's all he enjoyed?'

'Abuse? No, I don't think so, or rather, I don't know. Those were days of innocence, days when an eleven year old had no more knowledge of life than a six-year-old today. No one had a television. Few read newspapers, or could read at all. Radios were so big they'd fill the room and the batteries had to be sent to the local garage to be recharged. Programmes, of course, were controlled by the State, and listening to pirate or foreign channels was punishable by imprisonment. The only movies available were propaganda. Father Emanuel made no secret of his political loyalties and Franco made sure that the church was restored to the heart of village affairs. Everyone had to go to church on Sundays and no one could marry unless they'd been baptized.' He paused. 'They called her the Priest's whore, but that was unfair, given her age.'

'Could they have been in love?'

'Is it important?'

Fernández paced the small, white-walled kitchen.

'It might be. If the attachment went beyond lust or infatuation, and if there was a child, we may have a motive for the murder of both our fathers and the execution of three men last week.' He stopped and stared down toward the vast plains that stretched towards the sea. 'You say she was fifteen?'

'More or less.'

'I need to look at every photograph you have.'

'All of them?' Perpiñán laughed. 'Then you'd better make a start.'

They placed the photographs on the table - black and white, sepia, and colour, coincidentally charting the development of photography since its earliest days. They were ruthless in their selection, and discarded anything that didn't fit their criteria: Los Mineros 1939 to1975. They were methodical, and resisted the temptation to scrutinize each image in turn and they sorted them so that they could begin to make sense of the history of each and the era it recorded.

As wind whipped across the campo, Perpiñán helped gather prints together and they retreated inside, clearing the table and placing each stack in some semblance of chronological order. Perpiñán fetched a bottle of brandy, tumblers, and a second magnifying glass. 'The brandy will help us concentrate.' He smiled and poured the first shot.

They worked into the evening and, by the time the brandy bottle was half empty, they'd sorted the images into several groups: families dressed for Sunday; the gathering of harvest; proud miners and their machinery; fiestas; football teams; church services; and the slaughter of a pig.

The wind brought more heavy clouds and the heavens opened and torrents washed litter through streets and ginnels and drenched the lower meadows and orchards.

As the evening drew in and a chill air nipped at their bare arms, they sat and stared at five photographs, each of which they'd placed under a magnifying glass time and time again.

The first was of Pedro Perpiñán, Rodrigo's father. His arm was draped casually over the shoulder of two friends, circa1948. They were in their twenties and their eyes were full of mischief. They wore their cloth caps at rakish angles, and had collarless shirts and braces to hold up loose-fitting trousers.

The second was of Pedro Fernández, circa1973, aged forty-seven, holding his infant son Antonio, outside their home, his wife, Adelina, straight-backed by his side.

The third was of Jésus Gonzales, circa1963. He was standing at the bar with a glass of beer in one hand and a propaganda broadsheet in the other. The photograph showed that the bar was full, but most men had turned their backs, whilst others were staring contemptuously at the fascist agitator.

Perpiñán snatched the photograph and spat on it.

'Careful, my friend…I may need that as evidence.'

Perpiñán stared intently at the photograph through his magnifying glass. 'Good God.'

'What is it?'

'Who's that?'

Fernández took the print from him. 'Juan Gonzales?'

'The same fascist shirt, the same arrogant expression, the same light shining out from his backside?' Perpiñán poured another brandy. 'Salud, Inspector. We have our murderer, aged, what, thirty-six, thirty-seven?'

They sat in silence, enjoying the sensation of brandy warming and befuddling them. They had made progress and it felt good. Most importantly, they had two more photographs that could prove invaluable in their search for the Priest's whore.

Their contentment was cut short by a mobile phone.

It was Leo Medina. 'We've got a problem, Sir.'

'What is it Leo?'

'Uniform are searching for a seven year old. A boy called Joaquin Alvarez. Didn't come home after school. He's been missing for at least eight hours, possibly longer.' Medina sketched in the detail, adding, 'There's another kid involved. Ricardo Castro.'

'And he's missing?'

'No. He returned home just after four this afternoon, soaked, clothes torn. He was limping from a bad cut and one trainer was missing. His aunt called us after seeing an appeal for Joaquin on the six-thirty local news.'

'Why have we been dragged into this? The Guardia should be able to sort it out.'

'The Comandante knew you were in the area.'

Fernández exhaled forcefully. 'So, what time did they leave school?'

'We're checking.'

'And Ricardo's story?'

'Hasn't said a word,' Medina said. 'There's concern he may be traumatised. It's complicated with kids, Sir. It's late, late for a kid of seven, anyway.'

'OK.' Fernández struggled to clear his head.

He looked across at Perpiñán and covered the phone.

'I could do with a coffee.'

He returned to Medina.

'Contact the Comandante. Explain the situation and ask him for additional help. Get Valencia Ramoz into the Incident Room and tell her to collate information that comes in from the search teams and volunteers. Tell her to make sure every barn and out-house is searched, as well as disused railway and old mine workings. She's to contact the police, get dogs out, and ask the coastguard to put a helicopter on standby.'

Perpiñán placed a coffee in front of him.

'What else do we know about Ricardo?'

Medina gave a summary of the statements taken from staff at the primary school as well as his classmates, neighbours, and his aunt. 'Where are you, sir? Do you need a lift?'

'No. I'll contact Doctor Santiago. If the missing kid's dead, we'll need her on site. I'll join you as soon as I can. Start with Ricardo. Get him to talk.'

*

The house was on the lower fringes of the village. A uniformed officer had been stationed at the front door and Leo Medina followed him into the hallway. From there, he could see down a narrow corridor and into a kitchen, where several skinned rabbits hung from hooks.

A stairway led to a cramped landing. A door opened and a woman with tear-stained eyes and her hair pulled off her face hurried down to greet them.

'Any news?' she asked.

'Mrs Castro?'

'Her sister. Ricardo's aunt.'

She gave a rundown of Ricardo's background and the reasons for his arrival on her doorstep a few months ago.

'Have they found Joaquin yet?'

'Not yet. Where is Ricardo?' Medina asked.

'He's upstairs. There's a policewoman with him.'

'There's a social assistant on her way.'

'Perhaps we ought to wait until she arrives?'

'A child's life is at stake,' Medina said, calmly. 'Any delay could be disastrous.'

'Perhaps I should be with you?'

'Yes, of course, but kids can play adults off against each another.' He sensed time slipping away. 'Look, Ricardo knows one of my boys. They're in the same class at school. It might help if I speak to him.' He could see she was wavering, as though she was unsure what her sister would want her to do. He began to climb the stairs. 'It'll be fine,' he said. 'Put the kettle on. We could be in for a long night.'

The police officer stood as Medina entered Ricardo's room. 'We don't seem to be getting very far, I'm afraid,' she said.

'Stay with us.'

He looked about the room.

Toys were scattered on the floor, Tintin and Asterix annuals, translated from the original French, were piled on a small bedside table.

He looked over at Ricardo and smiled.

'Hey. How y'doing?'

Ricardo had had a bath and was dressed in pyjamas, ready for bed. He smelt clean and fresh and was resting on two pillows. The duvet was pulled up under his chin, and his mouth was set in defiance.

'You know why I'm here?' Medina kept his voice quiet and soft.

Nothing.

'We need you to help us.'

Nothing.

'You're not in trouble.' Medina sat on Ricardo's bed, towering above him. 'We need to find Joaquin. Can you help us?'

Nothing. A stillness in the room.

Medina wondered what was going through the boy's mind. He'd been abandoned by his mother and taken in by an aunt who lived a million miles from the slums of Barcelona. Medina wondered if he'd taken a beating in the past, or been abused, and wondered how resilient he was.

He sat silently for several moments and then said, 'You know my son, Pablo?'

Ricardo stirred.

'He's in your class at school. You give the girls a hard time, from what I hear.' Medina smiled and picked up one of the Tintin annuals. 'He often talks about you. He says you're his best friend, told me you swap books and play football on the way home.'

Ricardo stirred, his legs curled up under his chin.

'Pablo reckons Joaquin's a bit of a baby.'

Ricardo snorted.

'Not one of your friends.'

'As if.'

'Doesn't even play football,' Medina laughed.

'Useless.'

'Clever though.'

Ricardo looked up.

'Yeah, s'pose so. He gets everything right in the tests Miss gives us.'

'Pablo says you're pretty smart, keep getting better marks than him in everything.'

''Cept in maths. Your Pablo's bloody good at maths.' Ricardo stifled a laugh. 'S'why I sit next to him 'til Miss sees us and moves me next to a stupid girl.' He looked at Medina. 'Your Pablo's my best friend.' Tears welled up. 'S'pose you'll tell him we can't play together?'

'And why would I do that?'

''Cause you think I did it on purpose.'

'Did what?'

'Joaquin followed me. I didn't want him to come.'

Medina sat quietly and watched the turmoil written on his face. Ricardo sniffed, wiped his nose on the duvet cover, and rested his chin on his knees He was staring midway between the two of them. 'I didn't kill him,' he muttered.

'He's probably fine, but we won't know until we find him.'

'I didn't kill him. He fell.'

'Where was this?'

'That old mine. We climbed down a ladder and went exploring. We thought we found treasure. But it wasn't. It was…'

'What?'

'I tried to help him but he fell.'

'Joaquin could still be alive. You can help us. Will you do that, Ricardo? Show me where you went?'

96

Ricardo eased the duvet off and swung his legs to the floor. 'Joaquin ain't the only one down there,' he said.

'What do you mean?'

'We found someone else.'

Sofia Castaño was sitting in a neighbour's doorway. She was stroking a cat when she saw a woman talking to the Mayor. She watched. He was listening intently and then hurried away from the Town Hall. Sofia thought something exciting might be happening and left the cat and scampered after him. By the time she reached the Plaza de la Libertad she was fighting for breath.

She rested, hands on knees, dragged muggy air into her lungs, and then scurried onto a terrace overlooking the village. From there, she could see the Mayor near the cemetery. He was hurrying towards a group of older kids who were looking at a sports car.

She watched the Mayor speak to them and, when most of the kids had gone, Sofia could see the car more clearly. It had a grill that looked like a snarling tiger and she couldn't wait to get home and tell her mama that her brother had driven down from Madrid and was in the village.

A collapse in the demand for iron and its plunging market value hastened the demise of the mining industry around Los Mineros, but it was a series of accidental explosions and cave-ins that proved to be its death-knell. The closures threw men out of work and their families onto the street and the mines never reopened.

Children in the village had been told a thousand times not to go near the abandoned mine workings or trample across the campo and risk falling into unmarked, vertical mine shafts. But, from what he knew of his background, Leo Medina wasn't surprised that Ricardo had chosen to ignore the warnings and skip school around lunchtime that day.

With dark clouds rumbling above and the first drops of rain splashing to the ground, Medina held Ricardo's hand as they made their way through a carpet of thick gorse that covered a spoil-heap. Stark against a backdrop of the surrounding hills, the ruins appeared sombre and dejected and the wind howled amongst them as though lamenting the dereliction.

As they approached the entrance, the rain became more insistent and sheet lightning rent the sky and thunder rumbled about them. They stood before huge wooden doors that sagged on rusting hinges and Medina noticed cart rails disappear into the darkness of the mine. He placed a hand on Ricardo's shoulder and smiled reassuringly. They made their way into the tunnel. Arc lights were blazing where Ricardo's torch had shone earlier that day, and they retraced the route the boys had taken and stopped at the top of a ladder.

'He's down there,' Ricardo said, tears staining his face.

Uniformed officers clambered down, followed by a medical team.

'Is Joaquin alright?' Ricardo said. 'Is he dead?'

'I don't think so.'

Medina took his hand. 'You mustn't blame yourself. It wasn't your fault. It was an accident.'

Ricardo nodded, but his head dropped. Medina knelt down; his eyes level with Ricardo's face. 'You said there was someone else down there?'

'Yes.' Ricardo moved to the top of the ladder. 'You want me to show you?'

They climbed down. Ricardo stumbled as he tried to see what was happening to Joaquin and then led Medina into the darkness.

As they approached the mouth of a chamber, Ricardo pointed at a raised platform lit by diffused light from a vertical shaft.

Medina felt his pulse quicken. He wondered what the boys had been doing in the mine and what they might have found beneath - what appeared to be - a shroud.

'Let's get you out of here.'

He handed Ricardo over to a uniformed police officer and watched him climb the ladder. Once he was out of sight, he joined Fernandez and Doctor Santiago.

They were listening to a paramedic's initial diagnosis of Joaquin's condition.

'He has sustained multiple fractures from a fall and lost a lot of blood from a wound to the back of his head. We'll need to secure him and evacuate to hospital.'

'A helicopter's on standby,' Medina heard Fernandez say, and then followed him and Doctor Santiago into the chamber and across to the raised platform.

Part of the polythene had come away and a cotton sheet had been exposed to rain that had funnelled down the vertical shaft. This made the cotton sheet translucent. Medina watched Santiago cut away the polythene and saw her glance at Fernandez before she peeled back the cotton. The young woman's head rolled to face them. Her eyes were open and her mouth was locked in a hideous grin. Her skin was pale and grey, and her matted blonde hair was stained dark. Medina recognised her instantly.

'She's female,' Santiago said. 'She's Caucasian. Her throat's been cut, but I won't know until after an autopsy whether the knife wound was fatal, or post-mortem.'

She pointed at bruising on her cheek and forehead.

'Probably inflicted by a man's fist. Several teeth are missing, but there's enough to cross-check with dental records. The jaw's dislocated.' She knelt to examine the arm and forefinger of the right hand. 'We'll take nail clippings and scrapings. If she put up a fight, we may be lucky, but don't hold your breath - DNA from under the nails often produces misleading profiles.' She stood up, took a pair of scissors from her bag and cut the cotton. As she eased the sheet away, she said, 'the body appears fresh, but bacteria will have begun to digest internal organs. Flies would have been attracted to her from the moment she died. They will have laid eggs around wounds as well as the mouth, nose, eyes, anus, and genitalia. I'll get a entomologist to check the rate and progress of infestation.'

'Time of death?' Medina heard Fernandez ask.

'Sometime between the last time she was seen and when she was found.' She looked at Fernandez. 'This isn't a TV drama, Inspector. I'll know more after I've carried out my tests. Even then, pin-pointing the time of death won't be easy.'

'Did she die down here?'

'It's possible, but unlikely.'

She spent several minutes examining the body, and then said, 'She was probably killed elsewhere, and then dumped down here. You know her?'

'No. No, I don't think so.'

She covered the body. 'I'll know more by tomorrow. If she's local, dental and fingerprint records will help provide a positive ID.'

'She's local,' Medina said, his voice strangled by emotions pitching up from his gut. He had tears in his eyes. He moved forward and looked intently at someone he'd known all his life. 'It's Laura. Laura Domingo.'

6

Fernandez made sure that Julieta Santiago had all the resources she needed and then checked the crime scene was secure. It was two o'clock in the morning before he got away and he cut a lonely figure as he walked through the deserted streets towards Perpiñán's home. He pushed through a half open door, apologized and slumped into the fireside chair.

'Trouble?'

'Bank manager's son's had a serious accident. He and another boy were playing in the old mines.'

'God, how many times do they have to be told?'

Fernández sucked in air and exhaled forcefully.

'Antonio?'

'We've also found the body of Laura Domingo.'

'Carlos's daughter? Engaged to José Castaño?'

'Yes. Her throat's been cut.'

Soon after the church clock struck four-thirty, another thunderstorm broke and torrential rain cascaded off the roof and on to the terrace. Fernández woke with a start to find his friend proffering a cup of coffee. They sat out the storm, drank more coffee and put the small hours to good use, studying two photographs they hoped would hold the key to last Thursday's murders.

The first photograph was a group portrait of a dozen or more teenagers, in pantomime costume, standing beside a billboard outside the village hall. The billboard heralded their interpretation of La Cenicienta, based on the story of Cinderella, the dates of the performances clearly visible...

Three nights only!
The 6th, 7th and 8th of December 1973.

A white sash, draped across the billboard, announced that the show was a sell-out. The youngsters appeared to be embarrassed by all the fuss. Buttons stood sheepishly at the end of the row in his tight-fitting pageboy costume and pillbox hat. The fairy godmother's tutu displayed her ample legs and thighs, and seemed several sizes too small. The two ugly sisters looked gaudy in layers of make up and Cinders smiled beneath a dislodged tiara. Her soft, round face was framed by dark-hair, and her eyes shone at the camera. The rest of the cast huddled round the central characters, grinning playfully.

Fernández knew adolescence could re-draw faces, altering features as an artist might rework a portrait. He also knew inexpertly applied make-up could disguise rather than enhance a face. This might make it more difficult to match the teenagers in the first photograph with those who appeared in a second taken in May, earlier the same year. This time the group stood outside the massive oak doors of the village church. They were smiling and carrying bibles or prayer books. The four boys looked awkward in suits and white shirts, whilst the girls appeared demure in white dresses, white socks, black shiny shoes and white bonnets.

In both photographs, the village Priest stood behind one of the girls. The same girl. And, in the photograph of the pantomime, lost but for the power of Rodrigo's magnifying glass, it was apparent that the Priest's right arm had slipped behind her back and his hand was resting on her hip.

*

The storm abated and the church clock struck eight-fifteen. Fernández made his way to the doctor's surgery and settled on a seat in the corner of a crowded waiting room. He took two photographs, a magnifying glass and a calculator out of a bag he'd borrowed from Perpiñán.

It wasn't long before questions started to demand answers.

Could Cinders have been the Priest's whore? Had the photograph caught them in a moment of intimacy or was the Priest simply pulling her into the frame? If she had been fifteen at the time, she'd be in her early fifties now, and if she'd been pregnant, her child would be in her mid-thirties. So, where were they?

He stared at the photographs knowing he couldn't even be certain that it was the Priest who'd fathered the child.

After an hour the doctor beckoned him into his room.

Javier Guzmán was a locum, covering for the village doctor. Young, handsome, and immaculately dressed in light trousers and green shirt with white collar, Guzmán looked incongruous in the stark surroundings. He took a file from the cabinet in the corner of the room. He glanced through it and confirmed that he had been on duty when Juan Gonzales was carried into the surgery a month ago. He used his notes to remind himself of the salient details:

Juan Gonzales collapsed and was unconscious when he was brought to the surgery. He'd been sent for a scan at the hospital in Almeria and was diagnosed with a malignant primary brain tumour at an advanced stage. Treatments that included radiology and chemotherapy had been discussed with the patient. He'd been warned that the symptoms he'd been experiencing - vomiting, headaches, problems with vision - would become more severe, and his seizures would become more frequent and life threatening.

Guzmán looked up.

'He refused medical care, returned home and, as far as I can tell, he didn't visit his doctor again. It's of little consequence now, of course, but, even if someone had been prepared to provide palliative care, he would have died before the end of August.'

'And could his condition explain why he decided to act so...quickly?'

'His act of vengeance had been a long time coming, from what I hear. He'd waited years. But, yes, I suppose you could say that his imminent demise concentrated his mind. But then he blew his brains out.' Guzmán closed the file. 'End of story.'

Fernández hesitated. He wanted to knock the smug smile from the doctor's face, but couldn't tell if he was being facetious or if his black humour was his way of coping with such tragedy. He decided to give him the benefit of the doubt, for now. 'It's not as simple as that, I'm afraid. I'd like a copy of his medical history.'

'Do you have a court order?'

'That would take time. Time I don't have.'

Guzmán sighed and shook his head. 'Very well, if you think it's absolutely necessary.'

'Grateful for your cooperation.' Fernández glanced at the tubular bandage that extended from just below the elbow and covered much of the doctor's right hand. 'An accident?'

'A precaution. I sprained it during a fishing trip last week. I've got a golf tournament in a few days. Look, I don't want to appear rude, but if there's nothing more, I really am very busy.'

'Tell me about the good Samaritans who brought him to you.'

'I hadn't seen them before. My visits to the village have been irregular and neither of them had attended surgery whilst I'd been on duty. For all I know, they live

104

in the village, or could have been passing through. If it helps, the woman spoke with an Andalucian accent. By that I mean...'

'I know what you mean, doctor.'

'Yes, I'm sure you do.'

Fernández ignored the condescension. 'The couple?' he asked. 'Can you describe them for me?'

'The woman was middle aged, silver hair tied back in a chignon, matronly, not unlike many Spanish women of her age.'

'Nothing that would help you pick her out in an identity parade?'

Guzmán laughed. 'You don't honestly think she had anything to do with the deaths in the campo, do you?'

'But you'd recognise her again?'

'Possibly, but I wouldn't put any money on the table. She'd probably have been quite attractive - handsome face, large eyes - but she's let herself go.'

'And the man?'

'Carried Gonzales into the surgery but didn't say much. He was younger, ten years, maybe less.' Guzmán pushed errant strands of pale, thinning hair from his forehead. 'They left soon after I'd stabilised him.' He shuffled several folders on his desk, tidied them into a plastic tray and looked at his watch. 'Now, if that's all, Inspector, close the door on your way out.'

Being dismissed irritated Fernández and he sat on the edge of the doctor's desk, lit a cigarette and blew a lungful of smoke into the air. 'You can make a copy of that medical report. I'll wait.'

*

105

In the stark confines of the morgue in the basement of the hospital, Doctor Julieta Santiago wasn't relishing the challenge presented by the body of Laura Domingo. The body was in an early stage of decay, and Santiago knew it would be difficult to be precise about the time of death. When she'd stripped Laura's clothing away, the extent of her injuries had become evident. She hadn't died in the mine. The telltale purple-blue tinge to the skin in the lower abdomen and thigh confirmed that during the first few hours of death she'd been lying on her side. She'd sustained injuries, post-mortem, to the head, legs and spinal column when she was dropped down the shaft.

'You OK?' she asked her technician.

'Yes,' he said, 'as long as I don't think of her as a young woman in the prime of her life.'

He turned away from her and back to the corpse lying on the slab.

'She deserves our very best attention,' Santiago said, 'and that's what she's going to get. Right?'

She examined the cut in Laura's neck. It had almost severed the cervical vertebrae. As she prepared for surgery, she said, 'Let's see what other tales she has to tell us, shall we?'

The body had been through a complete cycle of rigor mortis, indicating death occurred more than two days ago. Core temperature, confirmed on-site, was eighteen degrees, although the insulation provided by the cotton sheet and the polythene would have delayed the decrease from thirty-seven. DNA and fingerprints had been sent to Policia Nacional and would be cross-referenced on the national database and Interpol. A forensic entomologist had checked the progress and extent of infestation and had confirmed that eggs laid by flies in the first hours of death had hatched and larvae had begun to pupate. This indicated that they were more than forty-eight hours old.

Santiago settled on an approximate time of death, the furthest she was prepared to stick her neck out at this stage: more than two days, less than three.

They worked methodically for several hours before she left her technician to finish up and, after checking the time, she went to her office, made a coffee and closed her eyes for ten minutes before calling Antonio Fernandez.

Fernandez waited for a copy of Gonzales's medical record and then made his way towards the bar.

Brits had colonised the plastic tables on the roadside terrace. They seemed so lost in conversation they barely noticed him.

Inside, men stood silently.

Their despondency contrasted sharply with the bright sunshine that glistened on surface water left behind by the early morning storm. Fernández assumed that news of Joaquin's accident and the discovery of Laura's body had exacerbated the shock and trauma of Thursday's deaths. Certainly, the sorrow was palpable, as though it threatened to suffocate their natural optimism - untimely deaths, deaths on their own doorstep, too close to home. In the eyes of those who hadn't turned their backs on him, he thought he detected a shift in attitude and he hoped they'd begin to open up.

He ordered an café solo, placed his bag on the top of the bar and savoured his first sip of the strong coffee as it roasted the back of this throat.

He took a serviette from the dispenser, scribbled his name and the contact details of the Incident Room at the Town Hall.

'You think of anything,' he said, waving the serviette in the air, 'there'll be someone to take your call. Day or night.'

He took his coffee outside, and stood behind a chair at the Brits' table. 'Mind if I join you?'

They nodded, shuffled to make room for him and fell silent. He smiled. It wasn't the first time his presence had sent conversation into free fall. 'I was hoping you'd be more forthcoming,' he said.

'It's such a sad business,' an elderly woman said.

'Heartbreaking,' said the woman next to her.

They returned to their coffee.

'But the boy's alright? He'll live won't he?' a man asked from the other end of the table.

'It's too early to tell,' Fernández said.

'If there's anything we can do.'

'We know the family, of course.'

'The boy's father manages the village bank.'

'I think they'd prefer to be left alone,' Fernández said.

'But it was an accident?'

'Yes.'

'Is it true? A woman's body's been found?'

'Yes, but I know you'll appreciate that until she's been formally identified I can't comment further.'

'We'd heard, of course, but just couldn't believe it,' said a thin-lipped, thin-faced man. His eyes darted back and forth as he screwed up a serviette. 'I've lived here for twenty years and wouldn't swap it for the world. But when something like this happens, it shakes you.'

'I agree,' said an attractive man with a full shock of greying hair.

Fernández had read an article about him in an English language paper: Adam Wells, a well-known local artist. 'But,' Wells said, 'there've been tensions in the village for years.'

108

They nodded in agreement.

Fernández noticed Klaus Dagmar put down his toast and wipe his mouth.

'Tensions lie much deeper,' Dagmar said. 'The Civil War tore this country apart and Franco did nothing to heal the wounds. Corruption and nepotism are endemic and establishing the Rule of Law is one of Spain's greatest challenges.' He sat back and folded his arms.

Fernández rested his elbows on the tabletop and his chin on his fists. It would be tempting for him to dismiss their observations as ill informed, but they were not too far from the truth. There were those in Spain who still refused to accept that the Rule of Law applied to everyone.

He looked down the length of the table, scanning each face, and settled on Klaus Dagmar's before saying, 'We've set up an Incident Room at the Town Hall. We're treating the events of the past few days as separate investigations. The murder of a young woman. Last Thursday's execution of three men. And the murder of the man who killed them.'

'It was murder, then?' Dagmar said. 'And, I presume you're looking for someone in the village?'

Fernández raised his head as a cobra might before it strikes. 'I may not have to look any further than this table.'

'Look here, Inspector, you're not suggesting...'

Fernández got up and lit a cigarette. 'Juan Gonzales was murdered. Whoever pulled the trigger had not done his homework, an amateur who thought he'd committed the perfect crime, but forgot to check which hand his victim used to wipe his backside. The woman in the mine was dumped a few days ago. Whoever threw her body down the shaft had assumed it would be months, if not years, before she was found. He would have been right, but for two young boys.'

109

He turned on Klaus Dagmar. 'I won't be looking far from the village, but it would be a mistake to think that my investigation will be restricted to the local Spanish.'

He threw a euro onto the table to pay for his coffee.

'Have a nice day.'

Ana-Maria checked her reflection in the full-length mirror. Her white cotton robe was open and 'the bump' was beginning to show. She clamped the phone between her shoulder and neck and began to towel-dry her hair.

'Mama? I got your message. Is José with you?'

'No, he's not here. Why didn't you call back? I've spent the whole night worrying.'

'Oh, come on mama. José's a big boy now. He probably drove Laura back from Madrid after the match on Sunday and they've been making up for lost time.'

'If that relationship's based on lust, it'll not last.'

'I'm sure they're very much in love. You'll remember what it was like, in those early days, you and Papa? You probably couldn't keep your hands off each other.'

'We were very young...'

'And oh, so innocent, Inocenta?' Ana-Maria laughed, and glanced out at the beach and the calm sea sipping at golden sand.

'You shouldn't tease me. I've got enough to worry about. I never know where Sofia is. José's in Madrid. You're putting your baby at risk...'

'Mamma?'

'You shouldn't drink, not when you're pregnant.'

'Mama, your grandson will be fine.'

'It's a boy then?'

'The scan confirmed it. I even saw his little penis.'

110

'Ana-Maria!' They both laughed.

Ana-Maria walked into her dressing room. Her full-time maid was changing the bed. She watched her for a few moments as she struggled with the mattress and then returned to her phone call. 'I've got some shopping to do and then I'll drive over to see you. Where did you say Sofia saw José's car?'

'Near the cemetery.'

'The Mayor hasn't had towed it away?'

'I've no idea. Probably been vandalised by now.'

The maid knocked on the door, apologised for disturbing her and asked for clean sheets.

'They're where they always are.'

'I'm sorry Ma'am, but I can't find them.'

'Then use a new set. They're in the airing cupboard.'

'Yes, ma'am. Thank you ma'am.'

Ana-Maria sighed and shook her head. She would talk to Paul about replacing her. Maybe they should employ a proper housekeeper and let her manage all domestic chores. It would cost, but if Paul landed the Almeria regeneration project they'd be able to afford a dozen housekeepers. She pressed the speaker button on the phone, began to apply her make-up and tried to reassure her mother. 'Paul is off to England tomorrow, but he's in the village today, supervising the restoration of the church. He said he was going to come and see you. I'll drive over. We'll come for lunch. Anyway, stop worrying. José and Laura will turn up.'

*

As the morning's civilian support began to filter into the Incident Room, Fernández sought somewhere he could draw breath.

He grabbed a coffee and escaped to a small balcony at the rear of the Town Hall. A collapsible chair had been propped up in a corner and he wrestled impatiently with it before managing to open it. He sat down, took a deep breath, and shut his eyes.

Ten minutes later, Jacinta Estrada stepped out onto the balcony to light up her first cigarette of the day.

'Good morning, Sir.'

'Let's hope so,' he said, easing out of the chair.

Estrada was smiling at him like a young mother at a lazy child. The daughter of Ecuadorian immigrants, she was short, with dark skin and jet-black hair platted into a braid. She had eyes that seemed to light up whenever she found anything remotely amusing, and her enthusiasm for her job was infectious. She'd been promoted after several years in the Vice Squad in Barcelona, and then trained to be a member of an elite firearms response team. In her spare time she taught self-defence to women who'd been abused. For personal reasons – a younger brother experimenting with drugs - she'd transferred to Almeria to be near him.

Fernández was delighted to have her on his team. He followed her into the Incident Room. Two whiteboards displayed photographs of Laura Domingo and Juan Gonzales, as well as Alberto, Bartolomé and Matias Ramos.

He watched officers and support staff bustling about their business. He hated the profligate circus of a large investigation - computers, civilian staff, meetings, superiors to update, and the media. He preferred to work alone, but his designation as Senior Investigating Officer meant that he was a reluctant ringmaster.

He'd delegated the day-to-day running of the Incident Room to Jacinta Estrada and, as he poured a coffee, she had some good news for him - Laura Domingo's murder had galvanised his superiors into increasing resources available to them. There would be more computer and technical back up and, most significantly, Estrada and Leo Medina were to be drafted in full-time.

Leo Medina came in and threw himself into a chair.

'OK?' Fernández said.

'Been better.'

'I'm sorry about Laura.'

'Such a fucking waste.'

'Just make sure we catch the bastard, right?'

'Yeah.' Medina's breath seemed to catch in his throat, and it was clear he was struggling.

'You did well with Joaquin.'

'Yeah. I took the parents to see him in Intensive Care. The next forty-eight hours are crucial. Mother collapsed at his bedside and had to be sedated. Father's determined to find who's responsible and won't be happy until he does.'

'Not our problem, thank God.' Fernández paused. 'I'm waiting to hear from Doctor Santiago...the results of Laura's autopsy.'

Medina shrugged, hauled himself out of the chair and went to make a coffee. Estrada came over and sat on the Inspector's desk. 'I've been reviewing missing person case files over the last couple of weeks. We're awaiting confirmation of a couple of items found on Laura, but I thought we ought to be absolutely sure before going to see her father.'

'It is Laura,' Medina said. There was a flash of anger in his voice. 'We...we dated, way back, no more than kids.'

'Has anyone reported her missing?' Fernández asked.

'Nothing on record, Sir.'

'I saw her on Friday night, at the fiesta,' Medina said. 'With Sofia, Ana-Maria's little sister. She'd told Laura about a game of hide-and-seek.'

'With Gloria?' Fernández said.

'Yeah. Then they got quite excited about a text Laura received from José.'

'Ana-Maria's brother?'

'Yeah, played for Real Madrid reserves on Thursday evening. Pulled off at halftime and made his first team debut on Sunday. That's what all the fuss was about. Laura left the fiesta soon after receiving the text and was due to fly up to Madrid early on Saturday morning.'

'Makes sense,' Fernández said. 'She was scheduled to dance flamenco at El Morato on Saturday evening, but didn't turn up.'

'It takes an hour to get to the airport,' Estrada said. 'So, where was she between midnight on Friday and the time she should have boarded the flight?'

'Check the flight manifests and airport CCTV. Ask Madrid police to bring José in for questioning. Let me know when they've located him. And contact the Public Prosecutor's Office and get a judge to issue a search warrant for tomorrow morning. We'll pay our friend Felipe Romero another visit.' He turned to Medina. 'You feel up to seeing Laura's father?'

'Yeah. I'd like to be there.'

The phone rang and he lent wearily across his desk.

'Yes?'

'I hope I didn't wake you, Inspector?'

'Doctor Santiago. What have you got for me?'

'An update on Laura's autopsy. We may never know for certain, but it looks like she was killed elsewhere. She was knocked unconscious by repeated blows to the head and body, and then someone slit her throat. The knife was sharp, long bladed. After she'd bled to death, she was wrapped in a sheet and the polythene, and then

114

dumped. She did not go quietly. If tissue found under her nails doesn't match her gene profile, it might help you secure a conviction. If you want to drop by at about six this evening, I might have more for you.'

He sensed that she had something else to tell him.

'Doctor?'

'When you're considering motives for such brutality, you should include impending paternity. Laura Domingo was pregnant.'

Carlos Domingo used to like mornings.

In summer, he'd be up at daybreak, work for a couple of hours before a breakfast of bread, cheese, and coffee. The winter months were slower, the days shorter. The olive crop would ripen and would be taken to the local cooperative press. In April, he'd check on his orchard of pomegranate, orange and lemon trees. In May, and throughout the summer, he'd take on itinerant help from South America or Eastern Europe, not knowing or caring if the immigrants were illegal. He hadn't found a buyer for the fruit or the cauliflower or the broccoli he'd planted under plastic sheeting. He'd hoped a big-chain supermarket would buy them. But they didn't, and the recession put an end to the good times. And now the farm was a one-man business, long days, grindingly hard.

Two months ago the bank manager had told him they could no longer extend his credit. The farm and all he had worked for was at risk. His health was also failing. If only Marta was here. God hadn't given them enough time for the number of kids they'd planned in the early days of their courtship, and when his wife had died soon after she'd given birth, Carlos had poured all his anger, passion, grief and love into nurturing their baby girl.

Laura did well at school, but she couldn't wait for his mud-splattered, series-one Defender to pull up outside the school gates so she could help on the farm. She'd learned to use a twelve-bore to kill foxes. She'd grown up around animals; had watched them mate and helped when they had their young. She blossomed into the most beautiful of teenagers, driving her father mad with her stubbornness and ardent defence of her independence.

She'd left school, had refused to go to on to higher education and for a couple of years she worked on the farm. But, eventually, Carlos persuaded her to apply to university, where she studied farm management and biodiversity. It was, he'd argued, an opportunity to profit from her experience and be part of the farm's future.

She'd enrolled, and was older than most students – a mature student, officially – and, with her good looks, wicked sense of fun, and self-confidence, she was very popular. She brought friends home. Boys with ridiculous goatee beards and young women who seemed strangely at odds with her - their faces plastered with make-up, hair streaked with gaudy colours. She encouraged them to help on the farm and, in the evening, they'd drink cheap wine and make music, kidding themselves that they could be the next 'big thing'. They'd even cut a demo, sent it to a record company and waited for the call that never came.

She had just finished her final exams and had intended to spend the summer planning her future when, three days ago, she disappeared.

Carlos had been over it a thousand times. She'd come home from the fiesta, earlier than he'd expected, packed, and left him a note on the kitchen table...

Off 2 Madrid. José in RM 1st team. L xx

116

He'd heard a car in the small hours, two o'clock, maybe, and had managed to clamber out of bed. But he was too late to see which taxi firm she'd used. It didn't occur to him, until a few hours later, that she'd left much earlier than necessary to catch a flight to Madrid. He tried to phone the airport, but got a recorded message asking him to 'choose from the following options' and he'd given up, confused.

Fernández stopped at the entrance to Domingo Farm.

Medina got out and pushed the gate open. A dozen piglets, a huge sow, and two German Shepherds greeted them. As the dogs barked and snarled and bared their teeth, a voice railed above them. It belonged to Carlos Domingo who filled the doorjamb of the farmhouse door. 'What do you want?' he said, cradling an axe he'd been sharpening.

'We're police officers, Señor.'

As Fernández showed his ID and introduced Medina, he noticed that the sow had manoeuvred itself between them and the farmhouse.

'You'd better come in then,' Carlos said. 'Don't mind her. She won't harm you unless you threaten her little ones or she smells fear. Then I can't be held responsible for what she might do.'

He disappeared inside. Fernández looked at Medina. He shrugged and, with mud oozing beneath his shoes, he strolled briskly across the yard towards steps leading up to the front door.

Fernandez followed but, when he missed the bottom step, the sow screamed and attacked. Off balance, he fell awkwardly and the sow advanced. Medina kicked out at her, pulled him to his feet, and bundled him inside.

'You just got to show them who's boss,' Carlos said. He took the kettle off the range and poured water onto instant coffee he'd spooned into three mugs. 'Sit down. There's milk and sugar.'

As Medina pulled one of the heavy wooden chairs from under the table, the farmer said, 'I know you...'

'Laura and I...we were close for a while. A long time ago.' Medina tried to smile, then averted his eyes.

Fernández took a mug and glanced round the kitchen.

Logs were piled to one side of the open fireplace, ready for winter. The range had been blackened by years of use and photographs clustered on an oak mantelpiece above the hearth. Two of them featured young women who were remarkably alike. He assumed the one taken in the orchard was Laura's mother, and the other, sitting on the top step outside the farmhouse door, was of Laura.

There were other photographs...Laura and her friends mucking out pigs, Laura riding on the back of an open truck, Laura at a party, Laura at a fiesta, and Laura on a field trip.

'May I?' Fernández said.

Carlos shrugged.

'Laura, and your wife?' He held the photographs, his heart shredding at the sight of the two women with their strong jaw line, long blonde hair, open-faces and eyes that shone with love and youthful vitality.

'This ain't a social call, so if you've got something to say...' Carlos said.

Fernández replaced the photographs.

'Yesterday afternoon, during the search for a missing boy, the body of a young woman was found in old mine workings outside the village.'

Carlos's eyes narrowed.

'We have reason to believe it's your daughter.'

Carlos looked down at the flagstone floor.

'No.' He shook his head, his voice barely more than a whisper. 'No.'

'We've recovered items…' Fernández paused. 'An initial examination suggests she died about three days ago.'

'Saturday,' Carlos said. 'The morning she left home and didn't come back.'

He moved over to the hearth and placed his hands on the mantelpiece. He leant forward, his head bowed, and fought for breath as his body began to convulse.

'We'll need to take a statement from you.'

'Can I see her?'

'Yes of course. We'll need you to make a formal identification.'

'I want to be left alone with her.'

'I'm afraid that won't be possible…' Fernández began, not anticipating the farmer's reaction.

Carlos charged at him, catching him on the side of his head and knocking him to the ground. 'I will spend time with her!' he screamed, and stood over him.

Medina pulled at the farmer's shoulders, tearing him away, and pushed him back against the mantelpiece. He stood between them. 'She's at peace,' he said, calmly. 'No more harm can come to her. I'll take you to see her.'

Carlos Domingo fell silent. He pushed past Medina and slumped into a fireside chair, unable to stop the tears as his life crumbled around him. Minutes passed before he said, 'You're sure it's her?'

'Yes, I'm sorry,' Fernández said. 'If I could make this go away, believe me I would.'

*

Throughout the day, news bulletins carried updates on Joaquin Alvarez's progress. He was, according to a hospital press release, still in a coma and still on a life-support machine.

TV news also featured maps showing the location of the mine and a diagram that pinpointed where Laura and Joaquin had been found. Soon after Carlos Domingo had confirmed that the body in the morgue was his daughter, a statement was issued and a recent photograph of her was released - a favourite of her father's that showed her blonde hair cascading onto her shoulders, her blue eyes, and her confident and infectious smile.

The final feature of the day's news was reserved for a profile on Real Madrid's rising star and included shots of José Castaño waving to the crowd as he ran onto the hallowed turf at the San Bernabeu on Sunday. It was, the commentator reminded viewers, his first outing in the all-white strip, in front of passionate Madrid fans. After the game, the press had hounded him for an impromptu interview and he stood, acknowledging the adulation of the crowd, and talked excitedly, breathlessly, into half-a-dozen microphones.

The chill of the church was a welcome relief for Ana-Maria as she pushed open the heavy oak door and stepped reverently towards the top of the nave. She crossed herself and genuflected, lifting her eyes from the cold stone floor to stare at the crucifixion. She spent a few moments lost in a short prayer, then crossed herself and pushed herself upright. It would be more difficult, she knew, as time went on, but if she maintained her fitness and ate well she'd soon regain her figure after the baby was born.

It was the first time she'd been to the church since the renovation had begun and hadn't expected it to be so quiet. 'Hallo?' she said. She moved along the nave towards the altar and stood before the font. They hadn't agreed on a name, but now that they knew it was a boy she'd settled on Enrique, after her father.

'Hallo?' she tried again and walked over to a massive tarpaulin that had been draped over the chancel screen and the entrance to the Lady Chapel. It was there, Paul had told her, to shield worshippers from the latest phase of the renovation.

She eased the tarpaulin back and peered into the dank gloom. The stairwell to the crypt had been demolished and a concrete ramp installed to facilitate access to the catacomb below. She walked a few paces down the ramp and listened. 'Hallo?' she called once more. She noticed a plastic cable with a light switch on one end. It was fastened to the ancient granite wall. She flicked the switch and the cavern below was bathed in harsh florescent light.

'Hallo.' Her voice sounded shrill and it seemed to disappear into the numerous passages and burial chambers that had been unearthed recently. Amid the rubble, there was a small Bobcat digger with its shovel suspended in mid-air like a praying mantis. The slurry of its feeding frenzy was strewn across the floor - stones, earth, blocks torn from tombs and the remnants of a pillar. Of five boreholes excavated recently, two were filled with rubble, two more with fresh concrete, and one gaped open and empty.

The silence of the church had tracked her into the crypt and cloaked her in a numbness that chilled and frightened her. She shuddered, but as she turned to make her way back up the concrete ramp, she stopped and retraced her steps to the edge of one of the boreholes.

There was something on the floor. It glinted in the fluorescent light. She knelt down, picked it up and blew dust from it.

It was a gold pendant - a stick man with his arms arched above his head. She recognised it instantly.

Indalo Man...a symbol synonymous with the area, especially in tourist shops.

'You're lucky I didn't lock you in.'

'Madre Mia, you startled me.'

'I've given the men a day off.' Her husband glanced at the excavation work. 'Thought they'd appreciate a long weekend. Schools have shut up shop and it'll give them a chance to get the kids settled at home.'

Ana-Maria had recovered her composure and said, 'Mama called. She was worried about José. His car was found near the cemetery yesterday.'

'I thought he'd be celebrating - ordering room service in a swank hotel in Madrid and getting Laura legless.'

'So, what's his car doing outside the cemetery?'

'You're sure it's his?'

'Well, Sofia saw it and...'

Paul Turnbull laughed. 'Sofia? Sofia wouldn't know a car from a tractor. Have you tried phoning his mobile?'

'Yes, of course, several times, but I haven't been able to get through.'

'He's probably forgotten to charge it. You didn't see my mobile earlier this morning, did you? Can't find it anywhere.'

'You'll have to get yourself a new one.'

'Maybe a Godsend. The Almeria regeneration should be given the go ahead in the next couple of days and I could do with upgrading. I fancy an iPhone.'

'Have you packed?'

'No. There's no hurry. I don't go until tomorrow. I'll drive down to the airport after lunch, tie things up in the UK and fly back, Friday afternoon.'

He threw a protective arm around her. 'You shouldn't be down here on your own. It's dangerous. What if you'd slipped and hit your head? You could lie here for days before someone found you.'

He kissed her forehead and led her back up the ramp.

'No more adventures. Promise?' He ran his hand over her stomach. 'How's junior?'

'Enrique. I thought we could call him Enrique, after my father. What do you think?'

Paul Turnbull pulled open the heavy oak door and harsh sunlight stung their eyes. 'Your father?' he said.

'He'd be so pleased.' Ana-Maria thought she detected reservation. 'There's no hurry. It was just a thought.'

'And what are you trying to hide from me?'

'What do you mean?'

'In your hand.'

'Oh. Oh, that. I found it on the floor.'

He took the pendant and examined it. 'I'll mention it to Father Gabriel, see if he knows anyone who's lost it. In the meantime...' He lent forward and slipped it round her neck, but had difficulty fastening it. 'It's damaged. I'll just see...' He stood beneath a light and adjusted the clasp. 'There, that should hold.' He slipped it over her head and kissed her gently on the lips.

'But, I can't wear it.'

'Why not? Better on you than on the floor.'

'Even so...'

'It's safer round your neck than in Father Gabriel's cassock.'

She lifted her face towards him. 'It's beautiful,'

'And so are you, my darling. Now, stop worrying. If someone claims it, I'll buy you something bigger and better. And, as for José...he'll turn up in his own good time, with the lovely Laura on his arm.' He kissed her forehead. 'Come on. Mustn't keep your mama waiting.'

'You think Laura's lovely?'

123

'Not when she stands next to you.'

She slipped an arm through his and they strolled from the church to her childhood home.

As they stepped into the living room, Inocenta turned from the television set, her face streaked with tears.

'Mama?' Ana-Maria hurried over and sat next to her.

She was trembling and her hands were shaking and tears streaked her face.

'What's wrong? What's happened? Where's Sofia?' Ana-Maria looked round, suddenly fearful. 'Mama, is it Sofia? Has something happened to Sofia?'

Inocenta looked up and said, 'It's Laura. She's been murdered.'

Fernández dropped Leo Medina and Carlos Domingo close to the doctor's surgery, and then made his way to the Incident Room. He sat at his desk and switched on his computer before glancing at the display boards.

'You all right, Sir?' Valencia Ramoz looked up from her monitor. 'Need a coffee?'

'Yes, thanks.'

'You might like to check the database,' she called as she spooned instant coffee into a mug.

'What's new?'

'SOCOs have been sifting through the rubbish tossed down the mineshaft. Nothing yet.

'No hand-luggage? Mobile phone?'

'Nothing.' She passed his coffee. 'And you can strike Klaus Dagmar off your list. Forensics have cleared him from any involvement in Thursday's murders.'

'Was never going to be that easy, was it?'

'But there is some good news…Interpol contacted the German authorities. Extradition is only a matter of time. He owes the taxman a substantial sum of money.'

'That's better than nothing, I suppose.' He sipped his coffee. 'Have they found José yet?'

'No.'

'Chase Madrid police.'

Ramoz checked reports that had come in over night.

'An Aston Martin was abandoned near the cemetery.'

'An Aston, here in Los Mineros? Did someone come up on the lottery?'

'It's got a Madrid number plate.'

'Probably a tourist who'd had too much to drink, got a lift back to their hotel. Any feedback from taxi firms? Anyone remember picking up Laura?'

'Nothing yet, Sir. Oh…last thing you want to hear, but there have been demands for an enquiry into security arrangements at Joaquin's school. The press have been demanding a statement.'

'Contact the Comandante in Almeria. Ask him to send someone from public relations.'

'We could ask the Mayor. Give him something to do,' Ramoz suggested.

'Cabrera's a politician.' Fernández forced a smile. 'Yes, OK. See if he'll keep the press at a distance.'

'How's Carlos?'

'No better than you'd expect.'

He looked at her, sighed and then leaned forward.

'Better start running background checks on Carlos and Laura.'

'You can't think Carlos…'

'I don't know what to think at the moment, but I want to know everything about them. What they grow, their markets, how they financed the farm, bank statements. Just how serious was her relationship with José Castaño.

125

Other men she knew, past and present...men who might hold a grudge.'

He paused, the image of Laura's shattered face at the forefront of his mind. 'You're right, I don't think Carlos had anything to do with her death, but he is part of her story, and I've a feeling we're only on page one.'

Carlos Domingo found the cobbled streets difficult to negotiate and welcomed the arm offered by Leo Medina on their way to the surgery. Carlos remembered Medina as the boy who'd dated Laura. He hadn't said anything when he'd taken him to the morgue, but Carlos knew that he'd broken all the rules when he'd left him with Laura.

Later, after he'd helped him complete the paper work, Leo Medina had driven him back. They'd stopped at the cemetery just outside the village and Carlos spent time at his wife's graveside.

Mercifully, the evening surgery was quiet and they only had to wait a few minutes.

Doctor Javier Guzmán glanced up from his desk and put his pen down. 'How have you been, Carlos?'

'How d'you think?'

'I'm really very sorry.'

'That's what everyone says. Don't bring her back, does it?'

'I'll prescribe something to help you sleep.'

'Got me twelve bore. That's all I need.'

'Don't talk like that, Carlos. It's not what Laura would want to hear, is it?'

'You talk like she's going to walk through that door. She ain't coming back you know.'

'I know, Carlos. I know.'

'You had them results back yet?'

They were on Doctor Guzmán's desk and it wasn't good news. He'd decided not to tell him. A few days wouldn't make any difference. Nothing would make any difference. It was only a matter of time.

'Not yet.' Guzmán finished writing a prescription. 'Go to the chemist and pick these up. They'll give you a chance to recover.'

'I don't need drugs.'

'They'll help.'

'All I want is to be here when they find the bastard that's done this. They will. They'll find clues, evidence.'

'I hope so, Carlos, but for now do as you're told and take this to the chemist. Unbutton your shirt and sit on the sofa. This shouldn't take long.'

'How is he?' Medina asked as Doctor Guzmán closed the surgery door behind him.

'He's a very sick man, on borrowed time. He has an advanced and extremely virulent form of prostate cancer. It's infected several other major organs in the body.'

'Does he know?'

'No. It's the last thing he needs. The test results came through on Friday and…what with Laura…' Guzmán appeared to stumble over his next few words. 'You, you knew she was pregnant?'

'Yeah,' Medina said. 'The autopsy.' There was something in Guzmán's voice Medina couldn't place. It wasn't embarrassment, but it was as if he was nervous - like one of Medina's kids, hiding something. 'How long had you known Laura?' Medina asked.

'As a patient? For about six months. I'm a locum. I qualified in Madrid and spent six months as an intern at a hospital in Los Angeles. I came here to put my parents' holiday apartment on the market, but selling it has taken longer than anticipated and I was asked to help out.'

'I'm interested in your relationship with Laura. You said *as a patient*. How else would you have known her?'

Guzmán laughed. 'OK. I'm not going to lie to you. You'll find out soon enough. We went out for a drink a few times.'

'When?'

'Couple of months ago.'

'Her father mentioned that she'd known several other men. Friends, nothing serious.'

'Doesn't surprise me. Laura was very beautiful, but our relationship was always going to be short-lived.'

Medina tensed. He took a half-pace forward and said, 'Was that supposed to be funny?'

'God, no. Just that, I'm returning to the States. My fiancée has completed her studies and we're due to be married in the fall.'

'You were engaged when you dated Laura?'

'And so was she.'

'And had sex with her?'

'It's what adults do.'

'You used her.'

'Oh, for God's sake, grow up. No one got hurt. She knew my situation from the start. If you want to know what happened to Laura I suggest you start with her fiancé.'

'But you continued to see her as a patient,' Medina said, 'despite your relationship with her?'

'That was her choice.' Guzmán got up, went through to the waiting room and stared to tidy the magazines and newspapers scattered by patients.

'She could have finished it at any time. Believe me, I'm as shocked and as upset as anyone by her death, but don't blame me for her murder.'

'It could have been you.' Medina snatched a breath. 'Did she say who the father was?'

'The father? I'd have thought that was obvious.'

'José Castaño?' Medina looked into Guzmán's face, trying to read it. 'Could be yours.'

'If she was as promiscuous, as you said…' Guzmán eyes flashed in anger, his mouth distorted and saliva seeped from the corners…'she may not have known who the father was.'

'A simple DNA test would settle things one way or another.' Medina stood up. 'Next time you phone your fiancée, you might like to tell her you're helping us with a murder enquiry.'

'You leave her out of this.'

'She ought to know the sort of man she's involved with, don't you think?' Medina opened the surgery door. 'I'll wait for Carlos outside. I hope you're not thinking of leaving us soon, doctor. We need to talk some more, you and me. I'll be in touch.'

Fernández drove to Almeria and parked three blocks from the hospital. He brought bread and stopped at a fruit stall, then dropped everything at his apartment.

It was six thirty. He was late, but he took the time to splash cold water on his face and run a comb through his hair, then left his apartment and walked to the rear of the hospital. He punched in the security code and made his way to the morgue where he found Doctor Santiago sitting at a small table.

'Sorry I'm late…'

'Don't be,' she said, without looking up. 'It's given me a chance to catch up with some paper work. Anyway, I don't have anything new to tell you.'

She signed the bottom of a form.

'If you want to wait, there's a coffee machine in the corridor. It takes a Euro. You may have to kick it.'

She sighed, pulled her hair away from her eyes and collected another form from the top of the pile. 'I'll be about ten minutes. Make yourself comfortable.'

'I can come back.'

'Whatever.'

'You OK?'

'Fine. Grab a coffee and I'll join you when I can.'

He decided to forgo a coffee, left the claustrophobia of the morgue behind, trudged up to street level, and stepped out into the evening. He walked back to the square below his apartment, nodded at the old men sitting beneath a ficus tree and chose a bench near them. He lit a cigarette and stared at two photographs he'd taken from Rodrigo Perpiñán's collection. He cursed when he realised he couldn't see any detail without the scholar's magnifying glass.

One of the old men sat down next to him and slipped a pair of cheap bifocals into his hand. 'Comes to us all, Inspector.' He smiled, his teeth stained by a thousand cigarettes, his breath sweetened by an early evening brandy. He leaned over and peered at the photographs. 'That's not you,' he said, confidently.

'Nineteen seventy-three,' Fernández said.

'Same year Admiral Blanco was assassinated.'

The old man eyes light up. 'Do you know, the bomb was so huge it left a massive crater in the road?'

'One more pothole, one less arsehole.'

'Yes!' The old man fell silent. 'The assassination triggered reprisals.'

'Yes, I know. A death squad came to the our village and three innocent people were executed - a bullet in the back of the head.'

'Los Mineros?'

'Yes.'

'Where those photos were taken?'

'Yes.'

'That's not the end of the story, though, is it?' the old man said. 'The Priest and the man who'd betrayed the villagers were killed.'

'And his wife.'

'I remember.'

'My own father was caught up in it.'

'Killed?'

'Throat slit.' This was the first time he'd uttered the words outside Rodrigo Perpiñán's home and he felt naked, suddenly, as though people walking past were staring at him - pointing and telling others that his father had killed someone and that he was the son of a murderer.

'That was a long time ago,' the old man said, taking back his glasses. 'And, you're too young for these. You just need to get some sleep.' He slipped the glasses onto the end of his nose, took the photographs, and studied them, nodding repeatedly. 'I recognize the church.' He tapped the Confirmation photograph. 'Time was, we'd drive out to see friends, have a few beers, see the New Year in, drink Cava and eat grapes in the church square at midnight. I was about your age when this photograph was taken.'

'Then you'll know Alberto Ramos?'

'Yes, we go back a long way.' The old man laughed. 'Why, what's the old bugger been up to?'

Fernández told him what had happened to Alberto, Bartolomé and Matias, and filled in the background.

The old man was shocked.

He needed several minutes before he asked, 'And you're sure Juan Gonzales was murdered?'

'Yes.'

'When you catch the man who pulled the trigger, tell the bastard they'd have been last in line if any of us had been there.'

'Under different circumstances, I could have been at the front of the queue,' Fernández said, forcing a smile, picturing the photograph on his mother's mantelpiece - his father holding his newborn son.

'You know why Gonzales killed Alberto, his son, and his grandson?' the old man asked.

'Alberto, yes...' His voice trailed off. 'Maybe they were just in the wrong place at the wrong time.'

'Possibly, but let me ask you this...' He shifted on the bench as though making himself comfortable before he continued. 'Family's the most important thing in a man's life. You'd agree?'

'Of course.'

'And he'll do anything to make sure his child's future is secure, especially now that they have a future to look forward to?'

'Of course,' Fernández repeated, unsure where this was going.

'It's why, in any dispute, no matter how serious, many families will involve all generations.' The old man smiled. 'Let me give you an example. My neighbour's dog craps on the step outside my front door and this goes on for some time. I speak to my neighbour, but the dog doesn't stop shitting. The next time my son and family arrive for lunch, I take down my hunting rifle and we walk across to the boundary. I call to my neighbour and then, in front of my son and my grandson, I tell him that if his dog comes onto my land once more I'll shoot it. It's a trivial example, I know, but the point is that all generations would be involved. The dog owner would know that, even if something happened to me, there would always be my son, and my son's son.'

'And, you're saying that's why Juan Gonzales had to kill them all?'

'If he hadn't, the younger men would have come after him.'

It made sense, Fernández had to agree, particularly if Gonzales hadn't planned to commit suicide. But it didn't explain *why* someone had killed Gonzales. He pulled his mobile from his jacket pocket and scrolled through the presets. He nodded and smiled at the old man as Rodrigo Perpiñán answered. 'Can we meet tomorrow?'

'Before ten. Otherwise I'll be in the bar.'

'I need to know who's bought photographs from you during the past twelve months. It could be important.' He cut the call and, as he lifted the photographs from his lap, he turned to the old man and said, 'I'm sorry, I don't know your name.'

The old man smiled. 'Pedro. Just like your father.'

'You knew him?'

'No. I'm sorry. If I had, I'm sure I'd have counted him among my friends. But I'm not going to lie to you.'

'Do you recognise anyone in these?'

The old man took the photographs and, removing his glasses, pulled them close to his face. 'I'd seen the Priest around the village, but not to talk to. Cinderella has something about her, don't you think?' He laughed. 'I can only put a name to one of the boys. He was probably a bit older than the rest, a couple of years maybe, and as-stupid-as-a-donkey, if you know what I mean?'

The old man fell silent, and took a handkerchief from his breast pocket and dabbed moist eyes. 'You said there was a fascist raid, about the same time as this photo was taken? I remember. They cut out his tongue.'

'Pepe?' Fernández took out his mobile. 'Excuse me,' he said, and pressed a preset. Jacinta Estrada answered. 'Has the judge issued that warrant?'

'Yes, Sir.'

'Arrange for officers from the Policia Local to be on standby at ten, tomorrow. See if you can locate Pepe, the goatherd. We'll meet at nine. Make sure everyone's there, including the Mayor.'

'Ana-Maria came to see you this afternoon, with her husband. She was distraught. She wanted to talk about Laura and her brother, José. She was insistent. She wouldn't talk to any one else.'

'Ring her, set up a meeting for tomorrow at eleven-thirty. Has José surfaced yet?'

'No, but the Madrid police have contacted us. He hasn't shown up for training since Sunday's match.'

'Probably got a hangover, sleeping it off somewhere.'

'I said much the same, but apparently he's teetotal.'

'OK, keep me informed.' He ended the call and turned to see Doctor Julieta Santiago walking up the lane towards the square - her fine hair dancing as the breeze picked up.

'You know, I always thought of you as a lazy bastard,' the old man said, grinning at him, 'sitting on your balcony for hours on end.'

'Don't miss much, do you?'

'I've spent a lifetime looking over my shoulder, and know where each part of the puzzle fits.'

'And, how did you know I was police?'

He lent forward, his face close to his jacket, and sniffed several times. 'I can smell a cop from half a league. Unmistakable.' He laughed. 'Time was, if you'd been Guardia Civil, I'd have spat on you. But that was a long time ago. And this,' he nodded at Julieta Santiago, 'is who you've come to see. Tell me I'm wrong.' He grinned and patted his knee. 'Don't be too hard on your father,' he said. 'Those were desperate times.'

Fernández introduced Santiago to Pedro.

He took her hand, kissed it and told her she shouldn't waste her time with a Police Inspector. She smiled, told him she would think about it and asked him if he'd care to make her a better offer. 'Twenty years ago, maybe,' Pedro said, grinning. 'But, if it doesn't work out, you know where to find me.'

They took their leave, found a table outside a bar and ordered a bottle of red wine.

She sat, as if lightheaded and weary, and propped her elbow on the arm of the chair. After a few moments, She dropped her forehead in the palm of her hand and closed her eyes.

Fernández sat in silence. Around them, the City was alive and the drum of humanity echoed across the square. He picked out an elderly couple. He was impressed by the effort they'd made to get ready. He watched them walk side by side without a word passing between them - their dignity more eloquent than a thousand words. She was dressed in a calf-length black skirt, a long woollen jumper, and sensible black shoes with a small heel. Her hair was tied back in a bun and her mouth was pinched and stoical. Her husband had put on a crisply ironed shirt, open at the neck, and a dark waistcoat. His shoes were polished and his moustache trimmed and lightly waxed. In their faces, he saw, just for an instant, the faces of his mother and father growing old together and, as they passed, he imagined they stopped and smiled at him. If they'd been holding hands, he might have believed it was his parents. They would have held hands, he was sure.

'Sir?' he heard a woman's voice. It broke the spell. The waitress was holding a bottle of red wine and two glasses. She smiled at Santiago, probably appreciating what it was to be exhausted, and readied to uncork the bottle. Fernández shook his head, put his index finger to his lips and took the bottle from her.

Santiago had turned away from him, her face in profile, her hair folding gently on her shoulders. As she dozed, he found himself studying her. He looked at her slender neck, and the light freckling on the pale skin of her cheeks. Her eyelashes curved gracefully, and she had faint laughter lines at the corner of her eye. He glanced down at the training shoes she'd discarded as she sat down. They were new and had been tied carelessly – the laces flopping to the floor. She'd told him why she wore them. The hours she stood during the succession of autopsies that constituted the bulk of her work played havoc with her back. He looked at a small tattoo - a red rose above the anklebone of her right foot, and wondered if it was symbol of a rebellious youth or a passionate love affair.

He was unaware she'd stirred and was watching him.

'I'm sorry,' she said. 'I must have dozed off.'

'I was enjoying the scenery.'

'So I noticed.' She didn't smile.

'Drink?' He opened the bottle.

'Thanks. I'm sorry about earlier.'

'I was late.'

'I shouldn't have spoken to you like that, I'm sorry.' She sipped wine. 'When I'm tired I get grumpy.'

'Don't we all? It can't be easy, holding down a career and bringing up Holly.'

'Thousands of women do. Mama's a godsend.'

They sat in silence for several minutes, sipped their wine and watched the world go by.

'Death doesn't keep convenient hours, does it?' she said and turned to face him. 'Is that why you've never married?'

'No. I'm not sure. Never had time, I suppose.'

'Ana-Maria's a lot to live up to, for any woman.'

'That was a long time ago.'

They fell silent again. He poured more wine into his glass and offered her a refill. She put her hand over the top of her glass, shook her head and looked at him, he felt, as though she was studying his face.

'Thank you for inviting us to meet your family.'

'Holly didn't have nightmares afterwards?'

'No, she's tough as old boots. It's in the genes.'

'What time did you get away?'

'Not long after you. Your mother was very generous.'

He stumbled over his next few words.'My family took to you.'

'Took to Holly, more like.'

He looked across the square as the words *I took to you* tiptoed to the tip of his tongue, but he hesitated and they vanished.

Santiago sipped her wine, and then placed the near empty glass on the table. 'I'd better be going.'

'I'll walk you home.'

She smiled, stood up and slipped her jacket onto her shoulders. 'I'm sorry, Antonio, but...'

'I didn't mean...'

'No. No, I know you didn't, but I have a daughter to get home to. Good night.'

Leo Medina held onto to his two boys a little longer than usual that evening. They'd asked him if they could pray to Jésus to ask Him to make Joaquin him better. Medina's wife, Roz, joined them and they sat on the rug in front of the hearth, the youngest sitting on her lap. His prayers were for the safety of his boys. He dreaded their adventures at the dawn of each new day, not knowing what it would bring, not knowing what fate had in store for them. It was what he dreaded most: not knowing.

The boys were allowed to stay up ten minutes longer than usual and he watched them play. They filled the house with laughter and wild imagination. There was, he thought, an innocence behind those mischievous eyes.

'You ok?' Roz asked.

'Yeah.' He sighed deeply. 'I guess so.'

'You want to talk about her?'

'Laura? No. I don't know. I just can't believe…'

'Seems such a waste.'

'She was engaged.'

'José?'

'Yes. And pregnant.'

'Oh, dear God. Does Carlos know?'

'No, no he doesn't.' He looked down and found his right thumb was rubbing the knuckles of his left hand. 'He only has a few weeks at most. Cancer.'

Roz took his hand.

'I love you,' he said, turning to face her.

'Yes, I know you do. But, I want you to be careful.'

'Afraid I might do something stupid?'

'Wouldn't be the first time. Catch the man who did this and let the courts deal with it.'

'Yeah,' he replied, looking over at his two boys.

'For their sake. And for my mine. I don't want to be a widow before my time or spend my days visiting you in prison, do I?'

Fernández paused outside Perpiñán's small house as the church clock struck seven-thirty. The sun was flexing it muscles and threatening another daylong assault, and bee-eaters vied with swifts for an early breakfast. He unlatched the heavy wooden door and found his friend standing in the hallway, dressed in nothing more than his shorts.

Perpiñán looked tired. 'Coffee's on,' he said. 'Help yourself.' And he wandered across the small lounge and up the stairs.

Fernández stood at the sink in the kitchen and waited for the kettle to boil. He heard Perpiñán in the shower, singing. There was a rap on the door. He opened it and found that a stick of bread, three croissant and two pastries had been left on the step.

'Thought you'd need something before your day starts,' Perpiñán said, drying his hair. 'Help yourself. There's eggs in the pantry.'

'The pastries look good.'

'The widow García drops them off every day.'

'In return for?'

'Man cannot live by bread alone.' Perpiñán smiled. 'How's your favourite pathologist?'

'It's complicated.'

Perpiñán took the kettle from the stove. 'It always is with you. You watch the good doctor dance, invite her to your family matanza, and now you tell me it's complicated?'

'We have more important things on our minds.'

'Yeah, right. You still have a preference for Ana-Maria, don't you? I saw the way you looked at her outside the church. She's a bit beyond reach, I'd say. Married, wealthy husband, kid on the way.'

He couldn't resist twisting the knife. 'Admittedly, Dr Santiago has baggage…'

'Baggage?'

'Her daughter.'

'Baggage?'

'But she is smart, successful, beautiful…It's been a long time, hasn't it? Ten years since Ana-Marie dumped you. How many women have you fucked since then?'

Fernández broke off a portion of pastry and took a cup of coffee onto the terrace.

Perpiñán followed. 'It's like riding a horse, you know - easy once you get back on. Besides, I'm sure you'll be in very good hands.'

Fernández sat heavily on one of the patio chairs. 'Can we get on with it?'

'If you insist.' Perpiñán smiled and pulled a file towards him. 'I have that list you asked for - people who bought photographs from me last year.' He handed him a copy. 'I've been keeping a record of each purchase. Had a huge tax bill a couple of years ago. They'd assumed I'd been cheating for years.'

'So, there is justice in this world.' Fernández smiled, and then scanned the list. 'Anyone we know?'

'Most are tourists. A couple of Brits. Adam Wells, the artist, wanted to use photos to provide inspiration for his next series of paintings. The Mayor sent his clerk to buy a dozen of my books and photographs showing buildings in the village for a display in the Cultural Centre. Paul Turnbull bought copies for the church restoration. And Javier Guzmán bought two copies of my latest pictorial history.'

'Doctor Guzmán?'

'One for his mother in Madrid and one for his fiancée in the States.'

'What do you make of him?'

'He needs some work on his bedside manner, but otherwise...' Perpiñán shrugged. 'Why?'

'He told Leo he dated Laura.'

'So, Guzmán could be the father of her child?'

'It's possible, but we won't know that until we run DNA tests. It's probably José's. When we find him we'll be able to match his DNA with the foetus removed from Laura.'

'You don't need José. Ana-Maria's his sister. They'll have the same DNA. Might save time, 'til you find him.'

'I'm seeing her later this morning.' He got up and went to the front door.

'Oh, and Father Gabriel,' Perpiñán called. 'He's on the list. Came to see me about three months ago.'

'Did he say why?'

'No, but he looked through the whole collection and bought a dozen photographs, including the ones you're interested in.'

The civilian night shift had finished at eight and their replacements were sifting through new information.

Fernández glanced at Leo Medina sifting through evidence-bags on trestle tables, and then grabbed a coffee and asked Valencia Ramoz to update him.

Doctor Santiago, she told him, had emailed the main findings of Laura Domingo's autopsy. Madrid police had asked for assistance in tracing José. Joaquin was still on life support and there was a possibility he'd suffered brain damage. Ana-Maria would be there at eleven-thirty, but her husband had been called to a meeting in Almeria and would be flying to the UK after lunch.

141

Fernández sat on the edge of her desk and drained his coffee. 'Val, I need you to run things here. I want Jacinta and Leo out on the streets for the next couple of days.'

'As long as I have you at the end of a mobile.'

'Of course.'

They both looked round when the door opened and the Mayor walked in. Vincente Cabrera was in his early fifties. He was short and barrel-chested, with a face that was dominated by a full moustache. He'd been elected for a second term, and represented the socialist PSOE. He'd cultivated an image of *incorruptibility,* and had made it clear he'd never accept backhanders or exploit construction applications. These were temptation - he'd been quick to remind potential voters - that had proved irresistible to administrations throughout Spain and had resulted in thousands of illegal builds. He'd campaigned for a clean up and laws had been tightened. As a result – and this was something he was proud of - developers, local politicians, lawyers and notaries all knew that, at the whiff of a scandal, the spotlight would turn on them and Guardia Civil officers, specialising in fraud, would be knocking on their door.

Fernández shook the Mayor's hand and brought him up to date with the investigations.

'So, what do you want from me?' Vincente Cabrera asked, his voice high-pitched and irritatingly abrasive. He accepted a cigarette but declined a coffee.

'Access to the your records, including details of all residents - locals, ex-pats, and immigrants - the register of births, deaths and marriages, building applications - especially those involving the Ramos family - crime statistics, disputes between neighbours, maps identifying the location of mining works in the area and any diagrams of their layout...' Fernández paused.

'Not much then?' Cabrera smiled.

142

'I'll assign one of the civilian staff to liaise with you. There may be other records we need to access as the investigations proceed.'

'How far have you got?'

'We're making progress.'

Cabrera pursed his lips. 'Don't patronise me. I can open doors for you. You're up against it. You've no idea who murdered Juan Gonzales, you've no idea who killed Laura Domingo, you've no idea where José is, and you've managed to upset most of the village, including the Brits for God's sake.'

'Then I'll need certain assurances from you.'

'You'll want me to guarantee that whatever happens in these four walls, stays in these four walls, right?'

'I don't want anything leaked to the press.'

'By that, I presume, you mean anything that might damage your investigation.'

'Information must be restricted and controlled.'

'Even if it's in the public interest?'

'I'll be the judge of that.' The hiatus was brief. 'We understand each other? You'll attend briefings, and carry out requests. I'll also expect you to keep the media at a distance.'

'That won't be easy.'

'That's the deal.'

Jacinta Estrada came in carrying a bundle of files. She smiled at Cabrera went over to her desk and turned on her computer. Fernández told her about his decision to hand the day-to-day running of the Incident Room over to Valencia Ramoz.

'Makes sense,' Estrada said.

'You'll be more of an asset on the street, but I want you to lead meetings.'

'Briefings?'

'Yes.'

'This one?'

'Yes.'

'Then let's not waste any more time.'

She stood before the whiteboards and said, 'OK let's get started.'

She waited for everyone to settle, welcomed Vincente Cabrera, brought everyone up to date with progress in both investigations and then turned to Leo Medina.

He stayed at his desk, reversed his chair and sat astride the seat. His face was glum, as though he was conscious of the eyes bearing down. He dragged a tray in front of him. 'We know Laura didn't check in at the airport. These items were found on her body.' He held up several plastics bags - her leather belt and jacket, her jeans, and a pair of trainers. He took a deep breath and continued. He faltered several times as he explained that forensics were examining other items and were hoping to have results back within a week.

'A week?' Estrada said.

'Over worked, apparently.'

'I'll ask Doctor Santiago if she can speed things up,' Fernández said. He noticed a few of the team nodding at each other, knowingly, and chose to ignore them. 'Leo, has anything else been found? Luggage, handbag, mobile?'

'No, Sir. Uniform and SOCO will search the area around the top of the mineshaft today.'

'Tell them to ring her mobile.' Estrada shrugged. 'It's worth a try. Batteries have a long stand-by life. If it was ditched, someone might hear it.' She turned to the meeting. 'Additional staff have been brought in. They'll crosscheck information and maintain the database round the clock. Any new exhibits will be displayed here.'

She walked over to the trestle tables. 'Of particular interest,' she said, 'is this.' She held up a pendant found around Laura Domingo's neck. 'Something you'll all be familiar with. It's an *Indalo Man*.'

She pointed at an enlarged photocopy and asked if anyone could explain the origins of this local talisman.

Medina put his coffee down, walked over and took the pendant from her. 'I helped my eldest research this for a project at school,' he said, his smile weak. 'I got a distinction.' He cleared his throat. 'Anyway, a team of archaeologists found a cave painting in the late 1860's. They named it after San Indalecio, one of the Saints who'd converted Spain to Christianity. It was forgotten until hippies invaded this area after the Second World War. They were regarded as evil – all that sex, drugs and rock-and-roll – and local families painted Indalo Man on their walls for protection.' He was just about to sit down when he turned and asked, 'Where's Carlos, Sir?'

'At home, I guess. Why?'

'I'm not sure. But, when we went to tell him about…' He was obviously struggling…'When we went to tell him about Laura, I thought I saw a pendant like this in one of the photos on his mantelpiece.'

'We'll pay him another visit later.' Fernández turned to Estrada. 'Anything else?'

'Laura's DNA. Samples were taken from the foetus and tissue found under her nails. The results will be available later. Again, Sir, if you could…'

'I'll talk to her.'

'It's possible,' Estrada continued, 'that her attacker was the father of her unborn, or we could be looking for two different men. We need a list of suspects.'

'I'll give you a name,' Medina said. 'Guzmán.'

'Doctor Javier Guzmán?'

'Laura and father were patients,' Medina said, unable to hide his bitterness. 'Guzmán dated Laura.'

'One of several, Leo,' Estrada said.

'The bastard's engaged, has a fiancée in the States.'

'Immoral, maybe, but not illegal.' Fernández turned to Valencia Ramoz. 'Bank accounts?'

145

Ramoz pulled a file from a tray on her desk.

'Carlos has an overdraft. The farm's been running at a loss for several years and he's borrowed heavily. He's been refused any further loans. Laura's account is typical of most students - overdrawn. But she opened a separate saving's account two weeks ago and made a deposit of a thousand euros.'

'Do we know who?'

'Adam Wells, the artist.'

'Do we know why?' Fernández asked.

'No.'

'Blackmail?'

Medina groaned.

'Why not?' Estrada said. 'She's pregnant.'

'Adam Wells is the father?' Ramoz asked.

'Doesn't have to be the real father, just someone she'd been with.'

'Oh, for God's sake!'

'Someone who'd rather their little secret wasn't leaked and has plenty of cash.'

'Laura had several boyfriends.' Fernández looked at Medina, knowing he was finding the going tough. 'She'd brought home a few. God knows how many she didn't.'

'What about Guzmán?' Medina said. 'We know they had an affair. She could have told him he's the father and threatened to tell his fiancée unless he give her a thousand.'

'If he did, it's not in her account, so he refused?' Ramoz said.

'It's not exactly a fortune, is it?' Estrada said. 'If she was blackmailing either of them, she'd have gone for more, wouldn't she?'

'Jacinta,' Fernández said, 'pay Adam Wells a visit. Then, call on the Ramos women. I want to know more about their coffee morning with Ana-Maria. Leo, see if you can prise anything else from our two-timing doctor.'

'But, I don't understand. Why kill her?' Medina said.

'Blackmail can turn ugly,' Fernández said. 'Maybe she went back for more? But, let's not be too hasty. We need to establish if both Guzmán and Wells have alibis and check them out.' He turned to Valencia Ramoz. 'Val, as soon as the DNA results come in, let me know. We'll also need DNA samples from Wells and Guzmán to establish paternity or rule them out.'

'There's another possibility, Sir,' Estrada said. 'I don't want to speak ill of the dead, but Laura could have tried to extort money from another man.'

'Someone else she'd been fucking, I suppose?' It was obvious, Leo Medina could no longer hide his anger as the denigration continued.

'Why not? It's not unheard off for young women to have several sexual partners on the go.' Estrada paused. 'Look, she knows her father has serious financial problems. She blackmails Adam Wells. OK, it's a small amount, but maybe she contacted someone else she'd been with.'

'José?' Valencia Ramoz asked.

Fernandez rubbed the back of his neck, walked over to the whiteboard and added *José Castaño*. Let's find him and bring him in.'

Carlos Domingo hated Almeria. He hated towns and cities, but he needed to talk to the funeral director. A neighbour had given him a lift and he'd spent an hour with a nice man who'd talked him through everything that would happen and made a note of his requests. He'd taken Laura's most beautiful dress and a photograph of his wife with Laura as a babe in arms and asked if they could be placed in the coffin.

147

When the funeral director was sure he had everything Carlos had left. He wondered in the cool shadows of the backstreets until he found a chemist. He handed over the prescription that Doctor Guzmán had given him. The pharmacist's assistant had apologized and told him that there would be a delay of about fifteen minutes. Would he like to wait or come back later?

Carlos told her he would come back.

He ambled aimlessly along the pavement - away from the harbour and up the Paseo de Almeria towards the Puerta de Purchena. He ordered a coffee at a pavement café and watched pedestrians pass by. He tried to focus, but all he saw in every woman was Laura - tall, blonde, her corpse lying on the pathologist's trolley.

Leo Medina had shown him her belt, jeans, blouse, and trainers. The pathologist's assistant had taken him by the arm and led him over to where Laura's body was lying under a white shroud. The assistant pulled back the sheet and Carlos had been unable to understand what his eyes were telling him - his beautiful little girl, still and lifeless. He'd tried to compose himself. He snatched at his breath and his chest threatened to burst with grief.

Leo Medina had asked him to confirm that it was his daughter. He'd nodded and said, 'Yes.' And Medina had taken the assistant to one side and, for a few precious moments, Carlos had been left alone with his daughter.

He would never forget Leo Medina's kindness.

The town teemed with tourists, shoppers and people hurrying to work. Carlos left his coffee, walked along a side street and stopped outside an electrical store. He looked at the bewildering array of TVs and other gadgets on offer. Anything technical baffled him. It was Laura who'd installed the software for the business, Laura who'd kept accounts and printed out a statement for him each month, and Laura who'd warned him that the years of plenty were about to end.

He walked into the shop and glanced at the bank of screens blazing across an entire wall, each tuned to the local news channel. He stood and watched the updates on the condition of Joaquin Alvarez, the young boy who'd been found near Laura.

One of the shop's assistants came over and asked him if he could be of any help.

'Do those televisions have sound?' Carlos asked. 'I can't hear anything.'

'Each of these sets has the very latest digital surround sound system, sir.'

'Then let me hear what they're saying.'

The feature included aerial shots of the village and the campo where the Ramos men were murdered. He watched as the news helicopter swooped across the hills and zoomed in on the disused mining complex where Laura had been found. He studied the campo from the helicopter's vantage and turned to the shop assistant. 'Can you stop the picture?'

'You mean freeze it, sir? Yes, of course. We have the latest, multi-channel-tuners.' The assistant took a remote and pointed it at a slim, silver machine below the bank of TVs. The aerial shot froze above the hills surrounding the village.

Carlos moved closer to study the detail, then turned to the assistant and said, 'Thank you. Thank you very much.'

*

They were on the way to the homes of Juan Gonzales and Felipe Romero and were accompanied by uniformed police.

'I'm concerned,' the Mayor, Vincente Cabrera, said. 'You've identified two suspects, Adam Wells and Javier Guzmán, on very slim evidence.'

'We have to start somewhere,' Fernández said. 'The elimination of suspects is part of the process. They're our first real lead. Who knows, we could be lucky.'

'You're keeping your team occupied, giving them a sense of purpose.'

'Time will tell, Vincente. Meanwhile, we have a couple of homes to search.'

They stood to one side as a crocodile of young children headed towards lush vegetation that had been turned into a nature area for kids to study mini-beasts, plants and trees. School was out, and this was summer camp, run by volunteers and oversubscribed each year. The kids were noisy - chatting, laughing, conspiring and giggling - and seemed to be without a care in the world. At the back, head down, sullen, his hand held by stern faced adult, Ricardo Castro had distanced himself from the rest of his classmates. They would probably have been told not to talk to Ricardo about what happened down the mine, but to involve him in their games. They weren't to blame him and had to remember it had been an accident. Fernández wondered if it was too soon for him to be back with his classmates, but he had no doubt that everyone would be praying for good news from the hospital and would be looking forward to the time when Joaquin would be back amongst them.

He watched them disappear, and then led the way to Juan Gonzales's home. There, he left officers to bag up anything they thought might throw some light on why three men had been shot.

He led the remaining officers to Felipe Romero's.

His dog was asleep in the sun by the front door and was quick to vent its anger at being disturbed.

Romero came to the door. A grubby, white t-shirt and black, nylon shorts covered his scrawny body, and his spindly legs seemed hardly able to support his weight. His feet bare and filthy.

Fernández stepped forward. 'You fired rockets during the siesta last Thursday at the time three men were being shot.'

'So what?'

'The Mayor ask you to disturb the siesta?' Fernández looked at Vincente Cabrera, who shook his head. 'No, I didn't think so. So, I ask myself, why would Felipe risk upsetting the village?'

'I must have lost track of time. Easily done.'

'Something you've never done before,' the Mayor said.

'I ain't done nothing wrong.'

'Then you won't mind if we take a look inside?'

Fernández handed him a search warrant and nodded at the uniformed officers. As they pushed past Romero, Fernández pulled several photographs from an envelope.

'You must have been quite a thespian...' He held the photograph of the cast of Cinderella. 'Were you type-cast you or did you volunteer to be the Ugly Sister?' He handed Romero the photograph. 'Enjoy acting did you? Cinders as innocent as she looks, was she? Or were you all sneering behind her back? Sneering at the Priest's whore?'

'Oh, for God's sake. I've already told you, I've no idea who the Priest was fucking.'

He showed him a second photograph. 'And here you are, outside the church. Your First Communion, I'd say. Cinders looks radiant, doesn't she? They say carrying a child gives a woman the warmest of glows.'

'I wouldn't know.'

151

'Given the times, she might have decided she needed a surrogate father for the child, especially after the priest was killed.'

'I've no idea what you're talking about.'

'You still turn your *face to the sun*?'

'Do I do what?'

'You'll know the words to the *Cara al Sol*? You'd have sung them often enough. You were a member of the fascist youth - the *Little Arrows*.' He passed him a third photograph, early 1973, taken in the bar. A middle-aged Jésus Gonzales had clambered up onto a table. He had a bottle in one hand, and appeared to be berating the men in the bar, most of whom had turned their back on him. Jésus was heavy, with an obvious beer gut. He was dressed in a dark blue shirt and clumsy trousers. Juan Gonzales must have been home from one of his missions and was dressed casually in white shirt and flared cords. Felipe was standing at the door, his right arm raised in what could have been a fascist salute.

'God, you must be desperate - dragging up photos of a drunken old man. You say this was taken in 1973? The Civil War ended in 1939, for God's sake.'

'My friend, for many people, 1939 was just the start.' Fernández produced the magnifying glass. 'Would you like to look more closely? See the expression on your face? What is that? Adulation?'

'There you go again, hiding behind long words. You might have the education, Inspector, but you don't have a fucking clue.'

'Here's a few more big words. Collusion. Conspiring, collaborating...whatever word you chose, it makes you as guilty as the person who killed Juan Gonzales. Do you really want to spend the rest of your life in prison?'

He moved close enough to smell the wine Romero had drunk that morning.

'It's time for you to sing, my friend.'

One of the uniformed officers came out holding a plastic supermarket bag, folded neatly and handed it to Fernández.

'You want to tell me what this is?'

'Savings. I don't trust banks. Greedy bastards. Look at the mess they've got us in to. There's no law against keeping money in my house.'

Fernández handed the bag to Vincente Cabrera, who peered inside, pulled out bundles of bank notes, checked a couple and counted the rest.

'There must be one and a half, two thousand euros here. Where the hell would you get this sort of money?'

Romero said nothing, shrugged and turned away.

'It's a small price to pay for your silence,' Fernández said as officers emerged. They were carrying bulging black plastic bin liners and Felipe Romero watched as his world was carted off.

'Don't make things worse for yourself, Felipe,' Vincente Cabrera said. 'If you know anything about last Thursday, you must tell us.'

'Think about it, Felipe,' Fernández said. 'Someone's paid you money to help them and you'll be the one going to prison, not them. You want to tell me who it is?'

Jacinta Estrada glanced around the studio. Clearly, Adam Wells was a prolific and very accomplished artist, although she didn't much care for paintings that simply represented a subject without telling a story. Cameras could do that, so why spend hours copying a landscape or a bowl of fruit?

But these, she thought, were exceptional.

She walked over to an unfinished work propped up on one of three easels. The canvas had been washed and an outline had been sketched in.

'To my untrained eye,' she said, 'this looks good.'

'It is,' Adam Wells said, without a hint of modesty, 'but I don't use acrylic very often. The paint dries too quickly in this climate, but students in my class wanted to explore the medium, so I thought I'd throw something together to demonstrate the technique.'

'You have many students?'

'My classes are oversubscribed. Mainly Brits. Mainly women.'

'But no-one with your talent?'

'Are you trying to flatter me, detective?'

'The thought wouldn't have crossed my mind.'

Adam Wells, Estrada guessed, had turned fifty, had dark hair that looked dyed, and a face that was tanned and creased warmly when he smiled. She grudgingly admitted that she could see why some women, most women, certainly those of a certain age, would find him attractive.

'You know why I'm here?' she asked.

'Routine, I presume, interviewing everyone who may have some insight into the dreadful events of the past week.'

'And you have an insight?'

'Only what I told the Inspector when he joined us at the bar yesterday. He upset quite a few folk, I can tell you. As if we'd be involved.'

'Does your art sell?'

'It used to. I've had exhibitions in London, Paris, and Madrid. These days there are fewer people able to afford them, but my books sell quite well. We get by. Why do you ask?'

'Is your wife as generous as you?'

'We like to support good causes when we can.'

'And she would count your mistress among the good causes she'd be likely to support?'

'Mistress?'

'Your pregnant mistress - Laura Domingo?'

The blood had drained from Wells' face and his eyes darted from Estrada to the studio door, as though he wanted to check his wife hadn't come in.

'Good God,' he stammered, 'you can't think that I had anything to do with Laura's death?'

Estrada pulled a sheaf of papers from her document case. 'This is Laura's bank statement. A thousand euros? Your wife must have had a good reason for giving Laura that amount.'

'My wife...'

'Doesn't know. Of course she doesn't. She'd throw you out, if she did.' She waved the bank statement in his face. 'You going to tell me what this is all about?'

A week ago, the Incident Room had been just that - one of the larger rooms adjacent to the Town Hall's reception area. Now it occupied most rooms on the ground floor. The building dated back to the middle of the nineteenth century and retained many of its original features, including ornate cornices and roses, as well as a tile-clad wrought-iron fireplace fashioned by the village blacksmith. The reception area was the hub of the investigation. Other rooms were used to conduct interviews and process those arrested. A bathroom was used to take DNA swabs, blood, urine, or hair samples. And, the doors to two rooms had been reinforced to provide lock-up facilities.

Ana-Maria was shown into an interview room and given a cup of coffee. Fernández was late but when he did arrive Ana-Maria rushed over and fell into his arms. She held onto him for several moments and pulled him tightly to her. He encircled her with his arms and rested his hands on her back. She began to sob, her body trembling. He felt her softness, and inhaled the subtle scent of her perfume and the fragrance of her shampoo.

As he remembered it – how could he forget – she'd been the one with more experience when they first met. He moved out of his mother's home, rented a studio apartment in Almeria and Ana-Maria moved in. Those heady days lasted two full summers, but she grew tired of the demands of his work and its meagre wage packet. He would never forget the evening, almost ten years ago, when they sat in a café, and she caught the eye of a young man who'd parked his convertible sports car in a bay opposite them. The driver smiled at her. She wasn't remotely interested in him – or so she said – but it was as though a world of new and exciting possibilities had opened up. It was a world that confined the young, flat-broke Antonio Fernández to history.

They stood in the interview room and held on to each other for several moments. Ana-Maria seemed unable to pull away and Fernández was reluctant to let her go. The outpouring of sorrow over Laura's death had taken its toll and dark rings underscored her eyes, accentuating her pain without actually diminishing the beauty of her eyes or their impact.

At last, she moved away from him and pulled a tissue from the box on the table. 'I'm sorry,' she whispered, her voice weak.

'Don't be. Those left behind can never find enough answers.'

'But murder?'

'Would it have been easier if she'd died in the plane on her way to see José?'

'At least we'd understand why. Oh, Antonio, what has happened? How could anyone harm Laura? She was so beautiful, so full of life, so...'

'You look tired.' He pulled a chair from beneath the table and steered her into it. 'Can I get you anything?'

'No, no. I'm ok.'

'I'm sorry I wasn't here yesterday.'

'It's probably for the best. I was a rag. I'm sure I don't look much better now.' She managed a thin smile but it soon faded.

'Do you feel up to making a statement?'

'A statement?'

'It's routine, but you were one of the last to see Laura alive.'

She dragged air into her lungs as though fighting for composure. After a few moments, she said quietly, 'She was at the fiesta. Leo Medina was chatting to her. She had a text from José. He'd made Madrid's first team.'

'Played well, apparently.'

'Did you see the match?'

'No. I was busy.'

'I saw some of it. Sofia couldn't sit through it all.'

'I'll need to talk to Sofia. She was with Laura just before she left the fiesta.'

'Sofia?'

'The investigation into last Thursday's murders is not making much headway and Sofia did say she'd seen an old man carrying a carpet.'

'She probably overheard the men talking at the bar, or Leo questioning them, and repeated what she'd heard.'

'That's possible, but a carpet was used to conceal the murder weapons.' He offered her a cigarette, but she declined. 'I'd like to talk to her and her friend, Gloria.'

157

'I'll ask mama. And Laura? What's happening?'

'Tell me about her relationship with José.'

'They've known each another for years, of course. Went to school in the village, same class I think. Leo knew them both. They're all about the same age. José signed for Real on his eighteenth birthday. He's been in Madrid for the past seven years, making his way through the youth and reserve teams. He had a setback last year when he broke his leg. He spent a few weeks at home, met up with Laura, and they went out a few times. Then, he went back to Madrid and that was that until about three months ago. He was playing in the reserves against Almeria. A group of us went to support him. He was substituted at halftime and came into the stands to watch the rest of the match. He and Laura got on well and have been together ever since.'

'But you haven't seen José recently?'

'No.'

'Or spoken to him?'

'No. I've tried his mobile several times. His car's parked outside the cemetery.'

'The Aston Martin? Forensics have towed it away.'

'You can't think that my brother had anything to do with Laura's death?'

'We know she left the fiesta early and went home to pack. She was scheduled to catch the early morning flight to Madrid. She didn't check-in. We're assuming that José tried to contact her, and drove down to find out why she hadn't turned up.' He paused, knowing his next few questions would be painful. 'Laura's father told us about her other boyfriends.'

'She was attractive. Men found her irresistible. But she wouldn't have risked her relationship with José.'

'You knew she was pregnant?'

'José was going to be a father?'

'Something we haven't been able to establish, yet.'

'But it would be his?'

'It would help if you'd allow us to take a sample of your DNA. Until we find your brother…'

'Are you suggesting there may be someone else?'

'We have a couple of names.'

'Men she may have..?'

'Our investigation is on-going.' He looked across the table at a pendant resting between her breasts. 'Do you mind? We found something similar on Laura.'

She fumbled with the clasp, but couldn't undo it. 'I found it in the rubble in the church. The clasp's broken. I can't take it off without damaging it. Paul's mentioned it to the Mayor, so anyone who's lost it…' She ran fingers over it absentmindedly. 'Laura and José bought one for each other. She was wearing hers on Friday evening.'

'Do you mind?'

'No, please.'

He lifted it off her chest and examined it. 'Thanks. Would you like another coffee?' She shook her head. 'Ana-Maria,' he said, sitting on the edge of the table and taking her left hand, holding it gently, conscious of her wedding and engagement rings, 'I need you to tell me everything that you remember about the fiesta and…' He hesitated '…I need to know why you chose Thursday to visit Consuela, Juanita, and Madalena?'

She looked at him. 'Mama baked a chocolate cake. She's known Juanita for…well forever, really.'

'They're friends?'

'Yes.'

'Why didn't she take it herself?'

'Antonio, what is this? Is it a criminal offense to share cake and coffee with neighbours?'

'I don't know,' he said, 'but three men carried their own lunch into the field that day and, as you were enjoying your cake and coffee, they were murdered.'

*

Doctor Guzmán had just reached the green when he saw Leo Medina striding down the fairway.

The morning's four-balls had gone well. Guzmán and his partner were three up and were looking forward to pressing home their advantage on the back nine. Victory would, if nothing else, guarantee a few beers courtesy of their vanquished opponents. He lent over his club and after several phantom strokes he struck the ball firmly. It skirted the rim of the cup and settled about two meters away. He stood back, cursed quietly, shook his head and watched as his opponent's ball disappeared into the hole. Their lead had been cut by one shot.

'At least you went for it,' Medina called, as he strode onto the green.

'What is it, detective?'

'We need to talk.'

'Can't it wait?'

'If it could, I wouldn't be here, would I?'

Guzmán stowed his putter and dumped his clubs in a buggy. He watched his golfing buddies drive to the next tee, and then turned and strolled towards Medina. 'So, what's so important that you disrupt my only day off?'

'We need to know Laura's due date.'

'And, by simple calculation, the date of conception?'

'It would help.'

'You still think I killed her, don't you?'

'You're in the frame.'

'Now, ask yourself...why would I do that? We had an affair, yes. It ended around the time she conceived, yes. I didn't want...complications, agreed. But murder?'

'You'd have access to a sharp bladed knife – not a scalpel, too clinical, more like a knife you'd use for gutting a fish or slitting a pig's throat.'

'Oh, come on!' Guzmán's temper began to surface, just as Medina had seen it bubble during their exchange at the surgery.

'You'd know how to slit her throat so that death was a certainty. You'd know how long it would take her to bleed to death. You wrapped her in a sheet and then in polythene, bundled her into the back of the car and threw her down the mineshaft.'

'Oh, for God's sake. I really don't have to put up with this.' Guzmán moved closer and stabbed a finger at his chest. He faltered as if anger made him stumble over words. 'I'm, I'm sick of your, of your accusations. I'll say it once more. I did, did not kill Laura.'

Medina nodded towards a car being winched onto the back of a breakdown truck. 'You'll need a lift home.'

'This is outrageous!'

'It's amazing how forensic science has advanced. Do you watch any of those documentaries on TV? They're amazing. Whoever murdered Laura didn't expect her to be found. The mines have been closed for years and...'

'Oh, spare me the history lesson.'

'But two little boys decided they'd skip school and we have a murder enquiry on our hands - an enquiry that strips away every layer of the victim's life, both personal and private. Those parts of their life that are already in the public domain and those they'd rather keep secret. Except, of course, the victim isn't able to complain about the invasion of privacy, is she? Her human rights have been taken from her and we're left to represent her.'

'Jesus. You're beginning to sound pomp, pompous.' Guzmán shook his head and began to stride towards the next tee, shouting, 'Now, if you've done harassing me, I do have a round of golf to complete.'

Medina sensed his composure was about to evaporate and he couldn't resist baiting him once more.

'We could do this back at the Town Hall in a nice, cosy interview room. We'll lay on coffee. Your lawyer can hold your hand...'

He waited until Guzmán approached the tee and his golfing buddies were within earshot.

'We'll be asking one, simple question...where were you in the small hours of Saturday morning?'

During the journey from Almeria, Carlos Domingo sat silently in the passenger seat of his neighbour's truck. When they arrived, he asked to be dropped outside the village bank and stood gazing through the window at the solitary teller.

The bank manager had refused his last request for more time and more money and Carlos couldn't decide whether it was worth asking him again - whether it was worth carrying on, whether it was worth trying to keep the farm going. He knew this doctor had lied to him. The test results were on his desk. Carlos had opened the file when the doctor went to speak to Leo Medina. He didn't understand most of it, but he knew what *terminal* meant.

He rested his head on the bank's window and rocked slowly, hitting his forehead on the glass.

'Carlos.'

The bank teller had stepped outside. 'You'll harm yourself.' She smiled and took his arm. 'Have you come to see me?'

'I've come to see him.'

'Señor Alvarez is very busy at the moment.'

'He'll see me.'

'Not without an appointment.'

'Then I'll wait.'

'Can I help you?'

He looked at her and said, 'You'd be about her age.'

'Laura was beautiful and very popular with everyone. We'll all miss her, dreadfully.'

'Can I see him now?'

She sighed. 'I'm sorry. It's all a bit difficult today. His son's very ill after that dreadful fall in the mine. I'll call you tomorrow.'

'I said I'll wait.'

'Tomorrow. I promise.'

'Carlos?' Fernández said, as he got out of his car. He noticed the relief in the teller's eyes as he took Carlos by the arm and steered him away from the entrance to the bank.

'You caught him yet?' Carlos asked.

'We've narrowed the search down to three suspects. Officers have been conducting interviews with two of them this morning. Come on. Let's get you home.'

He opened the rear door of his car, waited for him to get in and then climbed into the driver's seat.

Carlos stared out of the window. 'I was on me way to see you,' he said.

'What about?'

'Can you get copies of the stuff they show on the news?'

'Newsreel footage? I would imagine so. Why?'

'Can you get the shots of the campo they showed this morning? From a helicopter. Shots of the mineshaft and the hills where those three men were killed?'

'You going to tell me why?'

'I was watching the news in a shop this morning. I think I saw someone who could have seen the murders. What do you call it? A witness? Yes, a witness to the murders.'

'A witness to the murders on Thursday?'

'He could have seen what happened to my Laura as well, but he won't be able to tell you.'

163

'Carlos, you're beginning to talk in riddles. You want to tell me who he is?'

'Pepe. The goatherd. He hasn't got a tongue, so he can't talk. But he could've seen what happened.'

'You're sure about this?'

'Not 'til I see the…'

'Newsreel footage?'

'Could help you couldn't it, if someone saw them doing it?'

'It could indeed, Carlos. It could indeed.'

Fernández took his mobile from his jacket pocket and dialled one of the presets. After he'd passed on Carlos' request for the newsreel footage to Valencia Ramoz, she had some good news for him…Laura's DNA results were in.

'God, that was quick.'

'Doctor Santiago's magic, I presume. You should think of ways to thank her.'

He tried to ignore her. 'Get some coffee on. Did Ana-Maria leave a blood sample?'

'Yes. You can pick it up and take it to the lab on your way home tonight.'

'I'll call in and see Doctor Santiago.'

'Thought you might.'

'I don't pay you to think.' He smiled, cut the call and glanced in the rear view mirror as Jacinta Estrada turned the corner. He lent over, opened the front passenger door and she slid in beside him.

She turned round. 'Morning, Carlos. How've you been?'

He didn't answer.

Estrada looked across at Fernandez.

He shook his head and then passed her a small plastic evidence bag.

'See what he knows about this. When you get him home, you may find the press waiting for you.'

164

'That's all he needs. By the way, I was going to call a meeting at nine o'clock tomorrow morning. Thought we'd establish a routine - meet each day, plan the next step.'

'Good.' He got out of the car. 'I'm going to church. I need to have a chat with Father Gabriel.'

Carlos rolled down the car window and said, 'When they going to let me take her home? I'd like her home one more time before she's put to rest.'

'You'll need to discuss that with a funeral director.'

'I've already been to see him.'

'We'll try to arrange something later. The officer will take you home.' He nodded at Estrada who clambered into the driver's seat and turned the ignition key.

As he watched the car round a bend, his mobile rang.

'Yes?'

'Well, good morning to you, Inspector.'

'Doctor Santiago. Did the walk last night clear your head?'

'It helped. I've got the DNA results and the analysis of the sheet and polythene Laura was wrapped in. Can you come over this afternoon?'

'About four? I'll try not to be late.'

She laughed. 'I should be finished by then.'

'I'll have Ana-Maria's DNA with me.'

'Really? Who suggested you take a sample?'

He felt an edge in her voice. 'Well,' he said, 'she's José's sister and I thought we could use her DNA…'

'That's not what I asked.'

Her tone had changed, he noted, as if it had dropped by several degrees. 'Is there a problem?'

'Yes, for Christ's sake. I can't keep track of forensic evidence if I'm not kept in the loop. The forensics is very much my responsibility, Inspector. Who the hell suggested that you take a sample from Ana-Maria? More to the point, who the hell authorised the procedure?'

165

He heard something in her voice he hadn't heard before and hadn't even considered that it might be an issue. It was the way she said *Ana-Maria*, as though she was resentful of her or, if not resentful…then what? Threatened by her, jealous of her? He wasn't sure, but the last thing he was going to do was admit to her that he'd taken forensic advice from Rodrigo Perpiñán. 'I'll see you at four,' he said. 'We can talk then.'

Estrada drove through the valley and turned onto a track that climbed towards Domingo Farm. Before they got there, she pulled into the entrance to a field, turned off the engine. She opened the glove compartment, took out the evidence bag Fernandez had given her and passed it to Carlos. 'This was found on Laura,' she said.

He looked at the pendant.

'You know what it is?'

'Indalo Man,' he answered. 'Cave painting, I think.'

'Leo Medina thinks he saw something like it in one of the photographs on your mantelpiece. Do you mind if I take a look when we get you home?'

He shrugged and handed back the evidence bag.

'Carlos,' Estrada said, 'this is gold. Expensive. Do you know where Laura bought it?'

'She didn't.'

She sensed he might not be able to hold it together for much longer. 'What do you mean?'

'Laura had lots of friends. They'd come and stay, sleep out in the barn. She'd play her guitar. They'd join in. Sing songs. They used to record themselves.'

'They made a demo?'

'I helped them. I pressed a button on a machine.'

166

He sighed. 'They'd count…one, two, three…and I'd press the button.' He looked at her. 'They'd work on the farm in summertime. I often wondered if they had homes of their own to go to. But they was happy, if you know what I mean?'

'I think I do, Carlos.'

'She had lots of boys after her.' He used the sleeve of his shirt to wipe away his tears. 'No-one serious.'

Estrada realised he had no idea Laura was pregnant. He didn't have television and wouldn't have bought a newspaper – he may not have been able to read - so he'd have missed any media updates.

She asked, 'Did Laura ever mention Javier Guzmán?'

'Her doctor. They went out a few times, I think.'

'Did she know a man called Adam Wells?'

'Never heard his name. Anyway, all that stopped a few months ago.'

'What do you mean?'

'The boy wearing that thing round his neck?'

'In the photo?'

'He's from the village. They fell in love. They were getting married. Bought each other that Indalo Man. Sort of engagement, I s'pose.' He started to sob and she realised this might be the first time he had cried since he'd heard about Laura. She got out, opened the rear door and slid next to him. She offered tissues and pulled him into her. She held him as his body shook. He resisted at first, as though unused to the comfort of a woman. But she persisted and, once he'd surrendered to her, she held him and waited.

Laura had been all he had. Now he had no one.

He stirred, took several tissues, blew his nose, and looked at her through tear stained eyes. 'I'm sorry.'

'Don't be, Carlos. You've been through a lot.'

'It was that pendant…Indalo Man. He's holding a rainbow above his head.'

She could see that he was fighting a losing battle to regain his composure.

'It's meant to protect anyone who wears it,' he said, 'and bring them good luck.'

Fernández found Father Gabriel in the church. He was fussing over mess made by the contractors. Shoring up the foundations had delayed the completion of the renovation and, no matter how well the entrance to the ramp was screened, dust continued to leak into the main body of the church.

Beneath, Fernández could hear a Bobcat clawing at the foundations and he stood to one side as a procession of men carried buckets of rubble up the ramp. He watched them push past a side door and dumped their load into a skip.

'They do the best they can, I suppose,' Father Gabriel said. He pushed his spectacles back up the bridge of his nose. 'I'm here to check on progress. Would you like to join me, Inspector?' He walked uneasily down the ramp, his hand searching the wall for purchase. The basement of the church spread under its footprint and was supported by massive stone columns that sectioned the area into a honeycomb of chambers. The floor was cratered with fresh holes. Some had been left gaping, whilst others had been filled with rubble or concrete. Additional metal joists served to shore up the walls and ceiling.

The air was thick with dust.

Father Gabriel stepped cautiously through the rubble and signalled to the Bobcat's driver. The engine died and Paul Turnbull clambered out of the cab. He removed his helmet and mask and cast them to one side.

'Father,' he said, then looked at Fernández, 'I hope the Inspector isn't the sum total of the reinforcements you promised me?'

'I just wanted to satisfy myself that everything is on schedule?'

'As far as possible. Yes. But one of my drivers is sick so I've had to step in. I've got a meeting in Almeria and a plane to catch, but this remedial work can't be delayed much longer.' Turnbull looked over at Fernández. 'The church has weak foundations. Cracks began to appear in the walls when the building shifted. The original foundations were laid on Roman mine workings about a thousand years ago. The inherent structural problems weren't detected when they rebuilt it in the sixteenth century.'

'But the work you are doing will remedy that?'

'Yes. We're drilling boreholes and filling each with concrete.' Turnbull turned to Father Gabriel. 'Have the funds been agreed, by the way?'

'I'm waiting for confirmation.'

'A delay could prove costly.' Turnbull climbed into the cab, turned and smiled. 'It's good to see you again, Antonio.'

The Bobcat's engine gunned into life and Fernández followed Father Gabriel up the ramp.

They left the church and, as they walked up the main road towards the heart of the village, the Priest said, 'You wanted to see me?'

'Rodrigo says you bought several photographs of the village. Life in the early nineteen-seventies?'

'Yes.'

They walked to a terrace overlooking the plains and mountains. The priest sat on a bench and patted the seat beside him.

'Why?'

169

'Why?' Father Gabriel pursed his lips. 'Perhaps I should explain. After Father Emanuel was killed, Rome wouldn't allow the village to have its own priest. He was murdered and I think you're aware of the part your father played that dreadful night?'

Fernández sat, silently. He was struggling with both the accusation and its veracity.

'His murder shocked Rome, particularly because it happened so long after the terrible events of the Civil War.' Father Gabriel looked at him. 'Juan Gonzales was the only person who would talk to me about that night, in January 1974.'

'You knew he was going to kill Alberto Ramos?'

'Of course not, but after what he did last Thursday, you cannot doubt the depth of his despair and the anger he felt when he heard that both his father and his mother had been slaughtered.' He brushed a fleck of dust from his cassock. 'The assassination of Prime Minister, Luis Blanco, in December 1973 is still regarded as one of the first acts of modern terrorism. Those who plotted his death, those who carried out the attack, and those who harboured the perpetrators were, effectively, part of the same terrorist organisation.'

'You're saying my father was a terrorist?'

'That's what today's newspapers would say. Imagine the headlines...'*The hunt for the terrorists who killed the Prime Minister*'. What else would you expect those responsible to be called? Freedom fighters? ETA is still active, still committing acts of terrorism, still killing innocent people.'

The Priest looked at him.

'To take another man's life is no more excusable in war than it is under circumstances faced by your father. No matter how much we might argue that the cause was just.'

'But the death squad killed three innocent people that night and it was Father Emanuel and Jésus Gonzales who betrayed them.'

'And Teresa Gonzales? What part did she play? Did she deserve to die?'

Fernández turned away, his anger threatening to spill over. He was still struggling to justify what his father had done and wondered if he'd ever be able to come to terms with the barbarity of his actions.

Father Gabriel was staring at his sandals. 'I needed copies of the photographs because Rome has charged me with finding out the truth. I need to know everything that happened that evening, in January 1974. If I can uncover the truth then it may be possible to begin a process of reconciliation.'

'And the village would have its own Priest, full time?'

'Yes, but only if I learn *all* there is to know. And that means exposing your father and his accomplices.'

'Accomplices?' The word stung. 'And, your report will be made public?' Fernández said.

'That's for Rome to decide, but these days it's difficult to suppress matters that are deemed to be in the public interest. But, I'll see what I can do and, with your help, who knows what miracles we can perform, eh?'

'I'll make sure you have access to information once it's no longer sub judice.'

'I also need to know if there is any truth in the rumour that Emanuel fathered a child. I need to find the woman known as the Priest's whore and I think you might be able to help me, Inspector.'

*

171

Fernández left Father Gabriel and went to the Town Hall. As he entered the square, the old mayor called after him. 'Antonio. Can you spare me a moment of your precious time?'

'What can I do for you, Eduardo?'

'It's more a case of what we can do for you.'

'We?'

'Things have changed since we spoke at the funeral.'

'I'm forgiven then?'

'Passions were running high. You understand? We may never be able to come to terms with the deaths of Alberto, Bartolomé and Matias but we can understand *why* they were killed. Concentrate on finding out who killed Laura.'

'You must know I won't rest until both cases have been resolved.'

The old mayor was silent for a moment. He dropped his head and shuffled his feet, as though debating with himself. 'That's as we expected.'

'You keep saying *we.*'

'Since the funeral, we've been talking.'

'We?'

'We know Rodrigo has been helping you. We know that you've questioned Felipe Romero and taken things from his home. But, for most of us, nothing adds up.'

'Then, let's hope my arithmetic is superior.'

'Come on, Inspector, we're trying to help.'

Fernández took out a cigarette.

The offer was tempting and he'd be stupid not to take it. This was a sign that the men in the village had seen sense and their co-operation, no matter how begrudging, was exactly what he'd hoped for.

'Laura's murder changes everything,' Gomez said.

He accepted a cigarette and cupped his hands around the lighter's weak flame. 'We want to help.'

'You must know I won't tolerate any vigilantes.'

172

'Yes, of course, but you don't have the manpower to cover everything. You have the press on your shoulder, José's missing, and his fiancée's in the city morgue.' Gomez drew deeply on his cigarette. 'We're offering to help, in any way we can.'

'You think the men can be trusted not to step outside the law?'

'You have my personal assurance.'

'But, it's not your responsibility, is it?' He needed to channel the men's anger, and their frustration and their fear, and not allow it to run rampant, unchecked. He'd felt their volatility outside the church on the day of the funerals and knew this was something that could blow up in his face. He turned and faced the man who had been, for at least a decade, 'the law' in this community. If anyone could keep the men on a tight reign, it was Eduardo Gomez.

He stubbed out his cigarette. 'You're serious?'

'Yes.'

'Then you'll need to report to Sargento Estrada at the Town Hall. You'll be part of the civilian support. Go there now and she'll brief you.'

'I knew you'd see sense.' Gomez offered his hand. 'You won't regret this, Antonio. You'll see.'

As he walked towards his car, Aimee Douglas called after him. 'Hey, Inspector, wait up.'

As she ran towards him, he watched her encourage a stray dog to follow.

'You got a moment?' she asked. 'I've been thinking about what you said, about girls in the village who'd play with little Sofia.'

'You've found Gloria?'

173

'Not yet. Most kids of that age go to school. So, I could have missed her. Maybe she doesn't exist? Now, there'd be a mystery for you, Inspector.' She chuckled and, Fernández thought, she seemed happier than the last time they'd spoken. 'There isn't anyone called Gloria in the village, as far as I know. Least ways, I haven't come across her. I thought it could be an imaginary friend. So, I asked Sofia.'

He stopped abruptly. 'And?'

'Nothing. That's what's so strange. When I was a kid I told my friends I had a horse. I pretended I'd been mucking out his pen, grooming him, feeding him, taking him for a canter. A pack of lies, of course, but there you go.'

'But when you asked Sofia?'

'She told me she had a secret she'd promised never to tell.'

'Promised who?' He felt his pulse quicken. 'Did she mention anyone, anyone at all?'

'No. Like I said, she told me she had a secret. It was as though she was desperate to tell someone but was afraid to.'

'Afraid?'

'You know what it's like when you're a kid and you're worried because you've done something wrong?' Aimee looked at him, her face serious and worried. 'I'm not a trick-cyclist, but she's got some serious stuff going on in her head. She was so free-range, giggling, up to mischief. You know what I mean?'

'Yes, but?'

'So much has happened. Her brother's gone missing, his car's been found near the cemetery, his girlfriend's been murdered, her mother's upset - crying an' stuff - and those men were murdered near her home. All that's gotta do little Sofia's head in, don't you think?'

*

Leo Medina was first to arrive back at the Incident Room, but couldn't face outstanding paper work.

He seemed despondent.

'Leo?' Ramoz said.

'Yeah?'

'You ok?'

'Yeah.' He turned back to his computer.

'Kids glad to be out of school?'

'The youngest waited until he's on holiday to go down with flu and the eldest one's got a cough like he's smoking two packets a day.'

'Best get them to the doctor's.'

'Roz'll wait - see if they get any better.'

'You've told her about Doctor Guzmán and Laura?'

'She doesn't need me to keep her up-to-date. Gossip doesn't take long to get round, does it?'

'She coping?'

'Yeah, her mama's staying with us for the summer.'

'How did your interview with Guzmán go?'

'I'm not sure…but do you know what fucks me?'

'Leo?'

'He showed no sign of sadness or loss.'

'You think he killed Laura.'

'The only thing I'm sure about is that he's a piece of shit.'

'Does he have an alibi?'

'Says he'd been invited to a Lodge meeting on Friday evening, then toured bars on the beach.'

'I'll send Uniform down to the front - see if anyone can remember seeing him. Did he consent to a DNA sample?'

'Yeah. Said he'd drop by before surgery this evening. He didn't seem overly concerned. If he is the father, he's not going to have to worry about maintenance is he?'

175

Jacinta Estrada breezed in.

'Eduardo Gomez is waiting,' Ramoz told her.

'Yes, I know, I had a call. Do me a favour Val…give him a coffee. I'll see him after I've had lunch.'

'How's Carlos?'

'Fucked up. He tried to see the bank manager. I took him home. We were greeted by a couple of journalists.'

'I hope he set his dogs on them.' Medina muttered.

'No, but he did discharge both barrels of his shotgun at them.'

'You're joking.'

'We pulled up at the farm, went inside, and then, before I knew it, he'd taken a loaded twelve-bore outside and fired above their heads. By the time I got there, he'd given them a piece of his mind and they'd fled.'

'Probably did him a power of good.'

'We'll have to be seen to take action against him, just in case anyone files a complaint.' Estrada removed her jacket and tossed it over her chair. 'And Adam Wells?'

'Another piece of shit,' muttered Medina. 'He'll have some explaining to do when his wife puts two and two together.'

'Alibi?'

'Says they went to the fiesta on Friday, stayed until it was pretty obvious the band weren't going to play and went home about one.'

'And the only witness to that…is his wife?' Estrada shook her head.

'He doesn't want us to speak to her. I wonder why?'

'DNA?'

'Says, he'll come in before his art class this evening, hopes his cooperation will buy our discretion.'

'Any idea what time he's likely to be here?' Ramoz asked. 'It's my little one's birthday and I was hoping…'

'You go. Just don't forget my piece of cake tomorrow morning.' Estrada smiled, thinly.

176

She pulled several evidence bags from a holdall and looked across at Medina.

'You were right, Leo. The photos of Laura and José at the farm? Both of them were wearing pendants of the Indalo Man.'

She handed him evidence bags and he looked through the clear plastic at the faces of the young lovers.

'Need to find him, don't we?'

'Everything that could be done, is being done. In the meantime, check if anything useful has been found in the bags taken from the homes of Juan Gonzales and Felipe Romero. Let me know.' She watched Medina trudge out of the room, and then turned to Ramoz. 'Keep an eye on him.'

'I'm not surprised he's finding it difficult. Not sure if I'd cope half as well.'

'You and me.' Estrada handed her photos of Laura and José. 'Process these and put them with everything else we've found. And don't forget that coffee for Eduardo Gomez. I can't spend too long with him. I need to talk to our three widows.'

As she looked through the window of the morgue, Julieta Santiago could see that Fernández was sitting in the corridor - eyes closed, face tight in concentration, forehead furrowed, arms folded, and the fingers of his right hand drumming on a cool-safe.

She decided to leave him where he was and retrieved a recording she'd made during an autopsy earlier that day…a young man, twenty-three years old, had died of a heart attack.

She'd arranged to see the family, to explain that he'd had a congenital heart defect and could have gone at any

177

time. As she soaked up the family's anguish, she poured out more energy than she could afford and, in the end, the only way she felt she could cope was to walk away.

She grabbed a couple of files, tucked them under her arm, filled a paper cup with water from a dispenser, then walked along the corridor and nudged the Inspector's toecap.

He woke with a start.

'Have you brought her sample?' Santiago asked.

'Yes.' He handed over the cool-safe containing Ana-Maria's DNA. 'How'd it go?' he said.

'What?'

'One of your technicians told me you were with the family of a kid...'

'Yes...' She hesitated and exhaled forcefully. 'Heart attack. He was playing football on the beach, for God's sake.' She sat next to him, opened the cool-safe and toyed with the tubes in the micro centrifuge. 'Did you authorize this?'

'Yes.'

She sighed, threw back her head and blew a lungful of air up towards the ceiling.

'Is there a problem?'

'If we're to stand any chance of a conviction, the forensics will need to be watertight. I've seen too many lawyers drive a horse and cart between the prosecution's case and the truth. I don't want to lose this one. And besides, samples like this are usually a waste of time. Ana-Maria is José's sister. If he is the father, Ana-Maria would be the child's aunt. There may not be a sufficient match for the DNA to be used in court. I'll get the sample processed but don't hold your breath.'

He broke open a new packet of cigarettes.

'Not down here. Come up to my office.'

She led him up two floors. The room was sunny and a vase of flowers stood in the centre of a large table.

178

'There's an ashtray on the table. Browse through the files if you want to.'

'I'd prefer the edited highlights.'

'I'll get some coffee.' She threw the files on the table, removed her lab coat, and then picked up a kettle, and disappeared into an adjoining room that served as a kitchen and storeroom.

He walked over to the window, lit a cigarette and looked down at the hospital car park. She was right, of course. If forensic evidence was compromised, there'd be no conviction.

She carried a tray with two mugs, a cafeteria and a box of chocolates, to the table. 'Help yourself.'

'I'll pass.' He dragged on a cigarette and watched her bury herself in one of the files. 'Did you ever have an imaginary friend?' he asked.

'Yes. It's a phase most kids go through. They can be very real and any suggestion to the contrary can provoke a reaction - big pout, sulks, and a scornful affirmation of the adult's stupidity. Holly and Sofia share an imaginary friend.'

'Gloria?'

'Yes, how did you know?'

'Educated guess.' He pulled up a chair and sat next to her. 'So, you said you had something for me?'

She opened a file.

'We took three different DNA samples...Laura's. Deposits found under her fingernails. And her unborn child's. The child's DNA should help us identify the father.'

'Two men have volunteered samples. We're waiting to interview her fiancé.'

'Still missing?'

'He hasn't come forward or contacted anyone in his family. It's possible that he was the last person to see her alive.'

179

She sipped her coffee, took another file, flipped it open, and scanned it quickly. 'The sheet that was used to wrap Laura's body, is fine Egyptian cotton. And when I say fine, I mean expensive. There'll only be a few shops selling quality linen like this, even in Almeria. The killer must have worked quickly or in poor lighting. He overlooked a laundry ticket stapled to a corner. There's no company name, address, or telephone number. It's a ticket with a number on it, like a raffle ticket. But, we've immersed it in Ninhydrin and lifted a fingerprint. It's unlikely to be the killer's, but if you can match the print with someone at the laundry they might be able to identify the customer.'

'I'll ask Jacinta Estrada to organize visits to laundries and high-end retailer in Almeria.'

'It's a long shot.'

'It's worth a try.'

'We found traces of Laura's blood and hair on the sheet, as well as fibres from her clothing and particles of sand. We also found salt deposits.'

'Salt?'

'Sea water that had dried into the fabric.'

'A beach?'

'Most probably. The small amount of blood found on the sheet suggests she'd bled to death before she was wrapped in it.'

'So, he took her to the beach...were there signs of sexual intercourse or rape?'

'No, but they argued. He hit her, repeatedly, and then slit her throat.' She hesitated. 'Why would he do that? Why not break her neck or use a rock to smash her skull?'

Her face darkened and she pulled a box of tissues from the top drawer of a filing cabinet.

He watched as she composed herself and waited. She looked exhausted and he wondered why she'd chosen this particular vocation - one that took such a toll on her, day in, and day out?

She sniffed, wiped her eyes and said, 'we lifted several sets of fingerprints from the polythene and found traces of cement, sand, and lime. The polythene had probably been used to protect building materials from the elements. If you're lucky, there'll be traces in the car used to take the body from the beach to the mineshaft. But even if you do find traces, you may not be able to make it stick in court.'

'Because anyone could have found the polythene on a building site.'

'Finding her blood in someone's car would help.' She wiped her nose again, and threw the tissue into a waste paper basket. 'You still haven't told me why you think he slit her throat.'

He sighed heavily. 'I don't know. It could be his calling card or he could be a local used to slitting a pig's throat. He could have acted instinctively or during the frenzy of the kill. He may have wanted to protect his car by draining the blood and let the high tide wash it away - no trace, no evidence.' He hesitated. 'We're assuming she was attacked because she was pregnant and extorting money.'

'And, went back for more.'

'But, what if it wasn't as simple that?'

'What do you mean?'

'I'm not sure. I'm still wrestling with the murders in the campo last Thursday.'

'But we're getting closer to the truth? You know why Juan Gonzales shot the Ramos men?'

'Yes. But, we still don't know who shot Gonzales and tried to fake his suicide, or why Bartolomé was finished off.' He got up and walked to the window overlooking the car park.

'You OK?' She asked.

181

'Not really.' He continued to stare out of the window.

'What is it, Antonio? What's wrong?'

He dragged air into his lungs and was determined not to renege on his resolution and succumb to his emotions, but he wanted to tell her...

When he'd finished, Santiago joined him, linked an arm though his and said gently, 'I wish you'd told me before.'

'The timing's never been right, has it? It's why I found Sunday so difficult...when mama slaughtered the pig.' He hesitated. 'I'm sorry for keeping you out of this particular loop.'

She closed her eyes and shuddered and he slipped his jacket over her shoulders. 'Thanks,' she said, and pulled the coat tighter into her. 'And thanks for telling me about your father.' They stood for several moments, arm in arm, as though hypnotised by the mundane activity in the car park below. 'Do you miss him?' she asked.

'Never knew him. There are photographs, of course, and mama is full of stories. But there's always been...'

'Something missing? An empty place at the table?'

He shrugged.

'I've found it very painful,' she said. 'Not knowing.'

He looked at her.

'I'm adopted,' she said.

He was unsure what to say and felt inadequate.

'Mama and Papa love me and I love them. They've been amazing.'

'I would never have known.'

'No, you wouldn't. Why would you? But I'll always wonder. My mother, my birth mother, died before I had time to draw my first breath. It's why I'm so protective of Holly, I suppose.'

'And your father?'

'Left before I was born. History repeating itself.'

She sighed heavily and pulled him closer.

They stood for several minutes, as if finding comfort in each other.

'We should get back to work,' he said.

'Yes.'

He was unsure how she'd react when he said, 'I need to talk to Holly.'

'About?'

'What Sofia told her?'

'You think Sofia saw something, don't you?'

'I've been up against a brick wall of silence. I've heard nothing from the Ramos women and I was sure Juanita would remember something.'

'They've had a lot on their minds, Antonio.'

'Yes, I know. Jacinta Estrada has been to see Juanita today. She may have something new.'

'And Sofia?'

'Ana-Maria thinks she made it up or overheard it.'

'Highly likely, given her age.' Santiago returned to the table and gathered up the files. 'You can talk to Holly, but I'll want to be present.'

'Of course.'

She returned to stand beside him at the window. Her arm brushed against him and he caught her perfume. It was redolent of stale sweat and was, he felt, testament to her long hours and dedication.

'You must be shattered,' he said.

'Nothing a long walk or hot shower won't remedy.'

'Would you mind if I joined you?'

'In the shower?' She looked at him and there was a moment's hesitation before they tumbled into laughter. It was hesitant at first, as though neither could let go, and then, as though throwing caution to the wind, they both succumbed and, each time one of them tried to stifle the laughter, they burst out laughing again until their sides ached and eyes watered.

'God those endorphins are better than any drug,' she said, as she fought for breath. 'If we could bottle them we'd make a fortune.'

He looked at her - her face alive with joy – his mind sidetracked by the thought of joining her in the shower. 'I meant, for a walk.'

'I know what you meant. Just teasing.'

He snorted.

'Look,' he said. 'It might have been wrong of me to authorise Ana-Maria's DNA sample, but I thought it was for the best.'

'I know. We're on the same side. Just keep me in the loop in future. Please.' She glanced at him. 'Come on, let's take that walk.'

They made their way down the Paseo de Almeria and across the busy intersection to the harbour. Fernández glanced at the deserted quayside and was impressed by the range of craft in the harbour - container ships, cargo boats, barges, tugs, and pilot launches. Most were tied up for the night and he guessed they'd be manned by a skeleton crew.

'I love it down here,' she said. 'It gives me a sense of perspective. I come here when I can, sometimes alone, usually with Holly. I spend my days in the confines of a windowless morgue and this is such a contrast...ships registered in Panama, Luxembourg, Madeira, Japan, France, and Norway...each multinational crew sailing to the far corners of the world and visiting countries I've only ever dreamed of. If I wasn't so tired, I'd steal up a rope ladder, stow away and wake up in Rio.'

They passed the gangplank of a large container ship. It creaked with the rhythm of water lapping against the side of the quay. 'Another day, perhaps,' she said.

'What's stopping you?'

He retraced the few steps.

'Go on. What's the worst that could happen?'

'I could be arrested and spend the night in a cell.' She turned and began to haul herself up the steep gangplank. She slowed as she neared the entrance to the ship's cargo hold, then stopped, turned, threw her arms into the air and screamed, her joyous cry punching through the air. She sat down, pulled her knees to her chest and buried her head in her arms, looking for the entire world like a small, vulnerable child.

He'd taken a few steps up the gangplank when someone opened a door to the Harbour Master's office.

'What's going on?' A uniformed guard stood in the light of the doorway, his eyes set on Santiago hunched near the entrance to the hold.

Fernández hurried over to him, fished out his ID card and whispered, 'I'm with the Policia Judicial. This is a police affair. Leave it with me.'

'You want me to call for back-up?'

'No. No, I can handle it.'

'Cos I don't want no trouble on my watch.'

'You could cover me, just in case.'

As the official went onto the balcony overlooking the harbour, Fernández made his way up the gangplank, sat next to her and was tempted to put his arm around her, but didn't.

She looked up at him, tears marshalling in her eyes.

He handed her a handkerchief.

She blew her nose, took several deep breaths, looked at him, grinned broadly and offered the handkerchief.

'Keep it.' He smiled. 'You OK?'

'Yes, I'm fine. It's stupid, I know, but that's the first time I've done anything impulsive for years and it feels so good.'

'You want to walk?'

'No, I want to stay here forever.' She laughed and he felt her brush against him as she rocked with the gentle rhythm of the ship at anchor. 'If Holly could see me now. The number of times she's wanted to do this - to scramble up a gangplank and pretend to stow away - and I've forbidden it.' She snorted, her face etched with pain. 'She's missed out on so much.' She chewed her lip as she said, 'towards the end of my relationship with Holly's father things were pretty acrimonious. She's confused and blames herself for his disappearance, even though she never knew him.' She looked earnestly into his eyes. 'She's a child who needs a lot of affection and doesn't want to share her mother with anyone. She just needs time, I suppose.'

He put his arm round her. She sank into his embrace and tears began to defy her. He held her as she wept, stroking her hair as he imagined she'd stroke Holly's after she woke from a nightmare. He glanced across at the officer standing on the Harbour Master's balcony and signalled that all was well. He watched ships move eerily across the harbour and seagulls settled in for the night, perching on the high ledges of buildings that skirted the wharf. After several minutes he said, gently, 'Holly's not the only one who needs time.'

'She comes as part of the package.'

'I know.' He tilted her chin and kissed her gently on the lips. 'Of course she does.'

She lent forward and returned his kiss, tender, light, and warm, and then rested her forehead on his.

'So is this what happens when we call a truce?' She smiled awkwardly. 'It's been a long time.'

'You and me, both.'

'Is it Ana-Maria?' she asked without pulling away.

'Is what Ana-Maria?'

'We met at a Flamenco class, ages ago. I told her I was a pathologist and she asked if I'd come across you, in the line of duty. She told me about your time together. She seemed very fond of you.' She brushed hair from his forehead. 'She meant a lot to you, didn't she?'

He puffed out his cheeks and sighed. 'At the time? Yes. I thought we'd be together, forever. It never crossed my mind...' He laughed, hollowly. 'There's arrogance for you. I didn't believe she'd dump me.'

'Are you still in love with her?'

'It was a long time ago.'

'Doesn't answer my question.'

'Do you still love Holly's father?'

'That's not fair.'

'Of course it is.'

'So, you do still love her?'

He stood up, pulled her to her feet and they walked back down the gangplank. When they'd settled on the quayside, he said, 'I won't deny that when I saw her at the funeral on Saturday, I thought she was as attractive as ever. But...' He was unsure whether what he was about to say was, actually, the whole truth. 'Whatever I felt for Ana-Maria died a long time ago.'

Suddenly, the shrill tone of his mobile phone cut through the air. 'I'm sorry. There are times when I really hate this job.' He snapped open the mobile. It was Leo Medina.

'There's been an accident, Sir. A car's over-turned on the coastal track near one of the nudist beaches.'

'Then get Trafico out.'

'Thing is Sir, Sargento Estrada's already there and she thinks she's found where Laura was killed.'

8

Julieta Santiago had insisted on accompanying him and they'd stopped off at the hospital to collect her field bag and leave a note for her assistant.

Fernández used the delay to contact Jacinta Estrada, who updated him…

Emergency services had received a call from a young man. His girlfriend had been in the car on her own when it left the track. She'd been taken to hospital with a fractured pelvis, a broken leg, and multiple lacerations to her face and hands after being thrown through the windscreen. When Estrada arrived at the scene, the boyfriend had insisted on handing over a mobile phone, and then told her how they'd found it. Estrada arranged for him to be taken to see his girlfriend in hospital, and then she'd called out Trafico and Policia Local and sealed off access to the beach. An incident van and SOCO had arrived and tents had been erected to provide a rudimentary lab, a kitchen and somewhere for officers to rest before sunrise. At first light, they'd start the search. In the meantime, nothing had been disturbed.

It was twenty-past midnight by the time they drew up behind police cars that were blocking the track leading to the beach and they walked away from the wrecked car and found Jacinta Estrada and Leo Medina waiting for them outside a tent.

'OK,' Estrada said, 'we may have our first real break-through.' She held an evidence bag containing a mobile phone between her thumb and forefinger. 'A teenage girl found it buried in the sand. According to her boyfriend, it rang several times. The caller was a woman. Wanted to speak to Laura.'

She nodded at Medina.

'If this is where Laura was killed,' he said, 'it'll help establish a timeline for her last...' He hesitated. 'I saw her leave the fiesta, just after midnight. She went home, packed and was picked up by a taxi just before sunrise.'

'We don't know it was a taxi,' Estrada said. 'Local firms have no record of a fare that matches.'

'We can assume that whoever picked her up, killed her.' Fernández said.

'Laura came here,' Medina continued, 'probably willingly, which would suggest she knew her killer and felt she had nothing to fear.'

'The sooner we begin the search, the better,' Santiago said, 'If she was killed above the tideline, SOCOs will need to search for blood absorbed into the sand. If the tide's washed it away...' She shrugged. 'Her body was wrapped in a sheet that had been laundered recently. So, we should look out for a lightweight, plastic bag with the name of a dry-cleaners on it.'

Estrada turned to Fernández. 'Do you want me to stay here tonight?'

He nodded. 'Yes. Thanks. But, try to get some sleep. Make an early start at sun-up. You can update us at the scheduled meeting in the Incident Room.'

'I'll stay as well,' Santiago said. 'Any evidence you find could be vital. I'd like to be here.'

'Fine by me.' Estrada smiled and then picked up where she'd left off. 'OK. Laura was killed and bundled into the trunk of a car, driven to the mineshaft and dumped.'

Medina moaned, audibly. 'I'm sorry, but Laura was a friend, with her whole life ahead of her, and words like dumped, bundled...it's so fucking disrespectful.'

'Yes, you're right, I'm sorry.'

'Comes with the territory, Leo,' Santiago said.

'Doesn't make it any easier to listen to.'

The wind picked up as the night cooled and the tents began to flap. They retreated inside and accepted coffee from a uniformed police cadet.

Estrada held up the mobile once again. 'Leo,' she said, 'you want to give them the really good news?'

'OK. We know that there were several calls made to this mobile before the car accident. According to the boyfriend, it was a woman's voice. She wanted to talk to Laura. I've also been through the text messages and found these...' He scrolled through the sent messages and opened the one timed at ten past twelve, early on Saturday morning. 'Laura was at the fiesta. I'd been chatting to her. She received a text from José. He told her he'd been selected for Real's first team for Sunday. She sent this message:

Congrats!
Will ask Gloria 2 take me 2 airport.

Medina continued. 'Sofia had just told us she saw an old man and Gloria playing hide and seek. Laura spoke to Sofia, and then sent another text message to José.'

Got info on Gloria.
Should solve our problem.

'You're suggesting Sofia knows more about Gloria than she's said so far?'

'Must have done. The info..?'

'Whatever it was, it would help José and Laura solve 'our problem'...Anyone any ideas?' Fernández waited for suggestions but none were forthcoming. 'Well, we still need to find José. He was in Madrid, early Saturday morning,' Fernández said. 'In an Aston Martin, he could be here in under four hours.'

190

'I've also checked the phone's call-log,' Medina said. 'Calls were made from a landline in Madrid, just after one on Saturday morning. So...he drove down, killed Laura and got back to Madrid before anyone missed him.'

'A long shot, on the eve of the most important match of his life...' Fernández hesitated. 'Question is, why would he want to harm her?'

Carlos Domingo had been restless all night.

He was angry the police hadn't contacted him about the newsreel footage. At the very least, he thought, Leo Medina would have chased things up. He gave up trying to sleep and sat in the high-winged chair by an unlit fire and stared at the front door. He held his breath whenever he heard a sound and his faltering imagination contrived images of Laura...she'd open the door and tiptoe across the flagstones and when she saw him sitting there, she'd tell him she'd stopped over with friends. She would be, of course, completely unaware of the worry he'd been through and she'd take milk from the fridge, pour it over cereal, and sit cross-legged in the chair opposite him.

He was staring at the empty chair when the first rays of the sun broke the horizon far out at sea and reality dawned. He cried when he realised that Laura wasn't coming home...Not today. Not ever.

At that moment, he knew he had a choice. He could sit in that chair and wait for the cancer to take him, or he could get up off his backside and do something. He got up, pulled on heavy boots, slipped out the back door and stole silently across the campo.

The air was still and early-morning swallows swept across the sky, excited by the promise of breakfast.

As the sun's warmth began to bathe the land, Carlos headed towards the hills where the four men had been shot and where - over in the next valley - Laura had been found. He knew that the police would still be at both crime scenes and that scientists would still be sifting through evidence – evidence that would help detectives piece together what had happened.

He also knew that the media would be camped within striking distance. But he wasn't interested in the police, scientists or the media. He was looking for Pepe, the goatherd, and he knew he'd be somewhere on the hills searching for fresh pastures.

He caught sight of the goats as they ambled lazily over the sparse hillside. The dogs were yapping at their hindquarters and Pepe was meandering behind, carrying a makeshift staff fashioned from a thin branch.

Carlos didn't want to surprise him. He circled higher and waited until he was within twenty meters. 'Good morning, my friend. Do you mind if I walk with you?'

Pepe didn't acknowledge him. He walked past, head bowed, his eyes fixed on the ground.

Carlos caught up with him and said, 'You know who I am?' When Pepe didn't respond, Carlos looked up the steep path at the goats; their shorn backsides swaying inelegantly as each hoof found uneven footing. 'The girl they found across the valley, in that old mineshaft? She was my daughter. Her throat had been cut, no better than a pig.'

Pepe trudged after his herd.

'She's not coming back, I know that, but you can help me find him what did that to her.'

Still Pepe appeared to ignore him and Carlos grabbed him by the arm and pulled him round to face him.

'I'm sorry, but I don't have much time. I need to find the man who did that to my Laura.' He prodded Pepe's chest. 'You got to help me.'

Pepe's eyes widened. His mouth gaped open and a deep guttural noise rasped its way from the back of his throat. He turned and walked away, each footfall leaden and weary, as though he carried a heavy burden. Carlos stood for a few moments and then hurried after him. He caught hold of his shoulder and pulled him round. 'You can't walk away from this. I will not let you walk away. I need your help.'

Pepe shoved his hand away, screamed at him, turned and stomped after the goats.

'I was in Almeria,' Carlos shouted, 'and I passed one of those shops that sells TVs. They had the local news on, and that's when I saw you, with your goats, on this hillside.' He scurried after Pepe and caught up with him just as he reached the brow of the hill. The goats had hurried down the other side, driven by the sight of fresh vegetation.

Both men fought for breath as they stood looking down at the old mine workings and the SOCO tents that masked the entrance. 'You gotta help me,' Carlos said. 'I think you could've seen something. You could've seen the man who did that to my Laura.'

Pepe turned on him, sounds streaming from the back of his throat, louder, strident. He began to gesticulate, waving his arms and shaking his fists.

But Carlos persisted. 'I know you can't talk to me, but we can play a game, one of Laura's favourites.'

Pepe looked at him, then dismissed him with a wave of his hand and starting back along the track.

Carlos shouted after him, caught up with him, spun him, caught the collar of his shirt, and pulled him close enough to smell the milk he'd drunk that morning.

'You nod if I get a question right. You shake your head if I get it wrong.' Carlos looked deep into Pepe's eyes as he asked, 'Were you here on the day my little girl was killed?'

Pepe shrugged.

'Yes, or no.'

Pepe shrugged and screamed, his face contorting with anger as he wrestled himself free. He tried to turn away but Carlos pulled him back to face him. 'Did you see him with her?' He tightened his grip. 'You must tell me. You must tell me what you saw.'

Pepe wrenched himself free and pointed his makeshift staff at Carlos. His eyes were flaming with anger and frustration. Aberrant sounds spilt from him as his body wired to strike. Suddenly, he lunged forward and brought the staff down heavily. He struck Carlos on the forearm and, again, he struck and caught him on the side of the head. As Carlos stumbled backwards, he lost his footing, and rolled down the steep slope of the hill, through thick gorse, where his head jerked backwards and hit a rock.

He lay motionless.

Pepe looked down, tears streaming. He raised both arms, his staff in his right hand, his left fist clenched, his whole body shaking. His scream echoed across the valley.

Jacinta Estrada wondered if the aches and pains that accompanied every movement she made would ever ease. She'd slept fitfully on a thin bed of foam in a tent on the beach. She'd been conscious of a restless Julieta Santiago beside her, but at least they were able to begin the search as soon as the sun broke over the horizon.

After several fruitless hours scouring the shoreline, they'd driven away from the beach, along the coast road and then across the plain towards the mountains.

They stopped in a bar for coffee, thankful for clean toilets and cold tap water to splash on their faces, and arrived at the Town Hall just before nine-thirty.

They found Fernández and Medina in conversation with Rodrigo Perpiñán, and Valencia Ramoz poring over documents with Vincente Cabrera and Eduardo Gomez.

'Good to see a full house,' Estrada called.

She removed her jacket, rolled up her shirtsleeves and tidied her hair into a ponytail. 'I trust you all slept well.' She stood in front of the additional whiteboards installed to cope with developments in the investigations and looked at Medina. 'Leo? Any success with items confiscated during the searches yesterday?'

'Apart from the stash of money, there wasn't much at Felipe Romano's, but when I checked items taken from Juan Gonzales's I came across these. Thought they might be of interest.'

He handed over several handwritten diaries.

'Well done, Leo,' Estrada said. 'Have a word with one of the uniformed officers…ask him to go round to Felipe's hovel and bring him here. I think it's time we tightened the screws. Let's see how he copes without his daily ration of booze.'

She took the diaries and passed them over to Rodrigo Perpiñán. 'Something to keep you busy.' She placed the volumes on his lap. 'Let us know the moment you find anything.'

As Perpiñán left the room, she said, 'OK, first let me give you the good news. Joaquin Alvarez has recovered consciousness. He's been taken off life-support and has been moved into a general ward. The doctors are optimistic that he'll make a full recovery.' She smiled broadly as everyone applauded. 'Let's hope the rest of the day is as positive.'

She checked agenda items she'd scribbled down over breakfast.

'We'll need someone to read through documentation provided by the Mayor. Thank you, Vincente. This looks like a job for you, Valencia.' She handed the files to Ramoz. 'OK. We're still trying to locate Gloria. Laura's texts suggest Gloria could be an adult. Technicians are still analysing messages and calls, but for now we'll concentrate on the two texts she sent at the fiesta just after midnight on Saturday.'

She pinned enlarged copies on the incident board...

Got info on Gloria.
Should solve our problem.

Congrats!
Will ask Gloria 2 take me 2 airport.

'I've sent copies to police who are handling José's disappearance. The Aston Martin found on Monday has been traced to a company in Madrid who've confirmed it's leased to Real Madrid. José took delivery of it two months ago. Forensics have been through it, and found nothing that takes us any further forward - no mobile, no sign of a struggle.' She looked across the room, inviting Julieta Santiago.

'I'll contact the lab in Madrid; ask them to recover his toothbrush from his hotel. That should help us match the DNA from the car. Needless to say, resources at our disposal are stretched to breaking point and I'm not sure how long we can demand results from forensics.'

They sat in silence, as though measuring the impact of a slow down in scientific evidence.

'So, why didn't anyone see him?' Medina said. 'How come he drove here, parked up and walked through the village without anyone seeing him? If he drove down on Sunday after the match, he'd have gone home, wouldn't he, to his parents, or to the farm to see Laura?'

196

'Laura was killed early, Saturday morning,' Estrada said. 'If he killed her, he must have driven down from Madrid, then back, played, then came down *again* after the match on Sunday.'

'But *why* did he kill her?' Medina asked. 'We thought she could have been blackmailing him, but the second text suggests they were in this together.'

'So,' Estrada said, 'if he didn't come down here on Saturday, he's in the clear...but, then we have to ask ourselves...what's the connection between the *info* and their *problem*?'

'And, if José's in the clear,' Fernández said, 'that would turn the spotlight back onto Guzmán and Wells.' He turned to Medina. 'Leo, invite them in and check their alibis.' He moved to a whiteboard where he wrote the name *Gloria*. 'Gloria features in both investigations. Sofia saw an old man playing hide-and-seek...'

'But we can't be certain if her old man is our old man,' Estrada said. 'Gloria could be a friend.'

'Who was asked by Laura to take her to the airport?'

Suddenly, the door to the Incident Room crashed open and a uniformed officer stood fighting for breath.

'You'd better come quick. It's Felipe Romero!'

Romero's body was propped in a white plastic chair, his head hanging to one side, his eyes vacant.

'His neck's snapped like a chicken's,' Santiago said. 'That may not be the most scientific of descriptions, but accurate enough. Bruising here indicates someone came up behind him, placed a forearm round his neck, twisted, and pulled upwards.' She removed her mask and inhaled odour lingering at his mouth. 'He's emaciated and he'd been drinking. He wouldn't have been able to resist a surprise attack.'

The area had been sealed off, but news had reached the media. Reporters had hurried from the square and were craning for a shot of the corpse or trying to glean information from uniformed officers.

'How long's he been dead?' Fernández asked.

'Poor muscle mass will complicate diagnosis and the heat will have accelerated the process, but I'd say he's been through the eighteen hour cycle of rigor mortice.'

She checked the thermometer. 'Core temperature's stabilized at ambient.' She pulled up his t-shirt. 'This blue-green discolouration is an indication of the extent of decomposition. I'd say, twenty-four hours, given the heat throughout yesterday. Certainly no more than thirty-six hours, otherwise we'd see marbling, bloating of the face...'

'He was alive around ten yesterday. We were here, carrying out a search.'

'Anytime after that then.'

The Mayor, Vincente Cabrera, was listening intently. He turned to Fernández.

'If you'd arrested him yesterday...'

'Hindsight's a wonderful thing, Vincente.'

'Nonetheless, when this is all over...'

'Anything we had yesterday,' Jacinta Estrada said, 'was pure supposition. We had nothing to go on.'

'But, we do now,' Fernández said.

He rifled through Romero's pockets, but found them empty. 'Robbery seems unlikely and, unless this was a random act of violence, we must assume he's been silenced.' He looked at Cabrera. 'Felipe Romero was a member of the fascist youth movement. Juan Gonzales was a fascist. It would have been easy for him to have enlisted his help, especially for two thousand euros.'

'But Juan Gonzales didn't have that sort of money,' Cabrera said.

'Whoever killed Gonzales was the paymaster and knew Felipe could testify against him. As far as I'm concerned, Felipe's death confirms that Juan Gonzales was murdered by the man who finished off Bartolomé Ramos.' He turned on Cabrera. 'It's an ugly game we play, Vincente. Go ahead, make capital out of what's happened, but don't pretend to be so fucking superior.'

'But, a man is dead!'

Fernández pulled him to one side. 'And if we don't find his killer soon, there'll be more bodies littering the streets.' He raised his hand and held it close to the Mayor's face. He wanted to slap some sense into him, but withdrew it at the last moment. 'I need you to stay focused. Keep the media off my shoulder and help us make sense of the information you've provided.'

Estrada's mobile sounded and she moved away from the reporters, listened, and then waited for Fernández and Medina to join her.

'The girl who crashed the boyfriend's car is awake.'

'You want me to go?' Medina asked.

'No, I'll go. She might find it easier to talk to me, given what she went through last night. I'm not sure how much more she'll be able to tell us, but it's worth a try.' She checked that they weren't being overheard. 'That's not all. Carlos has been brought to the Town Hall.'

'What's he been up to this time?' Medina said.

'SOCOs reported an incident. Two men, arguing. Carlos was found badly shaken. He has a lump on the back of his head the size of a golf ball, but otherwise he's all right. He's refused medical attention but insists on speaking with you, Leo.'

'I'm on my way.'

Fernández watched Medina muscle his way through the reporters and Estrada follow in his slipstream.

'Can you arrange for Holly to come over and play with Sofia this evening?' he whispered to Santiago.

199

'I'll be here for most of the day.'

'Pedra could bring her. Inocenta might appreciate her company. She's having a rough time. What do you say?'

'I'll want to be there, when you talk to the girls.'

'Yes, I know.' His mobile phone rang. It was Rodrigo Perpiñán.

'I've got something for you.' Perpiñán sounded tense. 'From the diaries.'

'Where are you?'

'At home.'

'Stay there. I'm sending a police officer round. Felipe Romero's been murdered. It looks like Consuela was right…anyone helping with our enquiries is at risk.'

'I don't need a minder, but you need to look at what I've found.'

'I'm going to see Juanita, Bartolomé's wife. The coffee and cake story doesn't add up and I want to know what she's *not* telling me. I'll be with you in an hour.'

He snapped the phone shut.

Santiago was looking at him.

'This had better be good, Antonio. They're both vulnerable kids.'

'Yes, I know.'

He looked round to check no one could overhear them and noticed Vincente Cabrera remonstrating with the pack of media hounds. 'The text message on Laura's phone did more than confirm that she knew her killer.'

'She asked for a lift to the airport.'

'And must have been picked up by him.'

'Him?'

'How many women do you know who could shoot three men, fake a suicide, slit a young woman's throat, lift her into the boot of a car and throw her down a mineshaft? No, we're looking for a man and the text message provides us with the most crucial piece of the jigsaw…motive.'

'She was trying to extort money from him?'

'Possibly. Not because she was pregnant, but because she knew that he was Gloria.'

'So, it must have been someone she knew well.'

He looked at her.

'Gloria?' she said. 'One of Laura's nicknames?'

'Yes, but a nickname for someone she didn't like or didn't respect,' Fernández said. 'She'd have wanted to keep his identity to herself, but must have told someone – someone close to her, someone she could trust…'

'Like her fiancé?'

'Exactly.'

'But, how did Sofia know he was called Gloria?'

'Must have overheard her talking to José.'

'Sofia's big secret.'

'Where is he?' Leo Medina said, as he strode into the Incident Room.

'Carlos has gone.'

Valencia Ramoz looked over at him from behind her computer screen.

'He left, said he couldn't wait any longer.'

'He's OK, though?'

'Wouldn't talk about it. He did ask if we'd got the newsreel footage. I told him it hadn't come through yet.'

'Shit.'

Adam Wells came in.

'And what can we do for you?' Ramoz said.

'I had a call from the Sargento. She said that you had more questions. She offered to send a car to pick me up, but I didn't want any fuss.'

'Sargento Estrada is not here.'

'I'll take him,' Medina said. 'This way, sir.'

He showed him into an anteroom and suggested he sat down.

Adam Wells was quick off the mark. 'I just wanted to say how much I appreciate your discretion.'

'You mean your wife hasn't worked out what's going on yet?'

'I mean, I'm happy to help in any way I can as long as my...' Wells hesitated, as though searching for the most appropriate word.

'Infidelity?' Medina suggested.

'My indiscretion...'

'Perhaps you'd prefer disloyalty or betrayal?'

'Look,' Wells attempted defiance, 'I'm here at your invitation.'

Medina stepped closer to him and, towering above him, he leant across the table. 'You're here because you had an affair with Laura. She demanded money. You paid her, but she came back for more, so you murdered her.'

'That's preposterous.'

'You gave her a thousand euros.'

'She posed for portraits and nude studies. I'd completed at least five. She said she was happy for me to exhibit and sell them. That was part of the deal. Look, I've told Estrada this already.'

'*Sargento* Estrada.' Medina sat down, opening a folder in front of him. 'A thousand's a lot to pay someone to sit for you. Must have been a very special series of portraits.'

'They should sell well, especially now...'

'You're joking?'

'It was part of the deal.'

Medina looked up, unable to believe what he'd just heard. He shook his head. He was struggling to control his temper. 'You knew she was engaged?'

'Yes.' Wells shrugged.

'But that didn't stop you fucking her.'

'You make it sound so coarse, so vulgar.'

'She told you she was pregnant, threatened to tell your wife, demanded more money, and you panicked, drove her down to the beach...'

'Look...' Wells leaned forward. '...We are both men of the world, you and me. You must fancy playing away from home occasionally?'

Medina sprang from behind the desk and grabbed Wells by the collar. 'She's lying on a slab in the morgue. Her unborn baby's dead and her father's life's been shattered. Jesus Christ, I ought to rip you apart, you fucking cunt.' He pushed Adam Wells into his chair and watched as he toppled backwards, crashing onto the tiled floor.

Valencia Ramoz opened the door. 'What happened?'

'His centre of gravity shifted, and he fell.' Medina stood over Wells like a prizefighter, willing him to get up so that he could have another shot at him.

'I'll get Doctor Guzmán,' Ramoz said.

'Don't bother.'

'It's no bother, Leo. He's already here.'

'Has it occurred to you that you're exceeding your authority and contravening the Penal Code?'

Doctor Javier Guzmán lent back on his chair. 'And locking Adam Wells in a cell isn't going to endear you to your superiors. Your actions may even herald the end of a career that's only just started. You'll probably be queuing at a job-centre this time next week - suspended from duty, pending an enquiry.' The doctor sat forward. 'Not looking good, is it Leo? It's only a matter of time before my lawyer gets here.'

Medina spun the chair opposite him and sat astride it. He rested arms on its high back and chin on his hands, and looked at the man who had dated Laura, who'd fucked her and who may yet prove to be the father of her child. His eyes didn't flinch but, as his mind advised caution, his heart screamed for retribution. He knew Adam Wells would be unlikely to press charges and risk his wife discovering what he'd been up to, but Guzmán had trouble written all over his smug face.

Medina allowed the silence to linger and then forced a smile. 'We haven't found anyone to confirm your alibi. We've checked all the bars, restaurants, and nightclubs along the beach. We have a hundred hours of CCTV footage to go through. We've spoken to your friends at the Lodge, and circulated your car details to Trafico but, so far, we've found nothing. You must have had a quiet night.'

'Have you been down to the beachfront lately, on a weekend, in the small hours? Have you any idea the state some people get into? Most wouldn't recognise their own grandmothers.' Guzmán's face flushed.

Medina sensed anger simmering and allowed himself a slight smile. 'Your car…'

'My parent's car. I'm using it until I find someone to buy their apartment.'

'You'll remember it being towed away from outside the golf club? Yes, of course you do. The forensic report should be with us soon.'

'They won't find anything.' Guzmán folded his arms and sat back.

Medina sat on the edge of the table. 'You into home-improvement?'

'No, why? Should I be?'

'Oh, I don't know. The odd extension, a stone wall, a patio?'

'I did few things before putting the apartment on the market, mainly cosmetic.'

'Have you had cement in the back of your parent's car recently?'

'It's possible.'

'Sand? A young woman's body?'

'Oh, for God's sake. Now you listen to me…'

'If this is a confession, I'd better get something to record it on and a witness.'

'Charge me or let me go.'

'We could have up to seventy-two hours together, you and me, and your lawyer. The clock hasn't started ticking yet. You came voluntarily. You haven't been arrested, or charged. Just helping us with our enquiries.'

Guzmán stood up. 'Then I shall bid you good day. Enjoy what remains of your career.'

Medina barred his way to the door.

'Sit down. I haven't finished with you, yet.'

'But I've finished this ridiculous charade.'

He stepped forward and Medina put a hand squarely on his chest and gripped his shirt. 'You have motive… Laura threatened to tell your fiancée about your affair and the child you'd fathered. She demanded a substantial sum of money.'

'You'll have difficulty proving the child's mine.'

Guzmán nearly choked as Medina tightened his grip.

'Doesn't matter one way or another, does it?' Medina was close enough to smell the doctor's cologne. 'Once your fiancée hears that you've been fucking another woman…' He pulled him closer and whispered, 'Tell me doctor, is it ethical to fuck a patient?'

He released his grip and swung away, stretching the stiffness from his body, trying all the time to stop himself kicking the shit out of Guzmán. 'So, I hope we can agree that you had motive? Now, let's consider the opportunity… It was the seafront, wasn't it? Wandering

205

from bar to bar?' He moved away and perched on the other side of the desk - confident that he had the doctor's full attention. 'You rolled her up in an expensive cotton sheet. I'm sure we'll find others of the same quality when we search your apartment. You wrapped her in polythene to protect your parent's car and then you took the scenic route to the old mine shaft, where you dumped her body.'

'I'm not saying anything until my lawyer arrives.'

'Have something to hide?'

'I'm bored. Bored and irritated by your accusations. I've nothing more to say.'

'No alibi, doctor. More to lose than most...' Medina grinned. 'As you say: not looking good is it?'

Fernández found Juanita Ramos at the outhouse near the fountain. She'd placed a packet of soap powder on the ledge above a granite sink and was scrubbing a pale garment over a stone washboard. When she'd finished, she rinsed it in cold water trickling from a lead pipe.

'It's like stepping back in time,' he said, lighting a cigarette and watching her wring the water from a pair of trousers.

Juanita threw the trousers into a basket and wiped her brow, 'Are you going to stand there all day, Inspector, or make yourself useful?'

He drew heavily on his cigarette and stubbed it out. He stood alongside her and waited for her to hand him the shirt she was rinsing.

'Washing machine broken?' he asked.

'This,' she said, as she slapped the shirt on the stone washboard, 'is what my husband was wearing on the day he was shot.'

She pummelled the shirt into the stone. 'And this,' she added, her breath shortening as she grew more violent, 'is how I washed clothes when we were first married. There was no running water in the village, no sewerage, and no electricity.' She selected a vest from under the sink and after rinsing it she took a can and unscrewed the lid. 'For the blood stains...' She splashed the cloth liberally. 'My husband's blood. The blood of the man I loved.'

She pounded the vest against the stone washboard, and then lifted it above her head and lashed it against the granite sink.

It was, he felt, as though she was trying to flay the life from it.

Again she lashed it. And again, and again, until tears rolled down her cheeks and dappled the soiled foam in the granite sink.

He caught her shoulders and pulled her towards him.

He was trying to stop her from damaging herself, but Juanita pushed him away.

'Don't touch me,' she sobbed. 'Just, don't touch me.'

He stepped back and watched as her strength ebbed and she fought to regain her breath. It took several minutes but, as she calmed, she rinsed the vest, ran it through a mangle and tidied, ready to leave.

'Your Sargento Estrada didn't make any sense when she came to see us yesterday,' she said, standing before him, basket tucked under arm.

'Perhaps she wasn't meant to.'

'She kept asking us why we'd drunk coffee and ate cake with Ana-Maria.'

'Doesn't make a lot of sense, does it?'

'What do you mean?'

'It's troubled me. Why did Ana-Maria come to see you on that particular day? Why not the day before, or the day after?'

207

'It was her mother who'd phoned and asked if we'd like to try it.'

'So why Ana-Maria?'

'What do you mean?'

'Why didn't Inocenta bring the cake round herself?'

'No idea. Maybe Sofia was playing up. Wouldn't be unusual.'

He moved towards her and she backed away, a small movement, but one he hadn't seen before.

Something had changed. Something had happened to make Juanita wary. Maybe Estrada had touched a nerve. Maybe Juanita was beginning to realise that her husband had been singled out and that he hadn't told her everything.

'Here,' he said, gently, 'let me take that for you.'

She relinquished the basket. 'What now, Inspector?'

'Now, we're going to find somewhere nice and quiet and you're going to tell me all about your husband... everything, including those things you wish you'd buried with him.'

He spent an hour at the premises her husband rented and left with a promise that Juanita would go through Bartolomé's papers to see if there was anything that might help.

When he arrived at Rodrigo Perpiñán's, fresh coffee and a selection of pastries were laid out on the white plastic table. He helped himself and then closed his eyes for a moment, enjoying the sugar-rush from the pastry and the bite of the coffee.

'You ready for this?' Perpiñán said, placing the diaries on the table.

Fernández sat upright, drew his hands across his face and rubbed his eyes.

'You said these were taken from Gonzales's home?'

'Yesterday morning.'

'There are eight manuscripts in all, although the last one remains incomplete. Each diary covers five years.'

'Then Juan Gonzales could not have written them.'

'The diaries are his mother's. Teresa had kept them - religiously one might say - from the outbreak of the Civil War up to, and including, the evening she was killed, January 1974. It's a personal account and is quite remarkable, given that few people could read or write. She'd obviously been well educated. So, she couldn't have been from round here. A city, somewhere, maybe? It's subjective. That makes it unreliable as an historical record, but it's priceless as an individual's account of the effect that national events have on the lives of ordinary people. This is an important find, for both of us, and I must be allowed to add them to my archives once this is all over.'

'To do what?'

'Write a book, using them as the basis of her story.'

'And glorify the fascist movement?'

'You really think that's likely? I want to tell her tale. It has a resonance that deserves to be heard, a voice of the times in which our father's lived and died.'

'What relevance do they have to my investigation?'

Perpiñán took the last of the diaries.

He opened it with a reverence usually accorded rare museum exhibits and slipped on his reading glasses.

'This volume covers the period, 1970 to 1975. The last two years are blank, of course. I have photocopied several pages and highlighted certain entries.'

He handed over twenty A4 sheets. 'If the diaries are used as evidence, I beg you to look after them.'

'I'll wear white gloves if it'll put your mind at rest. Just tell me what you're so excited about.'

'The first page...February1972. I've highlighted the reference to a meeting attended by several of the main characters in your investigation - the author, her husband Jésus, her son, Juan, and the Priest, Father Emanuel.'

Perpiñán waited for him to locate the section and began to read from the diary...

They seem to have settled on our house for their meetings. They read through a copy of the ABC the doctor passes to them each day and tune into radio broadcasts from Madrid. There are reports of unrest, especially in the Basque area. The General is growing weaker. God bless Him and give Him the strength to carry on His great work.

Jésus is drinking more than ever. He will be seventy, next week, and refuses to guard his tongue. Juan is home for his son's birthday. He's away such a lot. The General's work is never done, he says.

'If we skip to 21st December 1973...page seven. This extract deals with the incident that brought the fascist death squad to our village...

Oh, Dear God, news reached us of the assassination of the Prime Minister, Admiral Blanco. He was leaving the San Francisco de Borga after Mass. When we met last night, everyone feared this would spark a new wave of anarchy and hoped the General's response would be as swift and as effective as ever.

Father Emanuel is devastated. He has his own health to worry about, poor man. He's just returned from a sanatorium near Valencia. They managed to stop the bleeding, but he'll always have to be careful if he falls or cuts himself badly. The condition is life threatening.

'Life threatening?'

'Father Emanuel was a haemophiliac. Only males are at risk, apparently. It's hereditary, I think. You'll have to ask Doctor Santiago.' Perpiñán grinned. 'How's it going, by the way?'

'What do you mean, how's it going?'

'So, it's still complicated then?'

'A work-in-progress.'

He looked at his friend and shook his head. 'I don't know. Our personal and professional lives clash, and we don't seem to have control over either.'

'I doubt your love-life's as complicated as our fascist Priest's...' Perpiñán glanced at the photocopies of the last diary and turned over several pages. 'Ah, yes, here we are. Page fifteen. January 12th, 1974. If nothing else, this confirms the Priest's whore was not a figment of the imagination...

Cinderella has her claws in him. She stole his heart months ago. Poor man doesn't know which way to turn, but she seems to have found her Prince Charming!

What a scandal, if the news ever got out. The Father is to be a father. Or is he? I wonder if he knows he has a rival for her affections and that he may not be the father of the child she's carrying?

Jésus calls her a whore, but that's unfair. A whore? She's just a kid, but it seems she not so innocent, now.

'Her final entry...'

'Wait. I'm sorry. Just wait a minute.' Fernández read through the last entry again. He traced each word and sat back, his face ashen.

'You ok?'

'Yes.'

'What is it?'

'Nothing. Go on. Her final entry.'

'Is on the morning of the 16th January 1974. The day the death squad arrived...'

At last! Juan has sent word that Special Forces have extended their search for the terrorists. He phoned to tell us that two men involved in the assassination have been seen near the village and a military convoy will pass through, later today.

Jésus has called a meeting.

I have a heavy heart.

It took Carlos over an hour to locate Pepe. The goats had stumbled across a patch of lush vegetation and were stubbornly ignoring all efforts to move them on. Carlos watched as Pepe hunched against a rock beneath the shade of an olive tree.

'This time I've come prepared,' he said, and pointed the twin barrels of the shotgun at the goatherd.

Pepe scrambled to his feet.

'I know you know what happened to Laura. I know you can't talk. I know everyone thinks you're stupid...' Carlos pulled back the shotgun's top firing hammer and placed his index finger alongside the trigger guard. 'But I need you to talk to the police.'

Pepe pointed at the goats and his dogs, shrugged and held out his hands, as if demanding to know what he was meant to do with his animals.

'Bring them with us,' Carlos said, and nudged the shotgun towards the path to the village. 'Let's see how well trained you've got them dogs, shall we?'

*

Jacinta Estrada spent an hour at the hospital where she interviewed the girl who'd crashed her boyfriend's car. She was out of danger, but told Estrada that she couldn't remember anything immediately before or after the crash.

Earlier, Estrada had asked the boyfriend why he'd allowed her to drive his car. He'd said he hadn't. They'd had a row and she'd driven off without his permission. Estrada asked him what the row been about.

'Nothing,' he'd said

As she made her way to the Incident Room, Estrada smiled several times. She guessed the youngsters would never forget last night - though not, she thought, for the reason that had brought them to the beach in the first place.

Her smile disappeared when, after she'd taken off her jacket and thrown it over the back of a chair, Valencia Ramoz told her about Leo Medina's interviews with Adam Wells and Doctor Guzmán.

She stopped outside the interview room and listened. Whatever Medina had done was her responsibility, but she didn't know whether she was more concerned about Adam Wells or Javier Guzmán. Both could cause serious trouble. Maybe the artist had rocked on his chair and tipped backwards? Maybe he had had help from the big, blundering Cabo? Maybe Leo should have been pulled off the case as soon as Laura's body had been found?

She tried the handle, but the door was locked.

'Leo, open up.' The door cracked ajar. She pushed it and watched Medina return to his seat.

'Ah, the cavalry.' Guzmán beamed. 'Feel the noose tightening, Sargento?'

213

'Is there anything I can get you?'

'Out of here? My lawyer? Either way, you can't keep me here against my will.' Guzmán's voice was edged with tension.

'So, there's nothing I can get to make your detention more comfortable?'

'Charge me, or I walk out of here. You'll pay for this, both of you. You'll be stacking supermarket shelves by the time I've finished with you.'

'We've established his motive,' Medina said, calmly.

'Like fuck we have.'

'That's quite a temper.' Estrada smiled. 'Hidden that well, haven't you? Until provoked. Is that what happened? Laura threatened to tell your fiancée?'

'For God's sake!' Guzmán shoved his chair away, moved from behind the table and closed in on Estrada.

Medina placed himself between the two of them and the two men squared up.

Estrada knew that Medina would be hoping Guzmán would attack and give him the excuse he needed. 'Leave us, Leo.' she said.

'I'm not sure I should.'

'I don't think Doctor Guzmán is that stupid.'

She waited, and when Medina had left, she went over to the only window in the room and stared at the Town Hall's square. 'You know, there's one thing that's been bugging me after you'd volunteered information about your affair with Laura…your total lack of sorrow, or shock, or sadness. Heartless is probably the best word I can think of - no, wait a minute - callous and heartless. But then, you weren't shocked, or sad, when you heard she was dead, were you?'

'I'll make you pay for this.'

'So you said.'

'You can't treat innocent people like this.'

214

'No, you're right. I'll wait until your lawyer's here. In the meantime, I'm afraid I'm going to have to ask you to empty your pockets, and remove your belt. We don't want you topping yourself as you plunge the depths of remorse, do we?'

She walked out, locked the door and stood for several moments, wondering what she'd say to Leo Medina. She found him slumped in a chair opposite Valencia Ramoz, toying with the gold pendant found round Laura's neck.

'Val,' Estrada said. 'Take everyone out for an early lunch and get me a pastry from the bakery.'

'What and miss all the action?' Ramoz pouted.

'Val?'

'OK. You want anything, Leo?'

'Yeah. A thick slice of justice, with lashings of penal solitude for one of our guests.'

He didn't look up from the gold pendant.

Estrada watched the dayshift leave and, when they were alone, she said, 'OK, Leo, in your own time. What happened with Adam Wells?'

'He should have listened at school. The teachers were always telling us to sit with all four feet of the chair on the floor, else we'd topple and crack our heads open.'

'So, that's your story?'

'Yeah.'

'Leo, this could be a disciplinary matter.'

'No. He'll remember it as I do.' Medina continued to study the pendant.

'And the good doctor?' Estrada said.

'Let him stew. Wait until his lawyer gets here. Lean on him, you said. I did and he's rattled.'

'Listen to me, Leo. You can't behave like that. We have to do things by the book. Even if you hit someone in self-defence, all hell would break loose.'

'Yeah, I get it. Don't worry.'

215

Medina eased himself out of his chair. 'Look at this.' He dangled the pendant before her. 'How much d'you think it's worth?'

It looked like solid gold, but she couldn't be sure.

'Probably expensive,' she said. 'Didn't Carlos say Laura and José bought them as a sort of symbol of their love?'

'Yeah. It's hallmarked, so it's probably kosher. But, there's something else. See if you can find it.'

She ran the pendant through her fingers, flipped it over to check both sides and found the hallmark but nothing else. She shrugged and handed it back.

Medina held the pendant by its head and turned it upside down so its feet pointed towards the ceiling. He grabbed a magnifying glass and handed it to her.

She studied the soles of the pendant's feet.

The letter L had been engraved on one.

The letter D on the other.

'Laura Domingo?'

'Could be, couldn't it?'

'So what?'

'Don't know, but I'm guessing José's will have J and C stamped on the feet.'

'Something else we'll have to check when we find him. Well done. You'll make a passable detective one day, but...' She hoped he'd have no doubt about how serious she was. 'Remember...everything by the book, understand?'

'Yes, Sargento.'

They sat at their desks. There was an unusual stillness in the room and the clatter of cicadas accompanied by sound of a woman singing a lullaby drifted through the window from across the square.

Medina sipped coffee and Estrada examined the pendant.

But the tranquillity didn't last long.

The door crashed open and Carlos pushed Pepe into the room, his shotgun planted firmly in the goatherd's back.

'Carlos?'

'He can help you.' Carlos used the end of the barrel to prod Pepe. The goatherd's face was suffused with anger - his eyes indignant, his mouth snarling, low guttural sounds mingling with spittle at the corners of his mouth.

Medina didn't move, but his initial amusement turned to fear when he realized that the gun was armed. He rose slowly, aware that any sudden movement might make Carlos trigger-happy.

Estrada tried to appear calm. 'You want to tell me what this is all about Carlos?'

'He needed a bit of persuasion to come and talk to you.'

'You don't need the gun, Carlos.'

Carlos turned the shotgun towards her.

'He knows what happened to my Laura.'

'Carlos,' Medina said. 'Don't do this.'

'He saw what happened, but wouldn't help.'

Estrada looked at the man she'd held in her arms, soaking up his grief, less than twenty-four hours before.

'I agree,' she said, 'we need to talk to him, but I can't do that with a shotgun aimed at my chest, can I?'

'Carlos,' Medina said, quietly, 'put the gun down.'

'You'll make him tell you what he saw?'

'Yes, we will, I promise.'

'He knows what happened.' Carlos lowered the gun. 'You want me to help you with him? He don't have a tongue, see? Cut out, it was. You have to play that kid's game with him.'

'Anything you can do, anyway you can help us - but I need you to give me the gun.'

217

There was a hesitation…then Carlos lunged forward and brought the butt of the shotgun down on Pepe's left shoulder. The blow knocked Pepe to the floor and Carlos stood over him.

'Carlos?' Estrada said, quietly. 'I'll take the gun.'

He turned and looked at her. He held the shotgun at arms length and appeared to be willing to surrender it but, as she moved towards him, he pulled it back. 'You will talk to him?'

'Yes, you have my word. Now, please…' She took the shotgun from him, handed it to Medina, helped Pepe to his feet and walked him to a chair. She took Carlos by the arm and led him out into the corridor. 'What you did in there was wrong. Someone could have been hurt. You could have had blood on your hands - my blood, or Leo's. You can't keep interfering like this.'

He looked at her and tears tumbled from his red-rimmed eyes. 'Sorry,' he said, quietly. 'When we catch someone, I'll rest easy.'

Estrada insisted that Leo Medina took the rest of the day off, to spend time with his family and calm down.

Guzmán's lawyer arrived. He spent ten minutes with his client, then demanded his release. Estrada explained why he'd been detained and mentioned his aggressive response to questioning. But she knew in her heart she'd have to release him.

'You have not heard the end of this,' the lawyer had assured her, and she sighed with relief as they pulled out of the Town Hall Square in the lawyer's Mercedes.

'One down,' Valencia Ramoz said.

'He's still in the frame.'

218

'Not for much longer, I suspect.' She passed her an email that had just come through from Julieta Santiago. Estrada scanned the information, got up, walked out of the office, down the hall, and unlocked the interrogation room where Adam Wells had been kept.

'About time,' he said and, as he gathered his personal belongings and slipped his belt on, he added, 'Look, I came here to help in your enquiries. That's all anyone needs to know, right?'

'What you tell your wife, is your affair. Now, get out before I change my mind.'

She watched him saunter across the square, then took out her mobile, waited for Fernández to answer, updated him, adding, 'DNA results for Adam Wells and Javier Guzmán have been emailed through. Neither matches the foetus.'

'Doesn't rule them out. Both had motive enough to want her dead.'

'The sooner we find José…'

Estrada hesitated as Ramoz handed her two more pages of information. 'The Aston Martin's been given a clean bill of health and the hotel in Madrid's confirmed José ordered room service at midnight on Saturday.

'He could have driven down, killed Laura, and driven back…but, looks unlikely, doesn't it?'

'Increasingly.'

'Let's wait until he turns up. Anything else?'

'God, this is so sad.' Estrada dragged air into her lungs before exhaling forcefully. 'When the mobile was found on the beach, a woman phoned several times. She wanted to talk to Laura. Her university tutor made the calls. She wanted to tell Laura that she'd passed her final exams, with distinction.'

*

219

As they lay in the quiet of their house - Roz sleeping peacefully, her head resting in the crook of his arm, her dark hair spilling over his chest - Medina stared at the ceiling as the drilling of the cicadas drifted through the open window and his boys stirred in the bedroom next door. He had come close to killing someone today. If he'd pushed Adam Wells with more force, or submitted to his detestation of Javier Guzmán, both could be lying on a slab in the morgue and he might never be able to lie like this again, with his family around him, with the woman he loved in his arms.

He hoped his 'inappropriate behaviour' would be overlooked and Guzmán wouldn't press charges.

But, as he lay there, he tried to convince himself that he didn't care if he had stepped over the line. He didn't care if he lost his job and had to go back to labouring on a building site. He didn't care what Fernández, or Estrada, or Santiago, or Vincente Cabrera, or what any of them thought. And then he heard Roz mumble in her sleep and realized that he did care. He understood suddenly what it would mean to be without her and the boys and as he pulled her to him and his eyes filled with tears, he grasped the simplest of truths…that, apart from his family, finding the man who killed Laura was the most important thing in his life. He'd have to behave. He'd have to keep his hands to himself and do things by the book - as Jacinta Estrada had insisted - but he *would* find the man who killed Laura and hoped someone would be there to stop him tearing the bastard apart.

*

She trusted Eva to cut well and to make sure her hair always looked immaculate, but when Ana-Maria looked at her reflection she wondered why hairdressing salons used such harsh, unflattering lighting? Was it the black cloak that drained her colour? Even she looked pale. She took her mobile from the smoky glass shelf below the mirror, dialled a preset, waited for her mother to answer, and smiled when Sofia took the call. 'Nena. How are you?'

'Mama says I'm a naughty girl.'

'Why? What've you been up to?'

'Nothing.'

'Is mama there?' The phone fell silent and Eva fussed with the foil she'd used to add highlights.

'Ana-Maria? Is that you?'

'Mama? Is Sofia sick?'

'I don't think so, but I'm worried about her.'

'Any news of José?'

'The men have searched everywhere and the police took his car away. You don't think that anything awful's happened, do you?'

'No, give it time. He'll turn up.'

'Antonio Fernández wants to talk to Sofia.'

'He's not still going on about the old man? Does he never listen? I told him she'd overheard Leo during the fiesta. You know how imaginative she can be?'

'He'll be here this evening. Holly's grandmother's bringing Holly over. It'll give the girls a chance to play together. Antonio seems to think Sofia has told Holly something.'

'About what?'

'Can you both come over, this evening?'

'Paul's in England for a couple of days. The Almeria contract's all but signed and he wants to make sure the UK side of the business can function without him.'

'But you'll be here?'

'Of course I will. We can ask Antonio if they've had the results of the blood test.'

'Blood test?'

'To confirm that Laura's baby was José's.'

'Of course it was his.'

Both women fell silent.

'You mean it could be someone else's?'

'They're questioning two other men who knew Laura. They've taken DNA from both of them and used my blood because José's...'

'But they can't think Laura slept around, could they?'

The hair dryer was wheeled into place and an assistant was waiting. 'They need to be sure, mama. I don't really understand the science, but because José and I have the same mother and father, it should be possible to check the baby's DNA against mine.'

'Oh, my God.'

The line went quiet, and Ana-Maria shook her head at the assistant to indicate that she wanted to complete the call. 'Mama?' She smiled at the assistant and shrugged. 'Mama? Look, I've got to go. I'll see you tonight. Mama? Mama? What is it? Are you alright?'

Fernández found Santiago at the morgue. She was struggling through a pile of paper work.

'Help yourself to coffee,' she said.

He retreated to the corridor where he found an empty bench and rolled up his jacket to use as a pillow. He stretched out and propped his feet on the handrail at the other end. He stared up at the ceiling as the mortuary door swung open and he caught the sound of a cutter being tested. He shuddered and closed his eyes. Perhaps it wasn't surprising, he thought, that she didn't always have time for pleasantries.

An hour later, an orderly with a loaded trolley outside the mortuary. Santiago came out, unzipped the cadaver's shroud, checked the identity of the corpse, and then watched the orderly push the trolley into the lab.

She woke Fernández and they took the stairs to her office. 'How's it going?' she asked.

He brought her up-to-date.

Then he added, 'Leo's struggling,'

'Laura's death's hit him hard.'

'Yes. Maybe I should pull him off the case?'

'Do, and you'll deny him an opportunity for closure. Sitting on the sidelines is not going to help him, or you. No one's likely to work harder than Leo to find Laura's killer.'

'I'll talk to him.' He rubbed the back of his neck. 'Do you have anything else for me?'

'There's another complication.'

'You're going to blind me with science, aren't you?'

'We need to talk about Ana-Maria's DNA. When a child is born, she inherits half of her DNA from her mother and half from her father. Tests produce a profile that looks a bit like a barcode. A person's barcode can be compared with someone else's…'

'To see if there's a match.'

'Matching a child's barcode to its mother and father is usually straightforward.'

'Which is why it was easy to eliminate Adam Wells and Javier Guzmán?'

'If either of them was the father there'd be a positive match.'

'And, when we find José?'

'It'll be easy to establish if he's the father. But Ana-Maria is the child's aunt and, as I suggested, the tests on the sample you gave me are inconclusive.'

'So, José may not be the father.'

He hesitated.

223

'If his wife corroborates his alibi, Adam Wells will be in the clear. And that will leave Javier Guzmán with some explaining to do.'

'Even though he's not the father?'

'Laura could have told him he was, and threatened to tell his fiancée.'

'José could be the father,' she said.

'I thought we'd just established that he couldn't be, because the barcodes don't match?'

'There isn't a *sufficient* match, not one that will hold up in Court. But, there is another possibility…'

'Keep it simple.'

'If José *is* the father…further DNA testing will prove that he and Ana-Maria are *not* brother and sister. Or, more precisely,' she said, 'they have different fathers.'

'So, Enrique?'

'Is not Ana-Maria's father.'

Her shrug was a small movement of resignation, but she hadn't finished. 'That's not all,' she said, quietly.

He got up, opened a window and the sounds of the city invaded.

He watched two men arguing over a parking space.

'Go on.'

'Tests we carried out on Ana-Maria's blood sample showed she's haemophiliac. At least, she's a carrier.'

He dropped his head as he recalled extracts from Teresa Gonzales's diaries.

'You OK?'

'Just another piece of the jigsaw.'

'We can come back to it later.'

'No, no it's OK.'

'Haemophilia is inherited,' Santiago said. 'If the man who fathered Ana-Maria was a haemophiliac, she would have inherited the condition.'

He stared out of the window.

'You wanted to talk to Holly and Sofia.'

224

'Yes. Yes, I know.' He sighed heavily. 'I'm just not sure *now* is the best time.'

'What is it, Antonio?'

'Rodrigo Perpiñán told me that if I looked under too many rocks, I'd find more than I bargained for.'

They sat in silence throughout the drive from Almeria and Fernández was grateful for the chance to banish images that tumbled through his mind. The harshness of the afternoon sun had relented and a warm breeze swept off the sea. Fair-weather cumulus clouds scurried across the tops of the mountains and bathed the hills in a patchwork of shadows.

As they approached the village, they saw a large herd of goats roaming over the lower slopes of the hills and Fernández made a mental note to remind him to bring Pepe in for questioning. He dropped Santiago near the Castaño's home. He watched her disappear among the labyrinth of narrow lanes, then parked at the cemetery and made his way to Perpiñán's home.

As he approached, he noticed that the front door was open. He stepped inside. The front room was deserted. He stood and listened. He crossed the room and pushed open the door onto the terrace. He assumed he'd find his friend, asleep, but the terrace was deserted. The chairs had been pushed under the table and everything was unusually tidy and clean.

He was about to leave when he heard the faintest of sounds from an upstairs window. He eased his Beretta from his jacket and slid the breechblock backwards, and set the trigger mechanism.

He went back into the sitting room and climbed the narrow staircase that led to the only bedroom. The door was closed. He stopped and listened, but couldn't hear anything. He raised the handgun, then placed his hand on the doorknob, turned it slowly, and in one swift, decisive movement, kicked open the door.

Perpiñán was sitting upright, his arms extended and trembling under the weight of the shotgun he was pointing at Fernández.

'For Christ's sake, Antonio, what the hell d'you think you're doing?'

Fernández lowered his gun. He rested against the doorframe, shook his head and began to laugh.

Relief flooded through him like the surge of cold beer on a hot afternoon.

'Do you mind?' Perpiñán placed the shotgun on the bed beside him.

Fernández looked at a shape beneath the bedclothes, a mop of greying hair betraying Perpiñán's lover.

'Antonio?'

'I need to talk to you.'

'Now? Can't it wait?'

'I wish it could.' He smiled. 'I'll be downstairs.'

'Oh, that's good of you.'

Whilst he waited, he collected Teresa's diaries, went to the terrace, opened the first and began to flip through it. After ten minutes, he heard muffled exchanges and the front door close. 'The widow García, I presume?' he said.

'None of your business. I should've let you have both barrels.' Perpiñán poured himself a brandy and offered the bottle.

'Maybe later.'

'This had better be good.'

'I wanted to look at the diaries again.'

'Because you couldn't face the truth the first time?'

Perpiñán sipped his brandy. 'Oh, come on, Antonio. You've seen the photographs. The reference to the Priest's whore in the diaries confirms her existence. The age profile fits. And as if that wasn't enough Teresa Gonzales didn't exactly disguise her name, did she? *'Not so innocent'*. The problem is, you won't admit that Ana-Maria, the great love of your life, is the illegitimate child of a woman who'd been fucking a Priest.'

Perpiñán downed the brandy and poured another shot.

'Inocenta, the Priest's whore, married another man and passed the child off as his.'

'It's more complicated than that,' Fernández said.

'It always is with you.'

'Ana-Maria's DNA was inconclusive.'

'Well, it would be, wouldn't it?'

'You've known all along? Then why the hell did you suggest I take a sample from her?'

'I knew you wouldn't listen to me, but I thought you might – just might - listen to Doctor Santiago and her *irrefutable* evidence.' Perpiñán sat down and lowered his voice, as though concerned the walls had grown ears, or the warm air would carry their conversation beyond his home. 'I was there that night. Remember? I was there. I saw the Priest and his whore.'

'But not her face. You said she had her back to you.'

'Yes, she did. But I realised who Cinderella was as soon as I saw Father Emanuel's hand on her hip. At first, I couldn't work out why *you* couldn't see it. Now, I know. You didn't *want* to see it. Or rather, you didn't want to admit that Inocenta was the Priest's whore.'

He paused, as though waiting for Fernández to accept the truth. 'It doesn't stretch the imagination too far,' he continued, 'to suggest that Inocenta may have been party to the murder of Alberto, Bartolomé, and Matias...that she didn't want the truth to be made public and may even have been involved in the attempted cover up.'

227

'The murder of Juan Gonzales?'

'Yes. For God's sake, what are you waiting for?'

'I need to be sure.'

'Who the hell are you trying to protect?'

Fernández looked at the campo as the village lights began to flicker into life. His head was swimming and he was struggling to stay focused. 'The diaries,' he said, 'suggested that Father Emanuel was haemophiliac. Ana-Maria will have inherited the condition from her father. But identifying her as the Priest's child doesn't make her mother guilty of murder.'

'You could pull Inocenta in and ask the questions that need asking.'

'And if she's had nothing to do with what happened last week?' Fernández spun round and faced him. 'You want me to ruin their lives, destroy their happiness and their reputation? I need something more than a few faded photographs, an old woman's diaries, and the results of a blood test.'

'You're protecting Ana-Maria. You can't run from the truth, Antonio.'

'I'm going,' he said, but as he stood up his mobile rang.

It was Julieta Santiago.

'Holly and Sofia have vanished.'

'What?'

'They were playing on the terrace. When Ana-Maria arrived, we went out to join them but they'd gone.'

'I'll be there as soon as I can. Phone Jacinta Estrada, tell her to get the local police out.' He turned to Rodrigo Perpiñán. 'Get down to the bar. See if Eduardo Gomez and his merry men are there. We need all the help we can get. One of our witnesses has disappeared.'

*

228

Leo Medina toyed with an empty glass and decided one more shot wouldn't hurt. He'd begun to feel mellow and enjoyed the sensation of the warm, smooth brandy as it slipped down. He held up the glass, ordered another and noticed Enrique Castaño in conversation with Carlos Domingo at the far end of the bar. It wasn't hard for him to imagine what they'd be talking about. Not wedding arrangements, for sure.

He looked at the publicity shots of José Castaño on the wall. 'And where the fuck are you, my friend?' He stared into the eyes of the Real Madrid star and remembered the hours they'd spent together. They were best mates and, it seemed, Laura was always there to tease them, to flirt, to flash her knickers and to promise but never deliver...not, that is, until they were a bit older and José had joined Real Madrid's youth squad - leaving the stage clear for the awkward adolescent Leo Medina had become. Looking back it was all so innocent, but even then Laura had a bit of a reputation. Of course, that made her all the more attractive to a seventeen year old.

Medina stared at the poster as he sipped his refill. 'And then you went off and left us, didn't you? Off to the bright lights, the flash cars, the money...'

He raised his glass and it must have seemed to those in the bar that he was saluting his friend. 'You were always a lucky bastard. I was never in the same league, of course. Then you and Laura got engaged.' Medina drained the glass. 'I didn't think it would last, to be honest.' His head dropped and tears began to muster in his eyes. 'And, it didn't, did it?' He stood up, unsteady on his feet and pointed the poster. 'You bastard! If you killed her, I'll fucking kill you!'

He threw the empty glass at the wall. It shattered and the disturbance brought the bar to a standstill. Enrique Castaño was quick to react, but Carlos Domingo slapped a hand on his shoulder, then nodded at Eduardo Gomez.

229

Gomez stood alongside Medina and folded his arms.

'Feel better for that?' he said.

'Bastard.'

'You've got no proof that José had anything to do with Laura's death.'

'If he did, I swear...'

The door flew open and Perpiñán stood fighting for breath. He looked towards Enrique Castaño.

'It's Sofia. She's disappeared.'

Enrique knocked furniture over, and barged his way out, closely followed by Carlos Domingo.

Ana-Maria led Fernández on to the terrace and they scanned the campo, hoping to catch sight of the girls. The light was fading and shadows played tricks, raising hopes and then dashing them as human shapes turned into a straggling bush or jagged cacti.

Santiago joined them. 'Inocenta and Pedra are out there, looking for them,' she told him.

He turned to Ana-Maria. 'What were they doing on the terrace?'

'Playing, rummaging through Sofia's toy-box. They must have climbed down the vine.'

'Sofia told Leo Medina that she saw an old man in the campo last Thursday.'

'Antonio,' Ana-Maria said, 'how many times? She heard Leo talking at fiesta on Friday night. It was late. She was tired. She would have been confused and repeated what she heard.'

'She told Holly about Gloria,' Santiago said.

'Oh, my God,' Ana-Maria said, suddenly. 'Oh, my God, I'm so sorry. She told me. Sofia told me. Just after lunch last Thursday.'

She looked at him. 'I'd taken her up to bed for siesta and she told me that she'd seen someone called Gloria playing hide-and-seek.'

'Can you remember exactly what she said? Her exact words?'

'She insisted I'd know who Gloria was...*you know*, she said, *Gloria*...as if by repeating the name I'd understand.' She hesitated. 'You think it was *this* Gloria who killed Juan Gonzales, don't you?'

'Yes.'

'But you don't know who Gloria is?'

'We're assuming it's Laura's nickname for him.'

'Him?'

'Odds on,' he said. 'We think Laura was blackmailing him to help José.'

'José was in trouble?'

'We don't know.'

'But,' Santiago said, 'we think that Sofia can identify Gloria and tie him to both investigations.'

Enrique and Carlos burst into the room.

'Where is she?' Enrique demanded.

'We don't know. Inocenta's out looking...'

Before Fernández could finish, Enrique and Carlos pushed past him, clambered over the railings and down the vine.

Jacinta Estrada arrived, closely followed by police officers, Eduardo Gomez, and a dozen men from the bar. She herded the extra manpower into the Castaño sitting room and began to organize the search.

'I can't just stand here,' Ana-Maria said, making for the door.

'It might be better if you stayed,' Fernández said.

Santiago brushed past him and followed Ana-Maria, but at the door she turned, and said, 'you just don't get it, do you Antonio?'

The bartender placed a coffee in front of Leo Medina, waited for him to pay, and then swept up the shattered glass that littered the floor beneath the publicity shots of José Castaño. Medina didn't need the coffee to sober up but he drank it anyway. He called Roz, just to hear her voice and know the boys were tucked up in bed. He told her he was heading down to the Castaño's to see what he could do to help.

He ended the call and stared at a poster alongside the shots of José - a montage of bullfighting photographs from Seville's *Plaza de la Maestranza*.

He snorted, regret and disappointment jostling side-by-side. As a child he'd dreamt of being one of Spain's great bullfighters and had plastered the walls of his bedroom with posters of men who'd risked their lives dressed in their *suit of lights*. These were his childhood heroes, but it was a dream that shattered when he grew too tall, too heavy.

He tried to focus on the photographs: the entrance of the bull into the ring; the novice matador taunting it with the *capote,* a large pink cape; the picador on his armour-clad horse, piercing the bull's back with a blooded pike; and the star matador confusing and frustrating the enraged bull, turning it this way and that.

He stared at the last two photographs that depicted the *pase de la Muerte*, the pass of death. The bull had turned for the last time and the matador had driven the sword deep into its withers and down into its heart. 'Oh, dear God.' Medina was unable to believe his eyes. His heart was hammering and his breath shortened as he took out his mobile and phoned Fernández.

'Yes, Leo. What is it?'

'Can you get to the bar?'

'You should be here, for Christ's sake. Two young girls are missing.'

'This is really important, Sir.'

Medina couldn't take his eyes off the title at the top of the bullfighting poster. 'I know who Gloria is.'

Fernández pulled Jacinta Estrada to one side.

'Stay here and coordinate the search. If the girls don't turn up within an hour, scramble a helicopter. Use search dogs and call mountain rescue. Whatever you do, keep the media well away from the area.'

'That's not going to be easy. We can't seal off a whole hillside.'

He placed a hand on her forearm. 'Do what you can. I'll be with Leo. If anything happens, let me know. OK?'

He opened the front door and was greeted by a flurry of flashguns, microphones and questions. He decided to make an impromptu statement.

'Two girls are missing, but we're hopeful of finding them soon. When we have any news, we'll pass it on to you, but I would ask that you do nothing to hinder the search. Thank you.'

He pushed his way through, ignoring questions, and walked briskly past empty police cars and up the road. He found Leo Medina waiting, impatient, alongside the cigarette machine in the bar. 'This had better be good, Leo.'

'Oh, it is, sir. It's better than good.' Medina paused, as though trying to organize his thoughts. 'Gloria's an adult. Right? Female? Unlikely, given the way Laura was killed. Laura gave everyone nicknames.'

'Scarpetta, Elliot Ness.'

'Exactly.'

Medina turned to photographs of the bullfight in Seville. 'Each demonstrates how the bull is forced to turn and turn again. It grows increasingly angry and frustrated with each pass.' He pointed at the matador holding the sword, ready to strike. He grinned at Fernández and then stabbed his hand at the top of the poster. 'Look at the title.'

'Pases de Gloria?'

'The Pases de Gloria. The turning of the bull.'

'Jesus.' Fernández stared the title, pulled his mobile and called Valencia Ramoz. He walked over and tapped on the bar. The bartender poured a brandy and then checked if Medina wanted another. He shook his head. When Ramoz answered, Fernández arranged for SOCO and Civil to meet him at the village church.

He cut the call and turned to Leo Medina. 'Find Father Gabriel. Ask him to bring a magnifying glass and wait for me outside the church. No one is to enter. No one. You understand?'

'Sofia!'

Most of the search party must have heard Inocenta's anguished cries, carried across the campo by a stiffening breeze.

'Holly!' Pedra's voice was harsher, more severe.

Both women knew that the odds on finding the girls had reduced dramatically. Darkness had cut vision down dramatically. It camouflaged undergrowth, rocks and mineshafts, and put everyone at risk. They also knew that no one would give up willingly, no matter how long it took to find the girls.

Enrique and Carlos had ignored the organized sweep and were scrambling among the rocky outcrops on the higher slopes, stopping occasionally to bellow across the valley.

Estrada was on the terrace, tracking progress through binoculars. After an hour, she phoned and was told that a helicopter would be there in fifteen minutes. It would make several passes, using its searchlight to try to locate the girls but, without night vision, it would then have to stand down until sun-up.

If the girls hadn't been located, the search and rescue coordinator told her, they'd probably survive, given it was summer and temperatures were high. Estrada didn't know how to respond to 'probably survive' and tried to imagine what might be going through the minds of Inocenta and Doctor Santiago. She tried not to think about the dangers the girls might face as they huddled together, trying to be brave, listening to every sound, and growing more anxious, more terrified. They not only had the dark to contend with, but also the wild boar, snakes, scorpions, mineshafts and deep crevasses.

She didn't have as much luck with her next call.

Mountain rescue were responding to an accident in the Sierra Nevada. They'd get to Los Mineros as soon as possible but, in the meantime, they advised her to bring everyone off the hills. 'It's too dangerous,' the team leader told her. 'The weather could close in and darkness brings its own set of problems.'

Three police dog-handlers arrived, their dogs yapping eagerly, pulling on their leads.

An hour later, she made the most difficult of calls and ordered civilians off the hill. The police officer who'd assumed control brought them together to explain what was happening… before the search was called off for the night, they'd make a final sweep, and double check all ruins, outbuildings, orchards, gullies and thickets.

One of men from the village echoed the sentiments of everyone involved when he said, 'Yeah, right, as if that's going to happen.'

'This is not up for debate. You're putting yourself and others at risk. You'll clear the campo and start again at first light.'

'There's two kids out there. You don't honestly expect us to stop?'

'My officers will continue to search through the night. A rescue team's on its way and a helicopter has been scrambled.'

The policeman stood his ground, but was relieved to see the Inspector striding towards them.

'Eduardo,' Fernández called, 'Get a dozen men and meet me outside the church. I'll explain when you get there.' He smiled at Pedra. She had put an arm around Inocenta - as if needing to warm and console her – and he had no doubt that she was trying to find some comfort for herself. 'I know it must be difficult,' he said, gently, 'but leave the rest of the night to the police officers.'

'You think it'll take the rest of the night? They won't find them?' Inocenta said.

'They'll be all right. Now, go home. As soon as they've been found, we'll let you know. I promise.'

He nodded at Pedra and watched as they joined the others. They dragged their heels, as if hoping they'd missed something and were desperate for good news before they crossed the police line and went back into the village.

He asked the officer where Enrique, and Carlos had gone.

'Last I saw them, they'd moved up the mountain, just below the escarpment.'

'And the two women?'

'Went off that way.'

He pointed towards a building site.

236

'Thanks. I think I know where they'll be.' Fernández borrowed a torch and made his way to the new-build. He ducked under the crime scene tape as the moon slipped from behind a cloud and stopped at the doorway. The area had been cleared of anything forensics might find useful, but the image of the four bodies was etched in his mind.

He heard Ana-Maria's voice as it drifted up from the basement. She was calling out the girl's names, her voice loud and strident. And then he heard Santiago's, softer, more fearful.

He stopped at the top of a skeleton-staircase leading to the basement and waited. Ana-Maria headed up the stairs, and he watched as she concentrated on each footstep, and called Sofia's name.

As she neared the top, she lifted her head and saw his silhouette. She swore, shone her torch in his face and strode up the last few steps. 'Jesus, Antonio, you think that's funny?'

'I need you to come with me.'

'They've found them?' Santiago asked; her face drained of any colour in the pale moonlight.

'No. Everyone's been pulled off for the night, except the police. A helicopter's on its way.'

'The girls are still out there and you expect us to walk away?'

He knew they'd want to continue the search, but he needed Ana-Maria at the church. 'It may be the hardest thing you've ever done,' he said, 'but I need your help. Ten minutes, that's all I ask.' He glanced at the Indalo pendant nestling on Ana-Maria's cleavage and, as he looked up, their eyes met. He smiled, awkwardly, and knew the next few hours would be immeasurably more painful than anything Ana-Maria had ever been through.

'I need you to show me where you found that,' he said.

'I told you. In the church.'

'Will you show me, please?'

'I don't understand.'

'Where's your husband?'

'He's in the UK. Flying back tomorrow. Why?'

'You must trust me. Come to the church. Please.' He turned and led her back as a helicopter swooped down and lit the campo with its searchlight.

'I'm sorry. I'm not going anywhere until you tell me what's going on. Sofia and Holly are out there, Laura's dead, and José's missing. And all you seem interested in is a couple of ounces of gold.'

'You can't just expect her to quit, Antonio,' Santiago said.

He ignored her, turned to Ana-Maria. 'I need you at the church. Now.'

'And I'm staying here until we find Holly and Sofia. For God's sake, Antonio, nothing can be more important than what's happening right here, right now. Whatever it is can wait 'til the morning.'

'No, I'm sorry, it can't.'

His voice had moderated but lost none of its gravity. He looked at Ana-Maria. 'Not if we're to stand a chance of finding your brother alive.'

He knew that if they'd continued to search, they may well have stumbled across Holly and Sofia within minutes of leaving the new-build. Sunday papers carried stories of searches being called off whilst victims were still alive, often no more than a few hundred meters from safety. Or they'd be found days later, injured, close to starvation, having lived off the land.

But, there was another possibility that nagged at him. The girls could have been abducted...enticed from the terrace, bundled into a car, and held somewhere. Or worse... As he led Ana-Maria through the village, the thought of two fragile bodies lying broken in a lonely grave tore at his heart. He'd almost convinced himself he wasn't dealing with an abduction...the girls had slipped away on some misguided adventure and the chances of the search party finding them were good. He'd almost convinced himself, but not quite.

'You going to tell me what's happening?' Ana-Maria called after him. 'Antonio?' She stopped as they entered the church square. 'I need to know, Inspector. I need to know what's going on.'

She stood with her hands resolutely on her hips and her chest heaving with exertion.

He noticed villagers pestering Eduardo Gomez and Guardia Civil holding back reporters. He saw Father Gabriel waiting at the church doors, Leo Medina by his side. He offered his hand to Ana-Maria. 'Come with me, please. I can't tell you here.'

As they passed through the church doors he nodded at father Gabriel and took the magnifying glass from Medina. Inside, he led her down the aisle, pulled back the tarpaulin, flicked on the light, and walked down the concrete ramp.

They stood among the rubble in the crypt. She looked into his anxious face. 'Tell me what you want me to do.'

'Would you mind?' He pointed at the Indalo pendant resting high on her chest. She tugged it and broke the crude fixing that held it round her neck. She handed it to him and he used the magnifying glass to study markings on the feet of the gold figure.

The initials J and C were clearly visible.

'I'll need to hold on to this for a while. Can you show me exactly where you found it?'

239

'It's José's isn't it?'

'I think it may be. Yes.'

'Oh, my God.' She backed away from him. 'You can't mean..?'

'I need to know where you found it.'

Ana-Maria scanned the crypt. 'Here.'

She stood close to a borehole. 'Antonio, please, tell me what's happening.'

'Laura was pregnant.'

'Yes, José's.'

'We're not sure.'

'But the DNA?'

'Because you're the baby's aunt, the tests were inconclusive. They would have been positive if the sample was taken from the father.'

'From José,' she said. 'Why can't you say it was his child?'

'We need to be certain.' He looked at her. Her eyes, he thought, were full of anger, fear and bewilderment.

'We want to interview your husband in connection with the death of Juan Gonzales.'

'In connection with…Paul killed Gonzales?'

'And, we think Laura knew what happened and tried to blackmail him.'

'He killed Laura?'

'We think so.'

'And José? Where's José?' Her voice lost its strength and her eyes brimmed with tears. Suddenly, she dropped to her knees and began to tear at rubble that filled the borehole. 'He's here, isn't he? He's here. Help me!'

She clawed at the earth, shovelling debris to one side, frantic in her desperation, her accusations raining down on him. 'You told me we'd be able to save his life.'

'There still a chance.'

'You lied to me. You know he's dead.'

'We won't know that, until we find him.'

240

'You know he's dead. I know you do!' She stopped and held her hand to her mouth. 'God, no, please tell me it wasn't Paul.'

'We think Laura phoned him and asked him to take her to the airport. When she didn't arrive in Madrid, José drove down and confronted him.'

'He killed José?'

'Yes, we think so.'

'Think, think, think!' She got up and moved towards him. She screamed and started to rain blows on his chest and arms. 'No, no, no!'

Alarmed by her screams, Father Gabriel ordered officers from Guardia Civil to keep everyone out and led Leo Medina down the ramp. They stopped at the entrance to the crypt. Fernández had taken Ana-Maria into his arms and they were sitting amidst the rubble, rocking back and forth. It was several minutes before he released her and Father Gabriel led her out of the crypt, back up the ramp, to one of the pews near the altar.

'Leo,' Fernández said, 'get SOCO down here, and tell Eduardo to get his men to help clear the rubble. Find the Mayor and tell him to keep the press away. Phone Valencia Ramoz and get her to contact the airlines. We need to know if Paul Turnbull flew to the UK yesterday and, if he did, what time he's due back tomorrow. And get someone to tell Carlos that Laura's funeral will have to be postponed.'

He accompanied Medina back up the ramp, pushed the tarpaulin to one side and saw Father Gabriel talking to Ana-Maria.

His mobile rang.

Ana-Maria lifted her head, tears dragging mascara down her cheeks, and he knew she'd be hoping for good news: that the girls had been found, safe and well.

It was Juanita Ramos.

He glanced at Ana-Maria, shook his head and turned away to take the call.

'How's the search for Sofia and her friend?' Juanita asked.

'Nothing yet.'

'Can we meet?'

'Now's not a good time.'

'Tomorrow morning, then?'

'What is it, Juanita?'

'I've been through Bartolomé's papers. I still don't understand why my husband was killed, but I think I know who pulled the trigger.'

9

By three o'clock in the morning the painstaking work of clearing the rubble had produced nothing. They'd dug down two meters without a trace of José and had started to excavate two other boreholes.

Valencia Ramoz phoned to confirm Paul Turnbull had flown from Almeria on Wednesday, and was returning on British Airways, leaving Heathrow at nine, stopping in Madrid and transferring to Air Nostrum for the one-hour flight to Almeria. Travelling business class on the first leg, Turnbull would have access to the business class lounge in Madrid and time for duty free shopping. What he wouldn't know, Ramoz explained, was that, throughout the journey, he'd have two plain-clothed Special Branch officers from London's Metropolitan Police shadowing his every move.

At four o'clock in the morning, the hunt for Holly and Sofia was suspended and soup, bread, and flasks of coffee were ferried out to the search party. It would be a fine day, if the first signs of dawn were anything to go by, and those left on the campo took the opportunity to rest.

The mountain rescue team arrival and the helicopter's involvement made everyone feel more positive.

Pedra and Inocenta had propped themselves up in the two fire side chairs in the Castaño sitting room and had fallen into a fitful sleep. Julieta, Enrique and Carlos were anxious for the search to resume, but even they recognised the need to rest.

Four o'clock in the morning was also the time when it was agreed that men who'd been helping in the church would go home and get some rest - those who had work, it was argued, could not afford to lose a day's pay.

At six o'clock, Guardia Civil briefed Policia Local - the over-riding priority was to keep media and anxious villagers away whilst SOCOs continued the search for José.

Ana-Maria lay on a pew, unable to sleep, her head resting on Father Gabriel's rolled up cassock.

Leo Medina went home and collapsed on the sofa. At nine o'clock he was due to relieve Jacinta Estrada – who, at that moment, was dozing on a white plastic chair on the Castaño terrace - and let her get home for a few hours.

Fernández made his way to Rodrigo Perpiñán's.

'I've been expecting you,' Perpiñán said. 'The village is awash with rumour…two girls kidnapped and José buried in the church.'

Fernández pushed passed him, time short. 'Did the widow García leave any pastries?'

'There's paella in the fridge. I'll put the coffee on.'

Fernández slumped on sofa in the sitting room. 'The kids haven't been kidnapped. Least ways, I don't think so…' his voice trailed off, momentarily, a strident voice in his head reminding him that there was no sign of them, *was there*? He dismissed the thought. Paul Turnbull was in the UK and there was no one else he'd consider responsible if it turned out that the girls had been abducted. 'We've a suspect under surveillance.'

'For which investigation?'

'Both.' He felt oddly reassured as he said it.

'Same man?'

'Yes. Problem is, with all the speculation, someone in the village might try to contact him.'

244

He looked at his watch. It was ten past seven. London was an hour behind. Ten past six.

In three hours, Turnbull would board the nine o'clock at Heathrow. Plenty of time for someone to warn him. Once he'd arrived in Madrid he'd have a couple of hours before the flight to Almeria - a couple of hours in which he might well turn on his mobile and collect messages; a couple of hours in which to engineer an escape from Spain's busiest airport.

Fernández closed his eyes.

Just after eight, he woke to find an omelette draped over steaming paella on the table in front of him.

'They're waiting for you.'

'Who?'

'You'd arranged to meet Juanita, Eduardo Gomez, and our illustrious Mayor.'

'Shit.'

'I told them you were in the shower. Not a bad idea, after you've finished eating.'

He got to the Town Hall, an hour late.

They took the Mayor's four-by-four and Fernández sat in the back studying documents Juanita had brought with her. 'Impressive,' he said, looking at the architect's drawings and site plan.

'It was a project that was going to make our fortune. A hotel with two hundred rooms, three pools, and five bars.' Juanita laughed hollowly. 'A nightmare from the moment they started the foundations.'

'It's been a regular feature in local papers,' Vincente Cabrera said. They left the road and drove down a track towards the coast. 'There have been objections from environmentalists, local residents, and land owners.'

'But it went ahead,' Eduardo Gomez prompted.

245

'Yes,' Cabrera said, 'but authorities are investigating the planning process. A final decision is due any day.'

'They suspect corruption?' Fernández asked.

Cabrera shrugged. 'Possibly.'

'It wasn't that long ago...' Eduardo Gomez said 'A developer would buy land and submit plans to the local Mayor's office. Money was paid under the counter, or one of the properties would be reserved for the Mayor, and the development went ahead.'

Fernández looked at Juanita. 'When you rang, you said you knew why your husband was killed.'

'It will be easier to explain at the construction site.'

The track wound its way through a steep sided valley and deteriorated dramatically as it neared the coast. As they rounded the final bend a huge, unfinished hotel towered above the beach and surrounding land.

They clambered out of the car and headed down to the beach. They stopped short of a sea sipping at rock pools and shingle. From there they could see the whole development with its glassless windows and gaping doors - each floor as forlorn and empty as the one above.

'Bartolomé was ambitious,' Juanita said. 'When he started out, he borrowed money from the bank, built homes in the village, luxury villas outside, and apartments along the beachfront. Business was good and we made money.' She hesitated. 'It would be easy to blame the recession but, in truth, his problems started ten years ago, when he went into business with an ex-pat who needed a Spanish partner.'

'To gain access to the town halls and their corrupt mayors, no doubt,' Eduardo Gomez said.

'My husband was a good man,' Juanita protested. 'Whatever he did, he did for his family. Just hear me out, before you start throwing stones. At first, the partnership worked well. Nothing was ever formalised, just the word of two men...a handshake as good as any contract. They were busy, repaid loans and had a good reputation. And then, this happened.' She pointed at the hotel. 'His partner used Bartolomé to get plans accepted, and then dissolved the partnership, cutting him out of the huge profits they expected to make.'

'But given the opposition to the hotel, his partner seems to have done him a favour,' Fernández said.

'On the face of it, yes, I'd agree. But last night, I found this.' She handed him a document and he spent several minutes reading it.

'*Rustico de Secano*,' he said, eventually.

'Let me see.' Eduardo Gomez put on his glasses and skimmed through it. 'It's about the land the hotel is built on. It was bought about eight years ago.' He looked at the document again. 'The land was *Rustico de Secano* - farmland. It would have been illegal to build on it. Permission to build on this land should never have been granted. The whole process was illegal. According to this, the site was bought for fifteen thousand euros.'

'A bargain,' Fernández said. 'And profits would have been huge.'

'But only if they got permission to build.'

'And by cutting Bartolomé out, he'd have doubled his profit.'

'Who's he?' Vincente Cabrera asked. 'Who bought the land with Bartolomé, then cut him out of the deal?'

'His partner.' Gomez handed the document back to Fernández and pointed at the signature. 'Paul Turnbull.'

'But what I still don't understand is...' Juanita's voice caught as she uttered the next few words. 'Why kill my husband?'

Fernández looked at the signature under Bartolomé's and glanced up from the document. Juanita had said she wasn't sure why her husband had been killed, but he could understand why she'd decided Turnbull had pulled the trigger.

247

'Turnbull is about to sign a contract worth millions,' he said, 'and Bartolomé saw his chance to recoup some of his losses. He threatened to expose Turnbull. If he showed this document to the authorities, the corruption would have destroyed his chances. Turnbull had to act and act quickly.'

Juanita bit her lip, fighting back her tears. 'But, why did all three men have to die?'

Fernández breathed out forcefully. 'Are you sure you want to hear this?'

'I need to know.'

'A few months ago, Gonzales collapsed. Turnbull found him, took him to the doctors. We're not sure what happened next, but Turnbull must have found out about Alberto's part in the murder of Gonzales' parents and told him. Gonzales, of course, had no hesitation and we can only assume that Turnbull convinced him to kill all three men.'

'But why?'

'He needed to silence Bartolomé, but knew his death would not be the end of the threat he posed. He had to kill Alberto and Matias...'

'Because they could have told the authorities?'

'Yes. I'm sorry.' He took her hands, aware of the bewilderment in her eyes, but felt she deserved to know, would want to know, the full horror of last Thursday. 'Turnbull convinced Gonzales to kill all three men, then he shot Gonzales. But your husband was still alive. Turnbull had to be sure and finished the job himself.'

*

248

Throughout the journey to Los Mineros, Fernández sat in the back of the car mulling over the evidence with which he'd confront Paul Turnbull. It could prove to be a long night.

Eduardo Gomez was sure that the mayor who'd taken Turnbull's bribe had died recently, but he agreed to use his contacts to draw up a list of those involved in re-designating the land. Vincente Cabrera offered to speak to political associates in Almeria and find out if the contract for the regeneration had been signed. Juanita sat alongside Fernández, her face turned to the window, her eyes vacant, registering little as the car sped along the coast road, across the plain and into the mountains. In her hand she clasped a small square of cloth from the shirt her husband was wearing when he was shot. She toyed with it, ringing it through her fingers and using it to wipe the silent tears from her cheeks.

Just before ten o'clock the car turned into the Town Hall Square. As Fernández clambered out, his mobile rang. 'Yes?'

It was Jacinta Estrada. 'They've found the girls. The helicopter's located them.'

'Where are they?'

'Way up in the hills.'

'They're ok?'

'Yes, we think so.'

'You think?'

'They're with Pepe. The goatherd. He's carrying one of them, making slow progress.'

'That's great. Just great.' He knew whatever he was feeling it would be nothing like the torrent of emotion that Julieta Santiago and Inocenta Castaño would be experiencing. He gave the thumbs up to Juanita, Eduardo and Vincente, then moved out of earshot. 'Does Ana-Maria know?'

249

'Not yet. I'll go to the church and tell her.'

'I'll meet you there.'

He paused. 'I don't suppose they've found him?'

'SOCO have cleared rubble from three boreholes, but found nothing. They've just started on a fourth.

'No sign at all?'

'You're sure José's there?'

'No. No, I'm not.'

'The Madrid police have come back to us,' Estrada said. 'They've uncovered a betting scam in the Capital. José got caught up in it. Had to borrow a serious amount of money.'

'How much?'

'Close to twenty-thousand.'

'But surely he could afford that?'

'Thing is, Sir, he was leading the life of a super star but I've been looking back through the information sent to us by Real Madrid.'

'And?'

'His salary is linked to the number of games he plays and goals he scores for the first team. He broke his leg last year. The Aston Martin's on loan, the club picks up the tab for his accommodation, and sponsorship clothes him and provides some of life's little luxuries.'

'So, paying off debts would not be as easy as it would for some of his more illustrious team mates?'

'Maybe loan sharks were after him,' Estrada suggested. 'And Laura tried to help solve the problem?'

'By blackmailing Adam Wells and Doctor Guzmán, and the man with the deepest pockets and the most to lose…'

'Paul Turnbull?'

Fernández rubbed the back of his neck.

'But she wouldn't have wanted José to know she'd slept around.'

'No of course not,' Estrada agreed. 'God, how stupid. She must have told Turnbull she knew he'd killed Juan Gonzales and demanded money in exchange for her silence.'

'And our only eyewitness is a six year old child.'

'Unless Carlos is right,' Estrada said, 'and Pepe knows more than he's saying.'

After the helicopter's scream scattered Pepe's goats it had taken an hour for his dogs - barking and snapping – to drive them back to the ruin where the girls sheltered over night. They made their way down the mountainside and half the village – or so it seemed - turned out to watch Pepe shrug off offers of help from police and members of the mountain rescue team.

Julieta Santiago fell twice as she hurried across the campo. She grazed her arm on a rock and managed to collect unwanted samples of coarse flora in her hair. She looked a mess (a jubilant, beside-herself-with-joy mess) and, unable to laugh or cry and as tears streamed down her face, she combined both in a passionate outpouring of love, relief and anxiety. By the time she reached the man who'd carried her daughter as he would a stricken lamb, she'd discarded any pretence that her job was important or that she was important. The only thing that was important was the tired, frightened, brave little girl who'd struggled in Pepe's arms when she saw her mother stumbling towards her.

On the Castaño terrace, Inocenta smiled as Pedra put her arm around her and they watched the tense standoff between Julieta Santiago and Pepe.

251

The goatherd appeared reluctant to release Holly but when she continued to struggle he relented and placed her gently on the floor. Santiago knelt down and Holly flew into her arms.

On the terrace, the attention of the two older women switched to Enrique and they watched him yelp with joy as he hurdled thickets of gorse and wild pampas grass and swept Sofia into his arms. He lifted her above his head, cried out and then cradled her to his chest.

Jacinta Estrada stood on the terrace alongside the two older women. She did not envy them their moment of relief and knew this moment of elation was no more than a respite for Inocenta Castaño.

For the Priest's whore, one trauma had run its course but another was about to begin.

Fernández found Ana-Maria in the church. She was monitoring the excavation of a borehole, her face lined with the twin agony of anticipation and denial. She'd wrapped Father Gabriel's cassock about her shoulders to stave off the chill. She'd watched rocks pass from one SOCO to another. Men from the village supplemented their efforts and the rubble was dumped in a skip outside the door to the southern nave.

As rocks were hauled to the surface, she leaned forward, looked into the borehole, held her breath, and scanned for traces of her brother.

Nothing.

But, nothing was good.

Nothing meant Antonio Fernández could be wrong.

Nothing gave her hope. Hope she clung to, resolutely.

Even when he stood behind her and spoke gently, it was as though he was part of her nightmare…

'They've found them. They've found the girls.'

His words didn't register at first and it wasn't until he touched her shoulder and startled her from her trance, that she grasped what he was saying.

'Yes, I know.'

'Both of them. Safe and sound.'

'Thank God.' She returned to her station, pulled a tissue from the sleeve of her blouse and wiped her eyes.

'I'll need to take your mobile,' he told her.

'My mobile? Why?'

'Have you tried to contact your husband this morning?'

'Yes, I tried, but here was no signal.'

'Your mobile, please, Ana-Maria.' He held out his hand. 'He'll be arrested when his plane lands this evening.' He looked at his watch. It was eleven fifteen. 'He's on the flight from London to Madrid. There'll be a delay before the flight to Almeria and I can't risk anyone contacting him.'

'Warn him, you mean.' She stood, as if transfixed, and he guessed she'd be struggling with the realisation that her husband may have killed Laura and José. But he was surprised when she managed to summon up vestiges of defiance. 'If you're so sure, why didn't you have him arrested in London?'

'It's easier this way. We'll have seventy-two hours to interview him before we have to lay the evidence before a judge.'

'You were always so sure of yourself, weren't you?' She turned on him, her eyes ablaze. 'You're enjoying this, aren't you? Ten years you've had to wait.'

She was right; he had waited ten years, but not to see her suffer. He wanted to hold her. He knew this would probably be the last time he would speak to her before her husband's arrest, but all he could summon was a simple, 'I'm sorry.'

253

He called over two Guardia Civil officers.

'Take Mrs Turnbull to the Town Hall and place her in a holding cell. Confiscate her mobile.'

'Like hell you will.' Ana-Maria pushed past him.

He nodded and the officers held her.

'Get your hands off me. I will not be treated like this!' As they led her up the ramp, she struggled, crying out once more, 'For God's sake Antonio!'

He ignored her protest and she was manhandled out of the church. He phoned the Incident Room, updated Valencia Ramoz and was told that Leo Medina had just started debriefing Pepe. He couldn't be certain had Ana-Maria had told him the truth about contacting her husband, and told Ramoz to alert officers tailing Turnbull.

'And keep an eye on Ana-Maria,' he said. 'Make sure she doesn't come to any harm.'

The girls had enjoyed a bath and being fussed over by Holly's grandmother.

Julieta Santiago checked her daughter's ankle and wrapped it in a crepe bandage. It wasn't long before they were dressed in striped cotton pyjamas and were sitting down to eat Sofia's favourite breakfast - honey pancakes and fresh orange juice.

It wouldn't be long, Estrada reckoned, before bed beckoned and she wanted to question the girls before exhaustion took its toll.

She glanced at photographs on the mantelpiece.

These had been happier days: the family on a beach before Sofia was born; a teenage Ana-Maria in one-piece swimsuit, posing; José more interested in the sand castle he'd made with his father.

Among the photographs there were several of Ana-Maria's wedding. It appeared to have been a lavish affair, with Turnbull escorting his bride down the aisle and out of the church, guiding her hand as she cut the cake, and helping her into a Rolls Royce.

Estrada waited until the girls had demolished three pancakes and were cuddled up on the sofa. She sat close by, reassured them that they weren't in trouble and then asked them to tell her exactly what they'd been up to.

They looked at each other and giggled. 'Well.' They giggled again and stumbled over who would go first before Sofia said, 'We were only playing a game.' They giggled once more, before the tale poured out of them…

They'd climbed down the vine, chased each other across the campo and slipped under the tape the police had put around the new-build - where those men had been killed - and then scampered higher up the hill.

Holly fell and hurt her ankle.

It was getting dark and they were scared. Holly tried to walk but her ankle hurt too much. And then, suddenly, hundreds of goats surrounded them. A man pushed his way through the goats, slapping their bottoms to make them move. He didn't say anything but, as the girls huddled together, he stroked their foreheads and brushed hair out their eyes.

Sofia told the man what had happened to Holly and he carried her to an old ruin, where he had water, some black bread and a soft blanket made of wool. It was dark. They heard people calling their names and asked the man to take them home. But he couldn't speak. He showed them his mouth. He didn't have a tongue.

It was really scary and they began to cry and Sofia asked him if he was going to hurt them or kill them, like someone killed Laura? The man shook his head and stroked their hair again. They asked if he would take them home? He nodded.

Now? He shook his head. In the morning? He nodded and smiled, and patted the blanket, and the girls held on to each other and cuddled until they fell asleep.

'Did he stroke you anywhere else?' Julieta Santiago asked.

'It's very important you tell us the truth,' Inocenta said.

The girls – Estrada was pleased to note - didn't need to consult and they looked, wide-eyed, at the women who'd encircled them unintentionally.

'He looked at my ankle,' Holly said. 'He rubbed a rag over the back of one of his goats. Then put it on my ankle. It smelt horrible.'

Both girls giggled, unaware that Estrada had decided the time had come to ask her questions.

'Sofia,' she said, and waited until she was sure she was listening, 'who was Gloria paying hide-and-seek with?'

The room fell silent and Holly took Sofia's hand.

'Sofia, we know who Gloria is,' Estrada said. 'It's not a secret anymore.'

Tears filled Sofia's eyes and she looked at Holly.

'They're tired. Can't this wait?' Inocenta asked.

'Sofia?' Estrada said, and then repeated her question.

'Señor Gonzales.'

'When was this?'

'Just before the fireworks.' Sofia began to sob.

Holly put her arm round her. 'I said it would be better if you told, didn't I?'

'Sofia?' Estrada took two wedding photographs from the mantelpiece.

'Can you see Gloria in any of these?'

Sofia nodded.

'Can you show me?'

*

After raiding the duty-free for malt whisky, perfume and chocolates, Paul Turnbull settled in Iberia's business class lounge. He only had hand luggage and asked if his case could be stowed in a locker behind the reception desk. It had been announced that Air Nostram's flight to Almeria had been delayed due to technical problems and one of the air stewardesses had told him that if there was anything the airline staff could do, he only had to ask - nothing was too much trouble. He'd thanked the tall, very attractive young woman, and had told her that he was sure he'd think of something.

He sat in the business lounge and flipped through several British tabloids and Spanish papers. The murder of Laura Domingo and the questioning of two suspects were featured in one; a *bungled burglary* and the death of Felipe Romero in another; and in a third he skimmed through a profile of Juan Gonzales, *Fascist Assassin.*

The back pages featured football's summer transfers and the legacy of London's Olympics. José Castaño, he noted, seemed to have slipped off the radar.

Turnbull had lunch and then checked his iPhone. He was about to call Ana-Maria when he saw the stewardess sashay towards him.

'I've got some good news,' she said, and sat down. 'The technical fault's been rectified and we'll be taking off as soon as everyone's aboard. You'll appreciate that there's no business class on this Dash 8 twin prop, but I'm sure we'll find a way of making your flight as comfortable as possible.'

'That's very thoughtful.' He grinned and glanced at her hand to check for a band of gold – less complicated if she was married.

'Is there anything else, Sir?' She raised an eyebrow and smiled.

'You'll be accompanying the flight?'

'Of course. We want to make sure you're delivered safely, don't we? Now, if you could make your way to the departure gate. As soon as we have everyone on board, we can taxi into position.' She pointed at his iPhone. 'You'll need to turn that off, I'm afraid.'

He was about to shut it down, when he asked, 'I don't suppose you'd like to join me for dinner this evening? Say eight-thirty?'

'What about your wife?'

'I'll text her, if you think I might be delayed?'

'I think it's highly likely,' she looked round, as if she wanted to be sure that she wasn't overheard, 'I know somewhere that's very intimate. To be honest, the food's not brilliant but they have rooms...' She smiled. 'I'll phone ahead, make a reservation.'

'I'll see you later, then?'

'Can't wait.'

Fernández was standing outside the bakery when his mobile sounded. It was Jacinta Estrada.

'They need you at the church.'

'Send someone to fetch Doctor Santiago. She's at the Castaño's. Tell them to be discreet.'

'I'll go myself.'

'Thanks. You'd better ask Father Gabriel to meet me at the church.' He closed his mobile and stood quietly for a moment. Even something as inevitable as that phone call hit him hard.

SOCOs had removed rocks and levered boulders onto the floor around the borehole before clearing away as much rubble and layers of dust as possible. At two metres, they'd unearthed the unmistakable light blue of denim and the heel of a training shoe. Their choice had been stark - proceed with caution on the assumption that they were dealing with a corpse or throw caution to the wind in the faint hope that he might still be alive. It must have felt like an eternity to those looking down from the rim of the borehole, but the officer in charge reacted almost immediately. 'Get down there and check.'

The young man was lying face down. A large rock had bridged across the crude burial chamber and had protected him from rubble poured on top of him.

They winched the rock from the hole before a SOCO was lowered and began to claw at the rubble. He filled several buckets and waited patiently for each to return empty. Suddenly, he stopped and moved an arc light to illuminate the body. He knelt and searched for signs of life. He checked for a pulse and then placed his ear close to the face. He looked up and shook his head.

'I'll let Inocenta know,' Father Gabriel whispered.

He hurried from the church.

Julieta Santiago arrived, unclasped her bag and asked to be lowered down.

She spent several minutes checking, but José was dead.

Fernández told the SOCOs to take a break and waited until they'd left. 'You OK?' he called down to her.

She looked up, her body trembling in the cold.

'It's so sad, Antonio, so achingly sad. Moments ago, Inocenta held onto Sofia as though her life would end if anything happen to her. Now she has this to face.'

He watched as she fought to regain her composure, but he couldn't wait too long – time, as always, of the essence. He lit a cigarette.

'This is a crime scene, Inspector.'

He stubbed it out. SOCOs began to drift back and a uniformed officer arrived to report that Enrique Castaño was at the church doors and was demanding to be let in.

'Don't let the press get near him. Bring him inside, but not down here. I'll tell you when we're ready for him.'

'Antonio,' Santiago called. 'There's nothing more I can do. I'll leave it for SOCO.'

'His father's here.'

'He'll have to wait. He can help with formalities once we've removed the body. Get me out of here.'

She was winched to the surface.

'It's not easy to asphyxiate a fit young man,' she said, 'He's been strangled?'

'There's no bruising, fingernail marks, or damage to the larynx, but there is petechial haemorrhaging in the eyes and face. Someone knocked him unconscious, hauled him to his feet, and crushed his chest...like a bear hug.' She removed her gloves. 'The girls are safe.'

'Yes, thank God.'

'Mother's taken them into the City. They'll stay at our apartment. We thought it better if Sofia was away from the press speculation and this...God knows what's going on in her mind. She's so young.'

'Let's hope we don't have to put her on the stand.'

'Can you secure a conviction without her?'

'I'm not sure her testimony would be reliable. Pepe's a better bet...I'm glad the girls are OK.'

'I know, but they haven't been a priority, have they?'

Santiago stepped aside as forensic officers prepared to seal off the site. 'You want me to tell Ana-Maria?'

'Yes. Thanks,' he said, stung by her accusation, but as he stared down at José's body he knew she was right: Holly and Sofia had not been at the top of his list.

He headed out of the church and several journalists tagged along behind him. They shouted out questions and demanded answers.

He looked at his watch.

It was three-thirty. Paul Turnbull was on-board the Air Nostram flight, bound for Almeria.

He stopped, turned and said, 'A press conference will be held in Almeria at five this evening.'

'Oh, come on Inspector, you can do better than that. Tell us what's going on. Give us something, for fuck's sake.'

Fernández lit a cigarette and dragged the smoke into his lungs. He glanced up at the barrage of cameras assembled in front of him, red lights betraying readiness to record. He considered his options. He needed to keep them away from the Castaño home and, knowing that Guardia Civil were in control at the church, he said, 'A body has been found in the crypt.'

He found Father Gabriel sitting with Inocenta.

She was looking at photographs of her son.

The Priest came over and whispered, 'I've told her about José. Enrique's gone to the church.'

'Thank you, Father. Can you stay?'

'Of course.'

Fernández sat down beside her and she looked at him, confused, but not yet able to cry. He placed his hand alongside the framed photograph she held, glanced at Father Gabriel and shook his head.

Now, he felt, was not the right time. Any statement made under these circumstances would be inadmissible or ripped apart by defence lawyers. Inocenta had only just got Sofia back after twelve frantic hours, and she'd only just been told that her son's body had been found, and he'd been murdered. But he had to be sure Inocenta was just that: innocent.

'Antonio?'

Her voice was surprisingly strong and startled him.

'Do you know who killed my son?'

'Yes. We think so.'

'It was him wasn't it? My daughter's husband?'

'Yes. It looks that way.'

'And it's all my fault, isn't it?' Tears, at last, began to trickle down her cheek. 'I was only trying to protect my family. Was that so wrong of me?'

'Now may not be the right time, Inocenta.'

'Now may be the only time we have,' she said. 'It was when I heard that Juan Gonzales had killed Alberto that I realised...' Her voice trailed off. 'It all began to make sense...the questions he kept asking me about Father Emanuel.'

'What did Turnbull want to know?'

'About that awful night, thirty-five years ago. He showed me photographs he'd bought from Rodrigo. He said he'd been drinking with some old men and they told him about Alberto. He asked me if I could remember what happened...As if I could ever forget...He knew the names of everyone involved, including your father.'

'Did Turnbull know you were pregnant with the priest's child?'

'Yes.'

'Do Enrique or Ana-Maria know?'

'Not yet.' She lifted her head and he was unnerved by the intensity of her eyes...eyes that were looking at the man who'd taken her daughter away more than ten years ago –living in sin, the neighbours had said, predictable, pious, hypocritical - trivial compared to what would be exposed during a trial. 'But, it's only a matter of time, isn't it?' she said.

'And you saw Paul Turnbull, last Thursday?'

'Yes. I was on the terrace, with Sofia. We watched him follow Gonzales towards that new-build.'

'You knew he was going to kill Juan Gonzales?'

'Of course not. I had no idea. We'd found Gonzales a few weeks back. He'd collapsed and we took him to the doctor. I went to see him a couple of times. Paul kept an eye on him.'

'And fuelled the old man's desire for revenge.'

She laughed, hollowly.

'Sofia thought they were playing hide-and-seek.'

'Yes. She told one of my officers. Unfortunately, we didn't take her seriously.' He hesitated. Time was short. Turnbull was hours away from custody and he needed to hear what Inocenta had to say. She reminded him so much of his own mother, fragile yet defiant, and wondered how his mother would cope if she'd just been told that he'd been killed? He wasn't sure how much more he could ask of her but, once again, her resilience surprised him. 'I heard the rockets,' she said. 'Is that when he killed them?'

'We think so. Evidence suggests Juan Gonzales killed Alberto and Matias, and shot Bartolomé, but he didn't die immediately. Turnbull shot Bartolomé and then turned the gun on Juan Gonzales and tried to make his death look like suicide.' He needed to clarify her version of events, but was desperate to leave her to mourn her son. 'You told Turnbull about Alberto?'

'No. The old men were brandy talking. They must have told him, but when he asked me, I couldn't bring myself to tell him that they were right. I suppose my silence simply confirmed what he'd been told.' Tears fell, unchecked, and she looked at him as though pleading for understanding, for compassion. 'I'm so very sorry,' she said. 'For your family and for Rodrigo's.'

'Inocenta,' Father Gabriel said, 'you were fifteen years old. You can't blame yourself for what happened thirty-five years ago or last Thursday.'

She looked at him, shaking her head.

'I may have been fifteen, but it wasn't all Emanuel's fault. They called me the Priest's whore.'

'It couldn't have been easy, for either of you.'

'We were in love.'

Father Gabriel took her hand. 'You were no more than a child.'

Inocenta pulled away. Tears scarred her face and her voice was weary. 'I was carrying his child.'

She sat, eyes distant, as though watching images of the past. She pulled a handkerchief from her sleeve and dabbed her face.

It was several minutes before she looked at him and nodded.

He took her cue. 'And Turnbull knew Ana-Maria was Father Emanuel's daughter?'

'Yes.' Inocenta sighed. 'Ana-Maria is pregnant and she's had tests. She had to explain to her husband that their son was at risk.'

'That he'd be a haemophiliac?'

'Yes. I'm not and neither is Enrique, so it didn't take long for Paul to work it out. The old men told him about Father Emanuel, about his illness and his trips to the sanatorium. He put two and two together. He told me he wouldn't tell Enrique, or the children, as long as I told him what he wanted to know.' She dabbed her eyes and blew her nose. 'But I didn't tell him, I swear.'

He had one more question. 'And who's idea was it to take cake round to the Ramos women last Thursday?'

'He'd seen Juanita and told her about the cake I was baking. She invited me round, but Sofia was playing up so I asked Ana-Maria to go instead.'

'Another one of Turnbull's lies,' Father Gabriel said. 'Keep the women occupied, out of the way, whilst he...'

'Will you ever be able to forgive me, Antonio?'

'Inocenta,' Fernández said, 'there is nothing to forgive.'

264

'You don't understand, do you? When Juan Gonzales returned to the village all those years ago, it was *me* who told him who'd killed his parents.'

His breath caught in his throat and tears welled up in his eyes. He was looking at the woman who'd condemned his father to death. He began to wonder how she'd coped – hiding from the truth, burying the secrets of that night, living with the enormity of her lies, and bearing their burden each day until the deceit caught up with her. He took her in his arms, pulled her tightly to him, and shuddered as her sobs soaked into him.

'I was naked when they burst in,' she said. 'They dragged Emanuel out of the house. Alberto stayed, told me what they were going to do. When Juan Gonzales heard about their deaths, he returned to the village, recovered the bodies from the mineshaft, and threatened to kill me if I didn't tell him who was responsible.' Tears streamed down her face, her words punctuated by sobs. 'I was scared. I had no one to turn to. I gave him your father's name and Rodrigo's, but I didn't tell him about Alberto. I wanted to protect him. He'd been so kind.' She appeared to be struggling. 'Juan Gonzales knew that someone else had been involved...' She stroked his cheek. 'I am so sorry, Antonio,' she said. 'So very, very sorry.'

The flight took an hour - just time for a couple of glasses of champagne with a man he'd met on his way to the departure gate – and Turnbull glanced out of the tiny portside window as the Air Nostram taxied towards the terminal building. The sun was exceptionally piercing as it bounced off the tarmac and he slipped on his RayBans.

He glanced round to see if he could attract the air-stewardess's attention. He wanted to confirm their date before leaving the aircraft.

She smiled at him from the crew-seat and then looked away.

The twin prop chugged towards the arrivals entrance and the pilot parked so that its nose faced the mountains in the distance.

Turnbull slipped his seat belt off and stood up to retrieve his hand luggage.

'Mr Turnbull?' the air-stewardess said.

'Yes, eight-thirty, there's a café…'

'If you'd accompany these two officers, please sir.'

'Something wrong?'

'Call it your Fast Track through customs.'

Turnbull's business class companion pulled open his jacket to reveal a modified Glock17 self-loading pistol. The plane's exit door eased open and two Guardia Civil officers took the short flight of steps into the cabin.

'I don't understand. What's going on?'

His head jerked round, but another passenger was standing in the aisle, barring access to the rear.

'The arresting officer will read you your rights.' The air stewardess smiled. 'Thank you for flying with us, sir. Have a nice day.'

She nodded at the Guardia Civil officers and watched as Turnbull was cuffed and led into the main concourse building. She smiled at the Special Branch officers who'd tailed Turnbull and accompanied the flight.

'Anyone know the Spanish for beer?' she said.

*

After she'd arranged for José's body to be taken to the morgue, Julieta Santiago had driven Ana-Maria into Almeria.

They were sitting on a wall overlooking scores of tiny craft moored in the fishing harbour, when Ana-Maria's mobile rang.

A senior officer from the Policia National informed her that her husband had been arrested and taken to their headquarters, where he'd be held until conditions for bail had been decided by a judge. She was informed that this process could take up to three days and that he was entitled to have a lawyer present. The police officer was apologetic. He told her that he couldn't discuss charges, and explained that she wouldn't be able to visit him until his case had been presented to the judge.

She told him she understood and, as she ended the call, a text message arrived. It was from her husband…

Miss u - still in uk - c u sat xx

Ana-Maria closed her mobile.

He was lying.

Again. Bastard.

But that was nothing compared with what he'd done to her brother.

'We'll give him something to think about, then get some rest,' Fernández said, placing a tray of files and evidence bags on a table in the middle of the interview room.

'How long can we hold him?' Medina asked.

'I'll talk to the Comandante, see if there's a case for an extension.'

'You think we've got enough?' Estrada asked.

'Never that simple, is it? We screw up and he'll walk. As things stand, the judge will probably grant bail.'

'And risk him killing again?'

'I want him off the streets as much as you do, Leo, but arresting him now means we're still waiting for forensic evidence and eyewitness accounts. If his lawyer is half-decent, he'll make the case for bail. There'll be conditions attached, of course - given the seriousness of the charges - but it's unlikely the judge will agree to a custodial remand. We have no proof he killed Felipe Romano, or Laura, or José.'

'Pepe's hard work,' Medina said. 'But I think he *did* see him kill Bartolomé and Juan Gonzales.'

'We'll need more than that. In the end, it might come down to who's the presiding judge.'

There was a knock on the door and they were advised that Turnbull's lawyer had arrived and was conferring with his client.

They used the lull to run through how, and in what order they would question Turnbull, and then waited for several minutes before they were ushered into the room.

Formalities out of the way, everyone was reminded of the charges: the murders of Bartolomé Ramos, Juan Gonzales, Laura Domingo, and José Castaño.

Fernández began by asking, 'How well did you know Bartolomé Ramos?'

'We'd worked on a few projects. Didn't last. He lacked the drive I need in a partner.'

'But, whilst it did last, you were involved in several deals, at least one of which, we have reason to believe, involved corruption.'

Turnbull consulted with his lawyer. 'No comment.'

Fernández placed a document in front of him.

'This is a document relating to the purchase of land. It's been signed by you and Bartolomé.' He drew on a cigarette as Turnbull glanced through the document. 'Even eight years ago the price you paid for the land was a bargain. It was so cheap, of course, because it was Rustico de Secano, land upon which it was illegal to build.'

Again, Turnbull consulted with his lawyer who spoke for him. 'My client fails to see what this has to do with the charges brought against him.'

'It's a matter of motivation,' Fernández began. 'Why would Mr Turnbull put a bullet through the forehead of a man who'd already been shot through the throat? Could it be that Bartolomé had threatened to inform the authorities in Almeria that the land was purchased illegally? The hotel in question hits the headlines every week, but it's not the objections to the hotel I'm interested in…it's the land.'

'No comment.'

Fernández glanced at Estrada. She held up an evidence bag. 'Is this your iPhone?'

'Not a crime, I presume?'

'Have you used it recently? To send a text to your wife, for instance?'

'I may have.'

'Still in London, eh? That'll take some explaining.' She produced another evidence bag. 'And this?'

Turnbull looked at his old mobile and Fernández noticed that his face blanched momentarily.

'If I'd known you had this, I could have saved myself a small fortune. Where did you find it?'

'In the crypt of the church, near where you'd buried the body of José Castaño.'

'My client,' the lawyer said, 'could have dropped it at anytime during the restoration.'

269

There was an uncertainty in his voice, as though he was beginning to suspect Turnbull hadn't been straight with him.

Estrada smiled.

'Yes. Yes, of course. You're quite right.'

She sat back and Fernández lent forward.

'We're processing the DNA taken during Laura Domingo's autopsy - her own and from the foetus she was carrying. A third sample was found under her fingernails. Now, if that was to match your DNA…'

'And, it may well.' Turnbull stood up, removed his gold cufflinks and began to unbutton his shirt. He eased it from his body and turned to reveal fading scratch marks on his back. 'The stuff of erotica, eh, Inspector? A young woman clawing at her paramour during sex?' Turnbull smirked. He replaced his shirt, but didn't bother to button it up. 'Laura needed money. I was glad to help. She paid me in kind. We had sex at my apartment last Friday, then she drove to Los Mineros for dinner with her father.'

'The same evening she went to fiesta with your wife?'

'Yes.'

'You were fucking another woman…'

'Inspector?' the lawyer warned.

He whispered something to Turnbull.

They watched as Turnbull patted his forearm.

'Friday was the last time I saw Laura. I was shocked by the news of her death, but had nothing to do with it.'

The lawyer rose and began to pack his brief case. 'Will that be all, Inspector?'

'Not quite.' Leo Medina leant forward. 'You like bull fighting, Mr Turnbull?'

'Cruel and barbaric.'

'I'm a huge fan. I'd provide a demonstration, but I'm sure you know how it goes?'

He picked up a copy of the bullfighting poster that he'd taken from the bar and slid it across the table. 'The Matador infuriates and frustrates the bull, making it turn, turn and turn again. There are several different passes, collectively they're known as the Pases de Gloria.'

Turnbull looked at the poster and then at his lawyer. He rolled his eyes and shook his head. 'Inspector,' the lawyer looked at him. 'We are grateful for the insight into Spain's national pastime, but...'

Fernández ignored him and asked Turnbull, 'Were you aware that Laura had given you a nickname?'

'Nickname?'

'Gave most of us nicknames, apparently.'

'Humour me.'

'She called you Gloria.'

Turnbull shifted in his seat. 'I'm sorry, but what has this got to do with..?'

'Pases de Gloria. The turning of the bull.'

'Inspector, this is not making any sense.'

'The turning of the bull. Turnbull.'

It was his lawyer's turn to laugh. 'Is that the best you can do? I really must insist that this interview as well as my client's detention are terminated immediately.'

'You know,' Fernández said, 'at first we couldn't work it out...Laura had arranged for *Gloria* to take her to the airport. She'd sent a text telling her fiancé that she had incriminating information about *Gloria*. And last Thursday, *Gloria* was seen playing hide-and-seek with an old man carrying a rug under his arm.'

'Are you telling us that you have eyewitnesses?' The lawyer asked.

'Two, actually. One is helping us as we speak. Can't shut him up. Talk, talk, talk.' Fernández extinguished his cigarette and lit another. 'We don't think that you killed Laura because she was trying to extort money from you or because she threatened to tell Ana-Maria about your sordid little affair. We think you killed her because she knew you'd killed Juan Gonzales.'

'And how would she know that?'

'Our other eyewitness told her.'

10

A week later

When Ana-Maria suggested they hold the funerals at the same time, neither father responded. It had been ten days since Laura came home from the fiesta, packed, and left around two in the morning. Since then her body had been locked in a refrigeration unit and Carlos had had to cancel her funeral several times. Enrique hadn't seen José for months - not since he'd played in a reserve match in Malaga...or was it in Almeria? He couldn't remember. But he'd never forget watching SOCO pull his son's body from the rubble. He'd been asked if he could confirm that the body was his son? He'd nodded, but when he'd asked if he could hold his son in his arms for a few moments, they'd refused. They'd told him that he might contaminate the site.

No, as far as Carlos and Enrique were concerned the funeral arrangements were not uppermost in their minds.

Fernández drove into the village and was pulled over by officers from Guardia Civil. He produced his ID and was waved through. He parked outside the bar and made his way to the church.

Flowers had been arriving all day and had been placed against the church wall. Many had messages pinned to the cellophane wrapping. As well as flowers, villagers had left teddy bears dressed in Real Madrid's all-white first team strip for José, and blonde dolls or cuddly toys for Laura.

Policia Local had cordoned off the square and both coffins, a single wreath on each, were unloaded from hearses and carried straight into the church. It was to be a private service, restricted to immediate family and close friends, and those who'd been invited were already inside. They'd turned to watch the cortège make its way towards the altar.

Fernández caught a glimpse of Julieta Santiago - her hair ruffled by breeze filtering through the church doors. She was near him, at the back, intent on the service, her face bearing her heartache. He glanced at Carlos Domingo, standing on his own, his head bowed, his face impassive. Inocenta and Enrique stood close to José's coffin and Fernández watched as they reached for each other and held hands. He saw Ana-Maria join them, and wondered if Inocenta had confessed everything? Whether she'd told them about her affair and that Father Emanuel was Ana-Maria's father? And, he wondered whether the confession had drawn them closer together or if the display of unity was for José's sake? He watched as Ana-Maria slipped her hand through the arm of the man she'd known all her life as 'Papa', and, as the service began, he saw Enrique draw his daughter and his wife closer to him.

In his apartment, Paul Turnbull ordered a pizza and then poured himself a malt whisky. He took the bottle out on to the balcony, sat on a sun lounger and ran through the case against him…

He laughed and shook his head when he recalled the nickname Laura Domingo had given him. He refilled his glass, held it up to the evening light and admired the whisky's depth of colour.

He ran the glass through his hands, took a draught, swilled it round his mouth, and swallowed.

His lawyer had insisted the police disclose the names of eyewitnesses. They'd refused and when he suggested the police were lying, his lawyer promised to pursue the matter.

He took a sip of whisky and put his glass down. He felt tired suddenly and sat back and closed his eyes.

Half an hour passed before he went through to the lounge. He turned on the TV and flicked through the channels.

The news included Laura and José's funeral.

He shook his head as he watched his wife and her family follow the coffins into the church. If his case did go to trial, he would make them suffer – all of them - the Priest's whore, the bastard child and the cuckold husband – and expose their hypocritical lives. He poured another drink and watched an update on the investigation into the murders for which he had been arrested. He raised his glass when he saw shots of his lawyer defending the judge's decision to release him on bail. And then he sat and watched profiles of the detectives leading the investigation. What he saw served to confirm what he'd thought all long…that he wouldn't need a high-profile lawyer. Not with a prosecution case based on evidence provided by an Inspector who'd been too busy trying to bed a scrawny pathologist and whose judgment had been clouded by copious amounts of brandy and a lack of detachment. Any decent lawyer would tear holes in the evidence they had against him. He smiled, and wondered if the best Inspector Antonio Fernández could come up with was that he'd killed Laura because she'd called him *Gloria*?

The shrill of the intercom cut short his solitude and he realised that someone wanted to talk to him from the street below. He pressed a button and was momentarily unsettled to hear her voice…

'Let me in,' she said.

'Yes. Yes, of course. I wasn't expecting…'

'No, but I am.'

He heard her push her way into the lobby, and opened the door and waited for the lift. Within moments Ana-Maria stood before him. She removed a headscarf, didn't say anything, and brushed passed him.

'How are you?' he asked.

'How the hell do you think I am?'

'I'm sorry I haven't been in touch.'

'I'm not.'

'I'm innocent, you know. I didn't do those awful things.'

'What else would you say?' She waited until she was calm before she added, 'my father was right. He knew there was something between you and Laura.'

Turnbull laughed, drained his glass and placed it on the coffee table. 'Enrique's not your father.'

'I know.' Her voice was ice cold. 'Mama told us that you found Juan Gonzales lying in the gutter. You took him to the doctor and then bullied her into betraying Alberto Ramos.'

'It'll never stand up in court.'

'I won't allow you to have your day in court.' Ana-Maria continued as though she hadn't heard him. 'After the funeral, I spoke with Inspector Antonio Fernández.'

'Recalling old times, no doubt.'

'You persuaded an old man to kill three men and then you blew his brains out. You killed Felipe because the police were about to arrest him and you killed Laura because she knew what you'd done.'

'You can't believe..?'

'You lied to me!'

She spun round and threw the glass. It shattered against the wall. 'How the hell do you expect me to believe anything you tell me? That pendant you gave me was José's. I wore that fucking thing round my neck.' She stepped closer to him; close enough to sense his brute strength. 'But what I don't understand is why you had to kill him?'

He raised his hand and she flinched. He grabbed her jaw and his hand clamped into her cheeks.

'If you're so sure I'm such a fucking monster,' he said, 'what are you doing here?'

She knocked his hand away.

'I won't allow you to have your day in court,' she said again, calmly, as though she'd run the words over and over in her mind.

'And what's that supposed to mean?'

'I won't allow you to humiliate my family.'

She forced a smile. 'Besides, there are others who want to talk to you.'

Turnbull heard the door open and turned to find a shotgun pointing at him.

'Time to take a stroll, Gloria'

They bundled him from the apartment, down the rear staircase, out the emergency exit and into Carlos's four-by-four. Ana-Maria took the wheel. Enrique sat one side of Turnbull and Carlos sat the other side and pressed the twin barrels of the shotgun deep into his ribs.

Throughout the journey Paul Turnbull protested his innocence. They ignored him and when they reached the farm, they stopped outside the largest barn.

Ana-Maria and Enrique hurried to open the barn door whilst Carlos pulled Turnbull from the car and, easing back the twin hammers, forced the shotgun into his neck.

'Don't give me an excuse to use this, because I won't hesitate. Now, move.'

Inside the barn, Carlos handed the shotgun to Ana-Maria and then tied Turnbull's hands behind his back. Enrique took a rope attached to pulleys and threaded it under the knot Carlos had tied. He pulled sharply and Turnbull's arms were forced upwards and his head and torso were forced forward.

'We'll be back in a moment,' Carlos said to Ana-Marie. 'We've got company for him.'

She watched them walk out of the barn, and then turned to her husband. 'You want to tell me why?'

'Ana-Maria. You must believe me. I didn't kill Laura. Why would I do that?'

'You were fucking her. I'm carrying your child and you were fucking another woman.'

'She flirted. I was flattered. But I didn't sleep with her.'

'That's not what you told Antonio.' She walked behind him. 'During your interrogation, you said that you were with her on Friday, just hours before she came to the fiesta. You boasted she'd left marks on your back.' She laughed, hollowly. 'Your sex was always about as subtle as a donkey's.' Suddenly, she struck him between the shoulder blades with the butt of the shotgun. 'You stupid bastard!'

'Ana-Maria, you've got to believe me.'

She stood in front of him and spat in his face. As he screwed up his eyes, she stepped back, held the shotgun high in the air and punctuated her next four words with strikes to his face and head. 'Don't. Lie. To. Me!'

She watched blood run from his nose and cuts above his eyes and felt a twinge in her womb and a sharp pain cut across her abdomen made her gasp and drop to one knee.

The door opened and Carlos and Enrique herded a large pig into the barn.

Enrique took the shotgun from Ana-Maria and helped her to her feet. 'You all right?'

'It's nothing, papa. It'll pass.'

Enrique nodded, searching her face for the truth.

She smiled, trying to reassure him. 'I'm OK.'

Carlos tied a rope round the pig's neck and passed it through another set of pulleys next to Turnbull.

'Carlos?' The injuries Ana-Maria had inflicted had distorted Turnbull's face. He spat blood from his mouth. 'Carlos. You must believe me. I had nothing to do with Laura's death.'

Carlos was examining his injuries. 'Thought that's what you'd say. I didn't expect you to confess.' He stood close enough to smell the trickle of urine that stained the dirt floor at Turnbull's feet.

'Carlos, you've got to listen to me.'

'I know you killed her.' Carlos took the shotgun and lashed it across Turnbull's face, opening fresh wounds, blood running freely from each cut.

Enrique stepped forward. 'You killed my son.'

'No, no. I swear.'

'He knew you'd killed Laura, so you killed him.'

'No.'

Turnbull's mouth had filled with blood.

'Enrique, please believe me. I didn't kill José, and I didn't kill Laura. Please help me.'

'You killed my son and threatened my wife. You have to pay for that.'

'Let's get it over with.' Ana-Maria's voice was calm, detached.

Carlos looked across at her.

'There's no point you being here,' he said. 'The cancer will come for me any day now.' He smiled and added, 'And, you've got this old man here, your mother

279

and that young sister of yours. They've been through enough. Having you sent to prison isn't going to help them, is it?'

Ana-Maria stood her ground.

'Killing this bastard was my idea,' she said.

'Maybe, but I have to kill him. He took my Laura from me.' He lowered the shotgun. 'Besides, you've got your little one to think about. Is it a boy or girl?'

'Little boy.'

Carlos smiled, unconvincingly, sadness coursing across his face. 'Go on, both of you. I can handle things from here.'

'It's for the best,' Enrique said, offering his hand.

'Papa?'

'It's for the best.'

She glanced at her husband and then followed her father out of the barn.

In the calm, Carlos lifted a large plank of wood, slid it though a metal guide on one side of the barn door, and then pushed it across the door and through a guide on the other side.

'Carlos! Please, I beg you,' Turnbull cried again, blood seeping into his eyes, clogging his vision.

Carlos ignored him and disappeared behind an old cloth curtain. Moments later, he dragged a small table in front of the curtain and placed a digital recorder on top of it. He pressed a button and then disappeared behind the curtain again.

He returned with thick hemp rope. He loosened the lasso round the pig's neck, tied its hind legs together, knocked it to the floor and then tied its front legs.

He spoke as he worked.

'That man you killed, the fascist bastard who carried out all those assassinations? Well, apparently, before he killed someone, he'd tell them why they had to die.'

'I didn't kill Laura, Carlos. What can I say to make you believe me? I shot Juan Gonzales. I shot Bartolomé and I killed Felipe...' He sucked breath through a nose that felt badly broken and was haemorrhaging freely. 'José turned up at the church. He'd heard about Laura. She'd told him I was going to take her to the airport. He put two and two together and came up with the wrong answer. We argued, he attacked and I struck him in self-defence.'

'You're a liar.'

'Laura sent me a text message, asking me to take her to the airport, but I swear...I was with another woman, someone I've been having an affair with for the last three years. You can ring and ask her. She'll tell you I was with her. I didn't find Laura's text message until I switched on my phone on Sunday morning. You've got to believe me. I didn't kill her.'

Carlos continued as if immune to his protestations.

But, he wanted to explain. 'You have to die because I can't wait. I can't wait to see how many years in prison you're going to get for killing my little girl. The cancer will take me long before the trial. And, even if I did last long enough to see you found guilty and sentenced, I won't be here in twenty years, when you get out.'

He took a long bladed knife from its sheath. 'People will tell you,' he said, placing the knife against the pig's throat, 'that a pig screams when its throat's slit...but it's only air gushing out.' He ran the blade gently along the length of the animal's neck. 'It don't die immediately.' He took rope and attached one end to the pig's hind legs and slipped the other end through pulleys attached to a rafter.

'Carlos! Please!' Turnbull was sobbing. 'I'll go to the police. I'll tell them everything. You have to believe me, I did not kill Laura!'

Carlos hauled the pig off the ground until it hung, squealing and struggling, its head and neck pressed into the floor by the weight of its body.

'After I've slit its throat,' he said, 'I like to hang the pig up. It helps the heart pump all the blood out. It'll spasm for a while. Even when it's dead, it'll spasm. It's as though it's still alive. But, it's only its muscles. They keep working. Amazing really, isn't it? It don't take too long before it's all over.'

'The woman's number.'

Blood flowed from Turnbull's mouth and nose and from the gashes above his eyes.

'The woman I was with. She'll tell you.' He began to recite a number.

'I don't believe you.' Carlos twisted the knife in his hand. 'You'd say anything to save your own skin.'

Then, suddenly, in one swift, violent movement, he plunged the knife into the pig's throat and its shrill scream filled the barn. He stood back and watched the butchered pig's blood soak into the dirt floor.

'Carlos!' Turnbull wept. 'For God's sake. No. The number, you must write down the number.'

Carlos dropped the knife, and grabbed the rope, and hauled the pig's carcass off the ground. He stood back as blood continued to spout.

Within moments, its body began to spasm.

Carlos picked up the knife.

'It didn't suffer too much, did it?'

He ran the blade along Turnbull's throat.

'Now it's your turn.'

*

'Going somewhere?' Julieta Santiago asked as she stood in the open doorway to his apartment.

'I'm due a few weeks leave.'

'And, you and me?'

'The girls, not my priority, you said, and I thought…'

'That wasn't fair, given the circumstances.'

'I'm not sure you were that far from the truth.'

He finished packing his suitcase, then sat heavily on the sofa. 'How long can you stay?'

'Not long. I'm taking Holly down to the harbour. I want to show her where I nearly stowed away and ended up in Rio.' She picked up an empty bottle of red wine. 'But, I've got time for a glass.'

'In the fridge.'

'I'll get it.'

He lay back on the sofa, stared at the ceiling fan and listened to noises from the square outside. He was still unsure about her – Julieta Santiago - the woman who'd removed his cigarette and taken charge of the crime scene the very first time they'd met. Each time they'd inched closer, it seemed to him, work got in the way, or Holly…not that Holly *got in the way. Oh, God, will it always be this complicated?*

She returned from the kitchen holding two glasses in one hand and an open bottle in the other. She put the glasses down and poured generous measures of Rioja but, as she handed him a glass, his mobile rang.

He shook his head and looked at her. 'I'm sorry.'

'Don't be.' She got up and left.

He sighed, cursed and flipped open the phone. It was Valencia Ramoz. 'Policia Local have traced the laundry where the bag with the raffle ticket came from.'

'And?'

'Forensics found traces of Laura's blood in a car.'

'Turnbull's?'

'Guzmán's.'

283

'Guzmán's. You're sure?'

'Forensics don't lie.'

'Fuck.'

'We've got CCTV footage showing him with Laura in a bar, three-thirty Saturday morning. Turnbull didn't respond to her text so she must have phoned Guzmán to ask him to take her to the airport.' Ramoz paused, as if waiting for a reaction but he was busy calculating the cost of this latest bombshell. 'There's something else,' she said.

'What?'

'I've just had a call from Policia Local in Almeria. The concierge at Turnbull's apartment contacted them. Turnbull had ordered a pizza. When it was delivered, no one answered the door. The delivery boy complained and the concierge opened up and found glass smashed over the floor.'

'And Turnbull?'

'Wasn't there. The in-house CCTV's been checked.'

'Anyone we know?'

'Two were unrecognisable - a woman in a headscarf and a man shielding his face ...'

'And?'

'Carlos was with them. He was carrying his shotgun.'

'Jesus fuck, that's all we need. Get Guardia Civil to Guzmán's apartment.'

'He could be at the surgery,' Ramoz suggested.

'I'll send Jacinta and Leo to check.'

'Where will you be?'

'My guess is that Carlos has taken Turnbull to the farm. Call an ambulance and make sure there's back-up on standby.'

*

Jacinta Estrada stood on one side of the door; Leo Medina was on the other. She glanced through the glass-panelled door of the waiting room, and then snatched her head back. 'We have a problem,' she said. 'One of your kids is in there. The eldest...'

'Pablo?'

'He's talking to an old woman. Which means...'

'That Roz and Rafe are in with Guzmán.' Medina pulled his Berretta from its holster beneath his jacket and pushed past her.

She grabbed his arm. 'Leo, wait...'

'That's my kid in there.'

She forced him back, slapped her left hand against his chest and stood between him and the surgery door. 'For God's sake. Guzmán's not some armed terrorist holding hostages. He's unaware we're here. He's with your son - just another patient at evening surgery. If we play this right, no one need get hurt. Go in brandishing your gun and God knows what might happen.'

Medina hesitated long enough for her to reason with him once more. 'Help me clear the waiting room and get Pablo and the rest to safety...'

'And then, I go in.'

'Let me call for back-up.'

'Fuck the back-up. I'm going in now.'

'OK, but I'll take that.'

Estrada pointed at his handgun. 'Unarmed, the risks to you and your family are reduced.' She looked at him, sensing they understood each other, but not sure what she would do if he refused.

He looked at her and balanced the Berretta in his hand as though weighing his options. She watched him run his hand over the cold steel before he handed it over and unbuckled his shoulder holster.

Estrada threw the holster behind a bush and slid his handgun between shirt and waistband at the base of her spine. She stepped to one side of the surgery door, and nodded. 'OK. We clear the surgery first. Then you get Roz and Rafe out.' She took out her warrant card, stood at the door and waited for Medina to open it. As he did, she slipped silently inside, pressed an index finger against her lips and held her warrant card in the air. He followed her, reinforcing the command to be silent and beckoning to his son.

Pablo got up slowly, confused.

Medina waved him over, took his hand and led him outside. Estrada cleared the rest of the patients. Deserted, the waiting room looked drab, its whitewashed walls covered in out of date posters, its woodwork peeling from years of neglect. The muffled sound of Guzmán's voice drifted through the frosted glass panel of his surgery door and was joined by the sound of Roz translating the medical diagnosis into child-speak.

Everything seemed calm and commonplace, giving Estrada valuable seconds to assess the situation.

She pulled Medina away from the surgery door.

'You go in and play the anxious father coming to check up on his kid. I'll stay out here until Rafe and Roz are clear.'

He tried to stay calm, tried to regulate his breathing, then knocked and eased the door open.

Guzmán looked up from examining Rafe's chest, his stethoscope still hooked around his neck.

Medina forced a smile and asked as light-heartedly as he could muster, 'Will he make it, doctor?'

Guzmán curtailed his examination, told Roz to get her son dressed, and then turned to his computer to print out a prescription.

Roz pulled Rafe's t-shirt over his head and Medina swept him into the crook of his left arm. 'I've come to apologise,' he said, addressing the doctor.

Guzmán continued to concentrate on the paper work.

'I had it wrong about you and Laura. We've made an arrest.'

Roz looked at him anxiously. Medina rocked his head to one side, placed Rafe on the floor and the boy held his mother's hand.

She took the prescription from Guzmán and led Rafe past the surgery door. As she crossed the waiting room and looked for Pablo, Medina imagined Estrada smiling reassuringly, her finger planted firmly against her lips.

Guzmán walked out from behind his desk and pulled open the top drawer of a cabinet.

'You've made an arrest?'

'Yes.'

'Doesn't make the harassment of innocent people any more excusable.'

'We've arrested Paul Turnbull.'

'Another travesty of justice no doubt. Don't mind trampling through people's lives do you detective? First Adam Wells, then me, and now Paul Turnbull. Doesn't matter, does it? Getting the right man isn't a priority...'

'We don't believe Turnbull killed Laura.'

Guzmán walked behind his desk, looked at Medina, and shook his head. 'My point entirely. Now, if you don't mind, I have work to do, saving lives, not ruining them.' Agitated, he began to clear his desk.

Medina glanced towards the waiting room and was satisfied Roz and Rafe were safe.

'Forensics have found blood. Laura's blood. In your car.'

Guzmán laughed. 'Evidence that's been planted.'

He leaned heavily on his desk.

'You know,' Guzmán said, 'this would be laughable if it wasn't so sick. You have fine, healthy kids. It's a pity you'll struggle to support them. Even construction work's hard to find, especially for a disgraced cop.'

'I apologised earlier,' Medina said, 'because although I always knew that you'd killed Laura, I thought it might have been a crime of passion, a fit of anger - killing her after she tried to extort more money from you. But it wasn't. It was cold, calculated, and quite deliberate. It's my guess you'd decided to kill her when you were sipping cocktails with her at that bar on the beach. What did you do? Slip into the kitchen, select a boning knife and hide it under your shirt?' Medina rested his hands on the side of the doctor's desk and lent forward. 'You see...if you stole the knife, her murder would have been premeditated and you'll go down for a very, very long time.'

Guzmán pushed himself away and collected patient files from the top of his desk. 'If you'll excuse me,' he said, his breathing shallow. 'I have a waiting room full of patients.'

'Actually, you don't, doctor.' Estrada was standing at the surgery door. 'Now, it's just the three of us.'

'Ah, the cavalry, yet again.'

Guzmán laughed and shook his head. Then, suddenly, he thumped the desk with both hands, scattering files to the floor. 'What do I have to say to make you believe me? What is it you don't understand? I did not kill Laura!'

Estrada looked across at Medina and nodded.

'Javier Guzmán, I'm arresting you on suspicion of the murder of Laura Domingo. You don't have to say anything, but anything you do say...' He completed the caution, moved towards Guzmán and placed a large hand on his shoulder. 'If you'd come with me, sir.'

Neither of them saw the glint of fluorescent light on the blade of the scalpel. Neither did either of them react in time when Guzmán lunged forward and pressed it into Medina's neck. 'Sargento, place your gun on the desk and step away.'

Estrada pulled her handgun from her holster and levelled it at Guzmán's head.

'This is not one of your better ideas, Doctor. Please. Don't make me use this.'

Guzmán pressed the scalpel deeper into Medina's neck and a thin trickle of blood seeped from the wound.

'Put the gun down, Sargento.'

'Shoot the fucker.' Medina's eyes glared at her.

'Your call, Sargento.'

Medina struggled.

'Sargento?'

She lowered the handgun. 'As you wish, Javier.' She calculated that the use of his first name would distract him momentarily and she placed the semi-automatic on the desk. 'I've done what you asked, doctor. Now, let him go.' She stepped back and glanced at Medina. It was a small movement and she hoped he'd understood what she was trying to convey...if he'd understood it might buy them precious seconds.

His life could depend on it.

Guzmán forced Medina's head back, lent forward and grabbed the Beretta.

'Smart move Sargento.'

He switched the scalpel to his left hand, pressed the handgun into Medina's neck, and slipped his hand under his jacket. 'Where's your gun?'

'I don't have one. When I'm trained...'

'You're not going to get that chance now, are you?' God, you're so pathetic. No wonder you couldn't satisfy Laura and had to settle for that mouse of a woman.'

Medina snapped.

He screamed and twisted violently.

He bulldozed Guzmán into the waiting room, caught him around the neck, lifted him in the air and slammed him against the wall.

As he crashed to the floor, Guzmán levelled the gun at Medina and pulled the trigger.

Nothing happened, but as he fumbled to disengage the safety catch, Estrada pulled Medina's Beretta from her waistband.

Guzmán struggled to his feet and raised his gun.

Both exploded at the same time.

Guzmán sagged and collapsed.

Estrada was thrown against the wall, left arm searing.

She screamed, scrambled across the room and kicked out at Guzmán. He rolled onto his back and, as he came to rest, his gun was pointing directly at her.

She didn't hesitate. She fired once more. She felt faint. Blood poured from her arm as the pain intensified, but she managed to stagger over to where Guzmán had fallen. She stood over him and waited. He lay motionless, but she felt she had no choice. She fired again, then turned her back on him and hurried over to Medina.

He'd slumped against the wall, both hands clutching his gut, shock spilling from his eyes as blood began to trickle between scalpel and fingers. He sank to the floor.

Estrada watched him slip into unconsciousness, grabbed a handful of bandages and packed the sleeve of her shirt, took out her mobile and waited a few agonising seconds before Valencia Ramoz answered. 'It's Leo. Get an ambulance. Where's the Inspector?'

'No idea. He's not answering his mobile.'

'Well, find him. And for God's sake, hurry.'

*

Fernández steered through the farm's open gate and into the yard. Days earlier, a sow had attacked him, as though sensing he'd brought the worst news any parent could hear. This evening, the farmyard was quiet. A few chickens scratched at the earth. The sow and her piglets penned up for the night. From inside the house, he heard the dogs bark, but even they fell silent.

He climbed from his car, listening for sounds, sounds of Carlos and Turnbull. He called the old man's name several times, and then walked to the farmhouse door and pushed it open. The dogs barked furiously at him, and snarled as he stepped into the parlour. 'Carlos?' he called and offered a clenched fist for the dogs to smell, hoping they'd back off. 'Carlos!'

Cautiously, he went up and checked both bedrooms.

'Carlos!'

He retreated and closed the farmhouse door. He stood on the stone step, surveying the yard, and shuddered as cool air swept down from the mountains.

Suddenly, a sickening scream shattered the silence.

He froze momentarily, and then hurried to the nearest barn and managed to prise the doors open a few inches. In a shaft of light, he saw a pig hanging upside down.

'Carlos!' he cried out. 'Carlos! Turnbull didn't kill Laura. Carlos! Listen to me!'

Again, he tried to force the barn doors open, but failed. He hurried back to his car, turned the ignition, and revved the engine. As he slammed into first gear, he heard an explosion. A shotgun. He slipped the clutch and accelerated. The car smashed into the doors and forced enough of a gap to enable him to scramble inside.

Late evening sun streamed through the opening and fell on Carlos's body. He was slumped on a chair, his shotgun on the floor, the back of his head showered across a crude cloth screen behind a table.

Fernández stood before him and fought back tears.

291

'Dear God, Carlos.'

He glanced at the pig.

It was still, its life-blood had drained into the parched soil, its head was hanging grotesquely to one side and a huge gash in its neck was moist with fresh blood.

Flies had started to gather.

Turnbull's body was suspended upside down, his face disfigured and swollen. Blood had pooled beneath him and whilst the flow had slowed, it was still trickling from a body in spasm.

Fernández looked at him. Turnbull's eyes stared back and blinked.

Fernández went over to the table, pressed the stop and rewind buttons of a recorder, and listened to the conversation between Carlos and Turnbull several times before turning it off. He carried the machine to Turnbull, sat down on a pile of logs next to him and lit a cigarette. 'We're going to listen to this, you and me,' he said. 'It would be inadmissible in a court of law, of course, but Carlos wanted to make sure I knew.' He played the tape and looked into Turnbull's eyes as his confession filled the barn. 'Carlos used to help Laura and her friends record music. He obviously remembered which button to press.'

He turned it off and pocketed the cassette.

'You know,' he said. 'I could thank you for bringing me closer to my father. I may never have known what he did, or what drove him to kill a man.'

He dragged on his cigarette and exhaled, forcefully, towards Turnbull's bewildered eyes.

'I might never have known how he died, or what my mother has had to live with all these years. I've been so wrapped up in myself and in my career...' He stubbed out his cigarette and lit another. 'I might have tried to justify what you did when you killed Bartolomé... providing for your wife and unborn child, making sure

292

you landed the contract, securing their future, removing anyone who put that at risk.' He dragged smoke deep into his lungs, lifted his head, and exhaled towards the rafters of the barn. 'But, you weren't concerned for anyone but yourself, were you?'

Turnbull's body shuddered.

A final spasm? Fernández wasn't sure.

Then several coins fell from Turnbull's trousers and dropped into blood pooled beneath his head. Fernández pulled on pair of forensic gloves, lent forward, dipped his fingers in the blood and picked up the coins.

'This is what it's all been about. Hasn't it? Money. Driven by greed.' He threw the coins across the barn and wiped his gloves on Turnbull's shirt.

He checked for signs of life - fainter now, almost indistinguishable from the final throws of death. 'But do you know what sickens me more than anything?'

He watched and waited.

'What sickens me is your callous disregard for those left behind... You've condemned the widows of Alberto, Bartolomé, and Matias to a life sorrow. Felipe may have been a drunk and dirt poor, but he was someone's son, someone's brother, someone's friend.'

His breath caught in his throat, his sorrow threatening to overwhelm him.

'And Ana-Maria and her family?' He gulped in air, his voice wavering. 'I hope to God you rot in Hell.'

293

11

Surgeons had performed a second operation to repair internal damage caused by the scalpel.

Fernández stayed at the hospital deep into the night and Estrada joined him at three o'clock in the morning.

A sling supported her left arm.

'How is he?' she asked.

'Not too good.'

'He'll pull through, though?'

'God willing. How's the arm?'

'Flesh wound,' she said. 'Perfect in no time.'

'There'll be an inquiry into both arrests.'

'Thought as much.'

'It's routine, but you might think through what you'll tell them.'

'I've got nothing to hide,' she said.

'They'll want to talk to Leo when…'

Her head dropped, shook it, and he could see the tears marshalling.

'You did all you could.'

'I know, but if we'd handled it differently…'

'You should be proud of the job you've done. Both of you. You had Guzmán in the frame for Laura. It was me who got it wrong. It was me who thought Turnbull killed her.'

'Leo will make a good detective. Please God, he pulls through.' She looked up at him. 'You want to go home, get some rest?'

'No, thanks. There are benches in the corridor. I'll take my chance on one of them.'

They dozed for a couple of hours. The hospital was quiet most of the time, lighting was at a minimum, and the nursing staff were calm and efficient, but at dawn the pace increased and it wasn't long before the business of caring was back in full swing.

At eight, Fernández fetched coffees from a vending machine and they sat, blurry eyed, and sipped espresso.

At nine, Roz arrived with her two sons and an elderly woman. She handed the boys over to their grandmother and they sat down next to Estrada whilst Roz went to check on her husband.

They watched as a man in a white coat came out of Medina's room, spoke to Roz, and then walked along the corridor towards them.

'Would you like to see your papa?' The doctor said, and they scampered along the corridor.

'Well?' Fernández asked, as soon as the boys were out of earshot.

'His condition remains critical, but there are signs of improvement. It's too early to tell but unless there's a relapse we're confident he'll make a complete recovery.'

'Thank God.'

'You want to see him?'

'Yes. Yes, of course.'

The boys had been hoisted onto the side of the bed - their eyes staring, fearfully, at the plethora of medical equipment hooked up to their father.

Medina smiled, and then lifted his hand and caressed his wife's face. 'You boys look after your mother, until I get out of here, won't you?' His voice was weak.

They nodded and Rafe began to cry. 'Are you going to be all right, daddy?'

'Yes. Everything's going to be just fine.' He looked across at Estrada. 'I owe you.'

'It was nothing.'

He tired suddenly, and closed his eyes and the boys looked anxiously at Roz.

'Best let him rest,' a nurse said to the children. 'He's in safe hands.'

Roz led her boys from the room and, as Fernández and Estrada followed, Medina's voice scratched across the room. 'Inspector?'

They turned.

'How's that cocky pathologist?'

They retreated to his local bar and ordered a couple of coffees and a selection of tapas.

'Word is you're on the move,' Estrada said, as she cut into a slice of fresh tortilla.

'I'm taking a couple of weeks holiday. When I get back, the Comandante has arranged for us to spend a month with London's Metropolitan Police, training with CO19, their armed response unit.'

'You said, us?'

'You and me.'

'Why?'

'When we return, I'll be putting a team together for the Serious Crimes Unit. Hoped you'd be interested.'

'A couple months in England?'

'Training's outside London, place called Gravesend.'

'Unfortunate name.' She smiled. 'Yes, I'd like to be involved...What about Leo?'

'Assuming he's...'

She stood up and gathered her jacket. 'I can't see him turning down the opportunity. I'll see you when you get back from your holiday. Travel safe.' She walked out of the bar and into a day that was already stifling.

Fernández turned to the TV and watched a feature on close-season activity in football's transfer market.

'You going to settle your bill?' the bartender said.

'When you learn to smile.'

He pulled a fifty-euro note, collected his change and, as he glanced at the television, he felt someone tug at his jacket. He looked down to see Holly and Sofia grinning up at him.

'Do you want to come to tea?' they chorused. 'We're making chocolate muffins.'

'The girls are planning to poison us all before we take Sofia back home,' Julieta Santiago said.

'Can't I stay one more night? Mama won't mind. She says it's good for us to play together.'

'As long as we remember to behave ourselves,' Holly said, and then grabbed Sofia by the arm and pulled her after her. 'Come on. Let's play chase.'

'Nothing much has changed there, then?' He watched the girls dash about the square.

'How's Ana-Maria?' Santiago said.

'Settling back into the village. She's decided to go through with the pregnancy.'

'You'll be by her side?'

'Hadn't thought about it.' He hesitated. 'The baby's not due for several months, but yes, I'll be there if she wants me to be.'

He searched her face for a reaction.

'I'm sure she'll appreciate that,' Santiago said. 'At least we've been able to confirm that José *was* the father of Laura's unborn.'

He sighed and lit a cigarette. 'Look, I'll come to tea, but only if you'll let me buy you dinner this evening.'

'Dinner?' She watched Sofia hide behind a ficus tree. 'I might enjoy that.'

He pulled an envelope from the back pocket of his jeans and pushed it towards her. 'Will Holly be OK for a couple of weeks whilst her mother's away?'

'Away?' She looked puzzled.

He tapped the envelope.

'Tickets for Rio. Wondered if you'd like to join me?'

She ignored the envelope, took a sip of coffee and then removed an evidence bag from a pocket inside her jacket. 'I found these on the floor of the barn, near where Turnbull had been strung up.'

Fernández looked at the remnants of three cigarettes.

'They're yours,' she said. 'When you phoned for an ambulance, one was on standby in the area. It took less than ten minutes to reach the farm. But it was too late. They couldn't do anything for him.' She tilted her head, raising an eyebrow slightly. 'You want to tell me why you waited so long before you made the call?'

He exhaled forcefully, looked at her, and then took a small cassette from his jacket pocket. 'Carlos made sure we had this before he turned the gun on himself. When you have a moment, doctor, listen to it. Listen to it several times, as I have done, and tell me whether you think Turnbull gave a damn about anyone but himself?' He stepped down from his bar stool. 'I'll see you here at eight this evening.'

He walked towards the door, hesitated, and then turned round. 'Oh, and don't be late.'

www.ingramcontent.com/pod-product-compliance
Lightning Source LLC
Chambersburg PA
CBHW020237180626
46810CB00006B/2244